LONG JOURNEY HOME

ASHLEY FARLEY

ALSO BY ASHLEY FARLEY

After the Storm

Scent of Magnolia

Virginia Vineyards

Love Child

Blind Love

Forbidden Love

Love and War

Palmetto Island

Muddy Bottom

Change of Tides

Lowcountry on My Mind

Sail Away

Hope Springs Series

Dream Big, Stella!

Show Me the Way

Mistletoe and Wedding Bells

Matters of the Heart

Road to New Beginnings

Stand Alone

On My Terms

Tangled in Ivy

Lies that Bind

Life on Loan

Only One Life

Home for Wounded Hearts

Nell and Lady

Sweet Tea Tuesdays

Saving Ben

Sweeney Sisters Series

Saturdays at Sweeney's

Tangle of Strings

Boots and Bedlam

Lowcountry Stranger

Her Sister's Shoes

Magnolia Series

Beyond the Garden

Magnolia Nights

Scottie's Adventures

Breaking the Story

Merry Mary

CHAPTER
ONE

I stand in the open doorway, staring out at the lush green grass of the fourteenth hole. I'm not a fan of golf. The game moves too slow, takes too long, and occupies entirely too much of my husband's free time. If it's just a silly sport, why do I resent it so much? Perhaps if he shared my love of fishing, we could go on outings together.

Leaning against the doorjamb, I close my eyes and imagine I'm lounging on the daybed swing on the veranda of my family's historic waterfront home. Joyful memories from childhood flash through my mind. Three little girls, my sisters and me, lazing in the shade of a sprawling live oak while our mother rocks our baby brother on the porch. Bare feet on weathered cypress planks as we race down the dock. Sailing our Sunfish in the calm waters of Catawba Sound. Rainy afternoons playing Crazy Eights beneath blanket forts in the cozy cypress-paneled family room.

Pungent aromas fill the air around me. The sulphury, rotten egg stench of the marsh at low tide. Sweet Ligustrum that marks the beginning of summer. Wood burning in the fireplaces on cool autumn afternoons. Our father's pipe smoke. Coffee percolating and bacon frying. Freshly cut grass and rain.

Pleasing sounds tickle my ears. The crowd roaring from an SEC football game on the television in the family room. Dishes clattering in the kitchen. Mama calling us to dinner. Our golden retriever, Bailey, barking at the mailman.

As the years progress, those memories darken, but I'm spared the heartache of those traumatic times by the slamming of the front door. Reluctantly, I turn away from the golf course and my trip down Memory Lane.

My breath hitches at the sight of my attractive husband in the doorway. Fifteen years of marriage, and he still has that effect on me. He's sweaty from the golf course, his dark cropped hair standing on end and damp navy polo and khaki shorts clinging to his toned body. He refuses to wear sunscreen, and his arms and face are bronzed with sunglass lines marking his temples.

"You're late." I glance down at my watch. I, too, had lost track of time, and it's already after six o'clock. "Shoot. We missed the ceremony. We'll have to hustle in order to make it to the reception before the wedding party."

Owen goes to the bar cart and pours himself a shot of whiskey. "What wedding? I don't remember you mentioning a social engagement for tonight."

I shorten the distance between us. "Are you serious? We've only been talking about Melissa's wedding since she got engaged last summer."

"Oh. Right. Melissa." He downs the whiskey. "You go ahead without me. You'll have more fun."

"But her mother is my best friend. How will I explain your absence to Hattie?"

Owen grunts. "Hattie hates me. My absence will thrill her."

"Don't be ridiculous. You know that's not true. Please, Owen, I've been looking forward to this night for a long time. I even bought a new dress." I twirl around, the pink silk dress billowing out around me. "We can drink champagne and dance under the moonlight." I walk my fingers up his chest to his lips.

"And when we get home, we can make love. It's been a long time."

Taking hold of my wrist, he kisses my fingers and drops my hand. "I'm not in the mood for socializing. You run along to the wedding, and I'll be here waiting for you when you get home." He loops an arm around my waist and walks me to the foyer.

"Don't bother. I'll be late." I snatch up my silver clutch from the console table beside the door and exit the house. What's the point of being married if I have to attend social functions alone?

Several of my neighbors are out in front of their condos, tending to their postage stamp yards and walking their dogs. I'm not on friendly terms with any of them, and before they can approach me, I hurry to my convertible and speed away. I was crazy to let Owen convince me to move from my sprawling 1920s Nantucket-style beach house into a one-story, two-bedroom condo.

Mariner's Landing, an upscale residential community, is located five miles west of our historic downtown. I was both the architect for the project and a primary developer. I collaborated with my brother, a custom home builder, to construct a combination of condos and single-family homes. The residences are situated around an eighteen-hole golf course and clubhouse that features a restaurant, swimming pool, and tennis courts. I appreciate the modern conveniences of the condo, but I miss being on the water and the unique quirks of my old home.

Church bells ring out as I enter town. The bells, announcing the union of a young local couple, are a tradition at Grace Episcopal Church. Melissa's ceremony has ended, and guests will soon be on their way to the reception. My husband does not know what he's missing. This coveted invitation to the wedding of the season is a symbol of social standing and importance in our small town.

Water's Edge is a hidden gem, a small town nestled deep in the South Carolina lowcountry between Hilton Head and Beaufort. The absence of a fancy resort keeps tourists away, although several charming inns offer quaint rooms in restored mansions to visitors who occasionally venture off the beaten paths to Charleston and Savannah.

The older buildings on Main Street exude a timeless charm, with their ornate facades, decorative cornices, and intricate detailing. Many of the businesses haven't changed in my lifetime—the barber, the butcher, the baker. The hardware store has expanded to take up an entire city block, and a gourmet market now occupies the old Sears and Roebuck building. New buildings reflecting contemporary design trends have also emerged. In these spaces are a coffee shop, clothing boutiques, and the florist.

On the waterfront, amid a host of new eateries, are the tried and true—The Clam and Claw, a family-style seafood restaurant, and The Turtle's Nest, referred to by locals as The Nest, a tavern where locals go to party on the weekends.

I cross over the Merriweather Bridge—a swing bridge named after my ancestor, one of the town's founding fathers—and drive to the southernmost tip of Sandy Island to the Sandpiper Club. I lose myself in the crowd migrating from the parking lot, through the clubhouse, and outside to the multilevel terraces where the reception is being held.

I grab a glass of champagne from the bar and survey the many delicacies on the food tables. A passing server offers a tray of bruschetta, but I refrain from popping one into my mouth. "I have a nut allergy," I inform her.

She retracts the tray. "Then you don't want these. We make the bruschetta with pine nuts," she says, and continues on her way.

I meander aimlessly through the crowd, feeling anonymous even though I know most of the people in attendance. A friend from church stops me, offering her condolences on my mother's recent passing.

I give Maria a sad smile. "Thank you. These past few weeks have been difficult."

Todd, Maria's husband, asks, "Where's Owen?"

"He's not feeling well." The lie slides easily from my lips. I'm used to making excuses for my husband's absence.

"I'm sorry to hear that," Todd says, giving me a look of pity. He knows my husband spends more time with his new golf buddy than his wife.

I excuse myself and make my way to the edge of the terrace where a refreshing breeze carries the citrusy fragrance from a nearby magnolia tree. The cool salty air wraps around me like a soothing embrace as I watch the waves gently lapping the white sandy beaches. The mingling scents of the ocean and the magnolia evoke a sense of tranquility. I especially love this time of year. Not only does the first weekend in June mark the beginning of the summer, for me, it marks the beginning of a new year.

The serenity fades, replaced by a deep, unsettling sense of unease. It feels as if an unseen storm looms on the horizon, sending chills down my spine and a sense of dread coursing through me.

"Mother Nature blessed us with the perfect evening." Hattie's voice startles me, and I'm surprised to see her standing beside me.

"For sure! It doesn't get any better than this." My eyes travel the length of her periwinkle off-shouldered, ruched taffeta gown. She's wearing more makeup than usual, and her strawberry hair is swept into an elegant updo with tendrils framing her face. "You look lovely."

Hattie fingers a tendril off her face. "I look like a prostitute. The makeup artist and hair stylist got carried away."

I laugh. "You're an elegant mother of the bride." I spot my brother talking to the groom, their heads close together. I wave at Will, but he doesn't wave back, even though I'm pretty sure he sees me. "Since when are Will and Carson friends?"

"Since Will hired Carson. My new son-in-law is the newest project manager at Darby Custom Homes." Hattie presses her hand to her chest as a dreamy expression appears on her face. "That sounds so strange. I have a son-in-law."

"You finally got the son you've always wanted."

"Yes! And as you can imagine, my husband is beside himself." Hattie tears her eyes away from her son-in-law. "I missed you at the church."

Only Hattie would notice my absence in a church packed with four hundred attendees. A sharp pang of guilt slices through me as I choke out, "I have no excuse, Hattie. I simply lost track of time."

She cuts her blue eyes at me. "Mm-hmm. Where's Owen?"

"He's wandering around here somewhere," I say, gesturing at the crowded terrace.

"No, he's not." Hattie moves in closer to study my face. "I can tell when you're lying, Ashton."

I squirm under her intense scrutiny. "Owen was late getting home from the golf course. I shouldn't have waited for him. I should've gone on to the church without him. I'm so sorry, Hattie. I feel awful about missing the ceremony."

Her shoulders soften. "I'm sorry for your sake. You should divorce him."

I cough up a laugh. "That's an extreme penalty for missing a wedding."

"This isn't about the wedding, and you know it. What did he do for your birthday?"

My face warms. "I'm sure he has something planned for tomorrow. Sunday is our special day," I say, even though I can't remember the last time we spent a Sunday together.

"*Today* is your fiftieth birthday. Not tomorrow. Owen should be here with you now." She takes my hands in hers. "I know you, Ashton, sometimes better than you know yourself. I can tell you're miserable. You're still young and beautiful. You can find someone new to share your next half century with, someone who treats you like a queen. If fear is holding you back, you're stronger than you think."

Irritation crawls across my skin. "Don't you have mother-of-the-bride duties to attend to?"

Hattie drops my hands. "You're right. I should mingle with my guests. We'll table this discussion until another time." She inhales a deep breath, drawing her shoulders back and holding her head high. "I'll need a few days to recover from the wedding, but then we'll celebrate your birthday. What say we break with tradition and spend the night in Charleston?"

I hesitate. My husband, not my best friend, should take me on an overnight trip to Charleston. "I can't get away right now. I'm swamped at work. Can we have our usual dinner at The Nest?"

"Whatever you want." She kisses the air beside my cheek. "I'll text you early next week, and we'll see what night works."

Tears blur my vision as Hattie disappears into the crowd. Every marriage has peaks and valleys. But mine has been on a downward trajectory for over five years. Why *do* I stay with Owen? We don't have any children to complicate a divorce. I still love him, but I'm no longer *in* love with him. I can see in his face that he's fallen out of love with me as well. Is Hattie right? Am I afraid of divorcing him? But why?

I elbow my way into a group of friends from my high school class. We've known each other all our lives, and I see them often at social engagements, but I'm not close to any of them. I regret joining them when I realize they're talking about celebrating their fiftieth birthdays, but walking away would be rude.

Sadie's blonde curls dance around her shoulders as she talks about the trip to Italy her husband, Terrence, has planned for the fall.

"That sounds fabulous!" Pam says, her green eyes bright. "Can you believe my tight-ass husband is splurging on a month in Nantucket in August? He's rented the most amazing cottage. I'm inviting all of you to come visit."

The small group lets out a collective cheer.

Amanda's left arm shoots out with fingers splayed. "Look what Harold bought me. While y'all are enjoying yourselves in Italy and Nantucket, I'll be admiring my upgrade."

Four sets of eyes stare down at the enormous solitaire

diamond. After a sufficient amount of oohing and aahing, Amanda retracts her hand.

"Should we tell them?" Leslie says, bumping shoulders with Diana.

"Tell us what?" Pam and Sadie ask in unison.

Giggling like a schoolgirl, Leslie leans into the group. "Shh! It's a secret, so don't tell anyone. Our husbands are throwing us a big bash in the fall. We're renting out an event barn, and we've hired a popular funk band to play our favorite oldies. You're all invited, of course."

"Wow! That sounds like so much fun." Sadie turns her attention to me. "What about you, Ashton? How're you celebrating your fiftieth?"

Heat creeps up the back of my neck. "I haven't gotten that far."

Pam frowns. "But isn't your birthday soon?"

"It's in July," I lie. "I have a lot of projects in the works at the moment. Owen and I will probably sneak away for a quiet weekend somewhere." I immediately realize my mistake. They will want to know where Owen is tonight. "Speaking of work, I see a client I need to have a word with. It was good to see y'all." I flash a wave as I slip away from the group.

I make a plate of food and locate a table under the tent. I feel like an awkward loser sitting alone, but after missing the ceremony, I should stay at the reception until the end. When the Motown band takes the stage, couples of all ages mob the dance floor. I envy my friends whose husbands are swinging them around, dipping them low, and holding them tight during slow songs. Owen and I used to love to dance. We often traveled to places like Charlotte and Columbia to hear our favorite bands. We have so few things in common anymore.

I steal a moment alone with the bride after the cake cutting ceremony.

"Let me get a good look at you." I spin Melissa around,

admiring the strapless organza dress with a sweetheart neckline and flounced skirt. "You're an angel, positively ethereal."

Melissa beams. "Thank you, Aunt Ashton."

"You're a married woman now. For heaven's sake, please stop calling me *aunt.*" While I'm not technically her aunt, she's more a niece to me than my own nieces and nephews.

Melissa giggles. "I'll try, but I'm not sure I can. That would be like asking me to stop calling my mom Mama."

"True. I'm honored for you to think of me as your family. By the way, I have something for you." I remove a drawstring jewelry pouch from my purse and hand it to her.

Melissa opens the bag and pulls out a bracelet with tiny pearls and a sterling heart charm. "I absolutely love it. Help me put it on." She hands me the bracelet and holds out her arm.

As I fasten the bracelet to her wrist, I explain, "Your mama and I gave each other matching bracelets for our birthdays one year. I still have mine." I finger the pearl bracelet on my wrist. "Hattie lost hers a long time ago. This one is as close to ours as I could find." I bring her wrist to my lips and kiss the heart. "Now, a piece of my heart will always belong to you."

Melissa throws her arms around me. "Thank you so much. I love you, Aunt Ashton."

"And I love you. Never lose sight of who you are." My own words hit home. I'm a hypocrite for offering such advice when I lost sight of myself a very long time ago.

CHAPTER
TWO

I wake on Sunday morning to find Owen sound asleep next to me in bed. He wasn't home when I got in from the wedding around midnight. I assume he went out for drinks with his golfing buddies. Which infuriates me when he refused to go out with me on my birthday.

I dress for church and leave the house without taking time for coffee. The streets are quiet as I pass through town on my way to the historic residential section. Towering live oaks, draped in Spanish moss, form a natural canopy across Pelican's Way, the curving road leading to Marsh Point. Tension leaves my body as I drive to the end of the familiar road and pull into the gravel driveway in front of my family's antebellum plantation-style home.

My ancestors built the house in the mid-1800s as a vacation home to escape the heat and mosquitos on their cotton plantation. Four spacious rooms flank the wide center hallway, which had allowed air to flow through from the front to the back of the house during pre-air-conditioning times. Five average-size bedrooms occupy the second floor, and outside, double-decker verandas stretch across the marsh side of the house.

As I enter through the front door, I hear one of Dad's Sunday morning news shows blasting on the television in the cypress-paneled family room at the back of the house. I drop my purse on a chair and walk down the hallway, calling, "Hey, Dad! It's me, Ashton."

I'm not surprised to find him ensconced in his favorite worn recliner, his cloudy eyes glued to the television. He's become frail in the weeks since Mom died, and he appears to have lost even more weight from when I last saw him a few days ago. Mom's caregivers made certain he received proper nutrition, but with no one around to cook for him, I suspect he goes days without a well-balanced meal.

I kiss the bald top of his head. "How're you doing today, Dad?"

"About the same," he says without glancing up at me. I wait for him to wish me a happy birthday, but he has either forgotten or he's too preoccupied by the news.

"You need a haircut," I say about the unruly gray hair growing in a horseshoe from temple to temple. I run a finger over his three-day stubble. "You could use a shave as well. Want me to see if your barber is working today?"

Dad smacks my hand away. "Stop fussing, Ashton. I have no use for a barber anymore."

"At some point, you're going to have to reenter the world, Dad. You can't just rot away in your chair. Your friends have asked to come see you. Why won't you let them?"

"I'm in mourning."

I let his comment slide, because this argument is old. He's using my mother's death as a crutch. She died from liver disease related to a lifetime of alcohol abuse. Mama was fortunate to make it past seventy. She'd been ill for a decade, confined to a bed for the past year, incoherent for six months, and unconscious the last weeks of her life. We've all had plenty of time to mourn. This isn't about her *death*. Dad's focus has been solely on Mom for so long, he doesn't know how to go on living without her.

I pull up a chair next to him and sit down. "Can I schedule a visit for us at Whispering Oaks? I understand their independent living facilities are top-notch. You can have your own one or two-bedroom unit, and you won't have to worry about the maintenance on Marsh Point." The house desperately needs work. The yard has become a jungle, and something inside the house breaks nearly every single day.

Dad responds by turning up the volume on the television.

I take the remote from him and mute the volume. "I'm trying to have a serious discussion with you, Dad. Will you at least consider Whispering Oaks?"

"Nope," he says, and presses his lips tight.

"You're being difficult. At seventy-eight years old, you still have a lot of living left to do. Many of your friends are at Whispering Oaks. You can take up golf again. Or find a new hobby."

"You mean like whispering to oak trees? Next thing I know, your mama's ghost will be calling me to heaven."

"Ha ha. Aren't you funny? You'll be going to heaven a lot sooner if you stay cooped up in this room, breathing stale air. Why is it so stuffy in here?" I get up and open the french doors on either side of the brick fireplace.

"Air conditioner's on the fritz again."

"I'm not surprised. We've been putting band aids on these units for years. We can't avoid replacing them any longer."

"I'll get around to it eventually. Damn place is falling down around me." Dad raises his hand and lets it drop back to the chair's arm. "Roof has a new leak in the master bedroom upstairs. The powder room toilet won't stop running. And the termite inspector was here last week. He recommends we replace the siding with HardiePlank."

"We knew that was coming. The siding is over a century old. Have you talked to Will about fixing these things?"

"What good is Will?" Dad grumbles. "He comes out to Marsh Point to use his boat, but he never enters the house. He's scared or something."

I've noticed this about my brother. Will avoids the inside of the house like the plague. He's afraid to face the same demons I keep locked in the deep recesses of my mind.

"Have you eaten anything today?" I ask, even though I know he hasn't. "Why don't I whip you up some breakfast before I head to church?"

"Good luck finding any food in this house," he mutters.

"I'll come up with something. But first, I'm going to check on the roof leak," I say on my way out of the room.

As I near the top of the stairs, I spot my sister standing near the bed in my parents' room. Why didn't Dad mention she was here? Does he even know? It would be like Carrie to slip in unnoticed. I don't trust my sister, and as I watch her inspecting something shiny on the bed, I have a sneaking suspicion she's up to something.

I press myself against the wall and peek around the doorframe. With only nineteen months separating us in age, my sister and I look enough alike to be twins, although her thick honey hair is long and layered, whereas I prefer the ease of my pixie cut. She's gained weight in recent years, the extra pounds settling around her midsection and on her thighs. In the absence of a career, I'm curious how she spends her time, aside from keeping up with her teenagers' busy lives. I don't have a problem with stay-at-home moms, but I worry about my sister's lack of interest in any extracurricular activities.

Squinting my eyes, I can see the glittering objects on the bed are pieces of jewelry. Mama's family's heirloom jewelry. Carrie glances around the room, as though making sure no one is watching her, before stuffing something in the front pocket of her white jeans. She drops the remaining jewelry, piece by piece, into a large cream-colored velvet bag.

I casually enter the room. "Hey, Carrie. What's up?"

My sister comes out of her flip-flops. "Geez, Ashton!" she says, gripping her chest. "You scared the devil outta me. What're you doing here?"

"Dad says we have a leak in the roof. I came to check it out." I eye the bag in her hand. "What's that?"

"Mama's jewelry." She opens Mom's top dresser drawer and drops the bag inside. "We need to clear out her things and divide up her valuables. Do you know if she has a will?"

I shrug. "No clue. I haven't thought about it."

"Let's ask Dad," Carrie says and exits the room with me on her heels.

I follow her down the stairs and into the family room.

"I'm curious, Dad. Did Mama have a will? If not, Ashton and I would like to divide up her jewelry."

I throw up my hands. "Don't drag me into this. You were the one rooting through her jewelry."

With a sigh, Dad reaches for the remote and turns off the television. "Your mother's attorney has been hounding me to schedule a meeting for the reading of her will. I guess I can't put it off any longer."

My sister looms over him. "Why have you been putting it off? Are you hiding something?"

"You're out of line, Carrie!" I say in a warning tone. "Mom has only been gone a month."

Dad grips the arms of the chair as he eases himself up to face her. "Truth be told, Carrie, I'm afraid reading your mama's will might open a can of worms none of us are prepared for."

Carrie and I exchange a look, and my sister asks, "Why? What's in the will?"

"I haven't a clue," Dad says with a grim shake of his head. "Eileen never discussed her personal finances with me. I'll contact the attorney this afternoon and schedule a meeting as soon as possible."

"You do that." Carrie spins around and strides across the room with her flip-flops smacking the bottoms of her feet.

I call after her before she reaches the door. "Wait, Carrie! Before you go. What's in your pocket?"

Carrie stops in her tracks, but she doesn't turn around. "What do you mean?"

"I saw you put something in your pocket when you were looking at Mom's jewelry."

"Carrie? Did you take something of your mother's without asking?" Dad shuffles over to her with outstretched hand.

Carrie fishes two pieces of jewelry out of her pocket, dropping them into the palm of his hand. I inch close enough to see the diamond tennis bracelet and sparkling emerald ring.

"Why should her jewelry go to waste when we could be wearing it?"

Disappointment is etched in the deep crevices of Dad's face. "I agree. But it's up to your mother to say who wears it."

Guilt sags Carrie's shoulders as she slips out of the room.

Dad wraps his bony fingers around the jewelry. "At least she has good taste. These are two of your mother's most valuable pieces."

"I'll make us some breakfast," I say and head off to the kitchen.

Dad wasn't joking about there being no food in the kitchen. I locate the end of a stale loaf of bread in the pantry, precooked turkey sausage in the freezer, and two eggs in the refrigerator that are a few days past the expiration date.

I've often daydreamed about the changes I would make to the house if given the chance. While I make his omelet, I imagine the new wall of windows overlooking a slate terrace and saltwater pool. My love of this old house drove me to study architecture. Over the years, I presented my mother with several remodeling designs, but she refused to have her life, such as it was, disrupted by construction. Maybe Dad will be inspired to make some changes once the house rightfully belongs to him.

After brewing a pot of coffee, I set the wicker table on the veranda with placemats, flatware, and a single stem blue hydrangea I cut from the bush near the porch.

"Dad!" I call out. "Breakfast is ready."

"I'd rather eat in here," comes his muffled voice from the family room.

Striding over to the open doorway, I order him to get up. "We're eating out here. It's a lovely morning, and you need some fresh air. You can spare your oldest daughter a few minutes of your undivided attention."

"All right. If you insist." Easing to the edge of the cushion, he picks up a cane from the floor beside his chair and uses it to hoist himself up.

"What's with the cane, Dad?"

He taps the floor in front of him with the cane as he moves toward me. "This cane belonged to my grandfather. It's made of solid mahogany and the handle is sterling silver." He presents the cane to me for inspection.

The wood is a lovely reddish brown, and the sterling silver handle is intricately carved. "Very nice."

"I found it in the closet. I figured I might as well use it."

"But there's nothing physically wrong with you. If you exercised more, you'd feel more limber. Even taking short walks around the yard is better than sitting in that chair all day."

Giving him back the cane, I hold on to his elbow while I walk him over to the table and help him get settled in the chair.

He examines his breakfast and then looks at the empty placemat in front of me. "Where's your plate?"

I don't tell him there was only enough food for one meal. "I'm not hungry. I'm fine with just coffee."

We bow our heads, and I offer a quick blessing, thanking God for the opportunity to spend this time with my father.

Dad forks off a bite of omelet and slides it into his mouth.

"Hmm. This is good. Not as good as your mom's omelets, but tasty."

I bite my lip to keep from laughing. Mom rarely cooked. She was usually hungover in the mornings and seldom came out of her room before noon. "I'm curious, Dad. Why did you stay with Mom all these years? No one would've blamed you if you'd left her."

Dad chokes on a piece of sausage, preventing him from speaking. He guzzles down some water and clears his throat. "That's a loaded question, Ashton." He sets down his toast and wipes his mouth. "You're a grown woman, and there's no point in lying to you. I stayed with Eileen out of a sense of obligation. She was a very sick woman. As you well know, alcoholism is a disease."

"It's also an addiction many people overcome," I say in a deadpan tone.

Dad freezes. "She tried. She went to rehab two times."

I look out over the marsh. "Obviously, two times wasn't enough."

"I honestly thought she'd finally beaten her addiction the second time. She stayed sober for over a year."

My ears perk up. This is news to me. "I don't remember that. What was different about the second time?"

Dad hangs his head. I sense he wants to tell me something, but he doesn't know how. A long moment passes and whatever he was going to tell me goes with it.

I reach for his hand. "What is it, Dad?"

He picks up his toast. "You kids were growing up, and you needed her. In hindsight, I should've hired a nanny, or a housekeeper."

I've often wondered why he'd neglected us during the most harrowing years. He lived in our guesthouse for a while, but then he moved off the property. I'm not sure where. He never invited us over. He popped in occasionally to check on us, but Mama usually ran him off. "Why didn't you? Hire a nanny or a housekeeper?"

"I was protecting your mother. I didn't want outsiders to know what went on inside this house."

"So you let the burden of taking care of my siblings fall on me instead," I say over the rim of my coffee mug.

Dad's eyes are shiny with tears. "That's the biggest regret of my life, and I will carry the guilt to my grave," he says and pushes his plate away, his half-eaten breakfast abandoned.

I get up from my chair and kneel beside him. "I'm sorry, Dad, for bringing all this up. I've paid a psychiatrist a small fortune, trying to retrieve the worst of my memories. If there are things about the past I should know, you need to tell me." I've never told him about the therapy, and if he's surprised, he doesn't let it show.

Dad palms my cheek. "I'm sorry, sweetheart, but when it comes to our family, the past is best left buried."

I HAVE a difficult time paying attention to the sermon in church. I can't stop thinking about Dad's warning about my mother's will. *I'm afraid reading your mother's will might open a can of worms none of us are prepared for.* What can of worms is he talking about? My mother inherited millions from her wealthy parents, who inherited it from their wealthy ancestors. She helped my father establish himself as a building contractor, and they lived a modest lifestyle on the money he earned building custom homes. Her stock portfolios have been growing all these years. Those millions may very well be billions. I'd assumed she would leave everything to my father except for her jewelry, which my sisters and I would divide equally. What does Dad know that we don't know? Is there something in her will that will make the rift in our family grow larger?

After church, I stock dad's refrigerator with his favorites from Fancy Pantry and spend the rest of the afternoon in my office. My architectural firm, which employs a small team of project managers and interior designers, takes up the entire second floor of a converted waterfront warehouse on Main Street. Sunlight streams in through windows in my back corner office, which offers a sweeping view of Catawba Sound. I'm currently working on several projects, including a large new contemporary home at the far north tip of Sandy Island. But my passion lies in restoration projects, and I lose myself in plans for remodeling an early nineteenth-century lowcountry-style beach house.

When I arrive home around six thirty, I'm surprised to see my husband's sleek sedan in the driveway and Owen at the kitchen island, preparing salmon steaks for the grill. He turns to face me with two flutes of champagne in his hands. "Happy birthday, baby."

I wonder if Hattie texted him a reminder. "My birthday was yesterday, Owen."

"Better late than never." He holds a flute out to me and I take it.

I look past him at the table, which is set with my fine china and a single red rose. Owen knows how much I despise red roses.

Owen follows my gaze. "Sorry about the rose. The selection at Fancy Pantry was picked over." Balancing the salmon plate in one hand, he opens the sliding patio door with the other. "Do you mind fixing our plates while I grill the salmon? The cornbread's warming in the oven, and the salads are in the refrigerator. I had them prepare one especially for you without nuts."

"Thank you for remembering," I say in a snarky tone as I take a sip of champagne. He'd better not forget about my nut allergy. To do so could be life threatening.

I adjust my attitude while I mix the salads and butter the cornbread. Holding a grudge because he forgot my birthday isn't helping anything. When he returns with the cooked salmon ten minutes later, our plates are ready and I'm wearing a smile.

We rarely sit at the table. I prefer eating at the island. The empty chairs between us are a reminder of what's missing from our lives. The glue that would hold our marriage together. The children I insisted I never wanted. The biggest regret of my life to date.

"How was the wedding?" he asks, placing his napkin in his lap.

"Lovely." I flake off a bite of salmon. "Everyone asked where you were. Where *did* you go, by the way? You were gone when I got home," I say and bring my fork to my mouth.

"To The Nest. Rich roped me into grabbing a bite to eat with him. I was hoping to beat you home, but the service was slow."

"Well, you missed a good time at the wedding. Some of my friends were talking about their fiftieth birthdays. Amanda got a new diamond. Sadie is going to Italy. And Leslie and Diana are throwing themselves a party. Your fiftieth is coming up in a few months. How would you like to celebrate? We could throw a party or take a trip?"

Owen's face crumbles as my point hits home. "We'll cross that bridge when we get there."

My phone buzzes on the table with a message from Dad. *We will meet with the attorney to discuss your mother's will at ten o'clock tomorrow morning.* It's not a group text. Dad is electronically challenged. And it's a summons, not an invitation. If we have other plans, he expects us to cancel them. Fortunately, I'm free.

I look up from my phone to find Owen staring at me. "Is something wrong?"

"We're reading Mom's will in the morning," I say, buttering my cornbread.

His face registers surprise. "No one told me she had a will. Did she leave you anything?"

"Who knows? I guess we'll find out tomorrow."

He spears salad greens with his fork. "Can I come to the meeting?"

"I'm not sure you're invited." I don't mind if he attends the meeting. If Mom has left me any money, I will give it to him to manage. Our marriage might not be on solid ground, but I trust him explicitly with our finances.

He eyes my phone. "Ask your dad. I'm curious to see what you got."

I set down my fork and wipe my mouth. "What I got was a dead mother, Owen."

"Don't be so sensitive, Ashton. You know what I mean."

I pick up the phone and thumb-type the text. *Are spouses allowed at the meeting?*

Dad responds immediately. *No! Only beneficiaries are included.*

"Dad says only beneficiaries are included. Sorry. You'll have to sit this one out."

"Nothing about your dysfunctional family surprises me." Owen stands abruptly and storms out of the kitchen, leaving me with the dirty dishes and an ugly red rose. There will be no cake to celebrate my half-century birthday. Not even a bowl of ice cream with a candle. Certainly not a trip to Italy or a month on Nantucket Island.

CHAPTER **THREE**

My siblings and I sit together on the sofa in the family room, lined up like convicted criminals awaiting sentencing. I'm in the middle with Carrie on my right and Will on my left. Carrie sits tall and rigid, a guitar string ready to snap. And Will squirms in his seat as he casts frequent glances at the french doors. Mama's attorney, the guest of honor, perches on one of our Chippendale dining chairs in front of us.

Virginia Morgan, who was several years older than me in school, wears her age well with her dark hair cut in a sleek bob and her skin free of wrinkles.

Virginia looks over at my father in his recliner. "Have you tried reaching Savannah?"

"I've been trying to reach her since Eileen died. So far, my investigator has found no trace of her."

I don't admit it to my father, but I've had a private investigator on retainer, searching for my youngest sister from the moment I received my first paycheck as an architect. *If* Savannah is still alive, she's changed her name and is living in a remote part of the world.

Virginia slides on a pair of clear frame reading glasses and looks down at the open file on the coffee table in front of her. "I left a message for Mary Macon, but I haven't heard from her."

"May May is always late." Mary Macon was my mother's closest friend and godmother to all her children. I nicknamed her May May as a toddler when I struggled to pronounce her double name.

We hear the creaking of the front door followed by a voice calling, "Yoo-hoo! Anybody home?" Seconds later, May May appears in the doorway wearing blue jean overalls with her long gray hair in a single braid down her back. "I'm sorry, I'm late. My truck wouldn't start, and I had to get my neighbor to give me a jump." She winks at Will, kisses my cheek, and pats Carrie on the head before plopping down in a wingback chair next to Dad.

"I don't understand," Carrie says. "Why is May May here?"

"She's a beneficiary," Virginia explains.

Carrie's eyebrows become one. "A beneficiary? You mean Mama left her something too?"

Virginia smiles at May May. "She left her a small gift."

As far as I'm concerned, May May should inherit the entire kit and caboodle as payback for her devotion to my family.

May May's green eyes sparkle like emeralds. "Isn't that sweet? I figured Eileen wanted me here to do damage control."

I'm curious what she means by *damage control* and what she knows about my mother's will. But since we're about to find out, I don't ask.

Carrie rolls her eyes. "Are there any other *beneficiaries* we're not aware of?"

"Only Savannah." Virginia picks up a stapled sheaf of papers. "Let's proceed. Do you mind if I dispense with the legalese and cut to the chase?"

"Please," my father says, nodding for her to continue.

"I will go in the order Eileen suggested. Ernest, you're up first. All liquid assets, including the cash in her banking accounts and her stock portfolios, will go into a marital trust for your benefit. Upon your death, that trust will pass to your children." Virginia's gaze shifts to me. "Ashton, in addition to all her jewelry, your mother has left Marsh Point, the house and the land, to you."

The earth falls out from beneath me. I'm completely dumbfounded, elated and devastated all at once. I'm barely aware of Carrie jumping to her feet in protest.

"This is insane. I don't believe you. Let me see that." Carrie snatches the document out of Virginia's hand, but Virginia grabs it back. "I have copies for each of you to take home. I will hand them out as soon as I'm finished."

Dad gives my sister a warning look. "Sit down, Carrie, and let Virginia finish."

With a huff, Carrie plops back down.

Virginia moves to the edge of her seat. "Before I proceed, you should know that Eileen gave careful consideration to her estate. And yes, she was sober for all our many meetings. Over the years, she told me a lot about your lives together. She loved each of you dearly. As for this will,"—Virginia waves the document in the air—"she knew exactly what she was doing."

"How do you know she was sober?" Carrie snaps.

"She insisted on doing a home breathalyzer test prior to our discussions. She knew there would be some hurt feelings, and she didn't want anyone questioning her sobriety or mental acuity."

"Who is the executor?" Carrie asks.

"I am." Virginia takes a minute to talk about how disbursements will be made. Sliding back in the chair, she crosses her legs. "So, as I was saying, Marsh Point and Eileen's jewelry will go to Ashton."

"I don't care what you say. There's no way Mama was in her right mind when she came up with that crap," Carrie says, jabbing a finger at the document.

"I have witnesses in my office who will vouch for her. I will provide their contact information for you if you'd like to speak with them." Virginia flips over to the next page. "Will, your mother has left you the boat slip at the end of the dock, and, Carrie, you will receive her sterling silver service."

Carrie is back on her feet. "I don't believe this! Ashton gets the house, and I get a teapot? How is that fair?" She stomps her foot. "Dad! Do something."

I risk a glance at my brother, who is fiddling with his phone, seemingly oblivious to the commotion taking place around him.

Dad's chin hits his chest. "Why did you do this, Eileen?" he mumbles to his dead wife.

"Ugh! I'm so done with this family." Carrie storms out of the house, slamming the door so hard a brass candlestick falls off the mantel.

Will gets to his feet. "I'm done here too." He leaves the house through the french doors, and I watch his tall frame lumber to the end of the dock where he keeps his twenty-five-foot center console fishing boat.

My excitement over inheriting the house vanishes. My mother was the source of this family's turmoil when she was alive. And she continues to drive us apart in death.

Virginia regains her composure. "Savannah, if we ever find her, will receive Eileen's record collection." She turns her attention to May May. "And Eileen has left you her journals." She fishes in her work tote and hands May May a stack of leather journals bound by a thick rubber band.

"Thank you." May May accepts the bundle, hugging them to her bosom like she embraced me many times as a child.

I experience a flashback of Mama stretched out on the chaise lounge in her bedroom with her feet tucked beneath her as she scribbles away in one of these journals. She's wearing makeup, her lips painted hot pink, and her hair, the rich mahogany color of her youth, is smoothed back with a yellow polka-dotted scarf. Her sundress is the same buttery shade of yellow, and a single strand of pearls rests on her collarbone.

Virginia gathers her documents, stuffing them into her tote, and stands to leave. Dad, May May, and I get up to see her out.

Virginia pauses at the front door. "Call me if you have questions."

I raise my hand. "I have a question now." I hold my arms out wide. "As you can see, the house is in a state of disrepair. Am I allowed to renovate while the estate is in probate?"

"As long as you have my permission as executor. Which you do." Virginia places a hand on my arm. "Coincidentally, I would get the jewelry out of the house as soon as possible."

"Don't worry. I plan on taking it with me today."

I wait until Virginia is gone before asking Dad, "Did you tell her about Carrie trying to take Mom's tennis bracelet and emerald ring?"

"Nope. That attorney has an eerie way of knowing what goes on behind the scenes." Dad turns away from the door and taps his cane toward the stairs.

"Where are you going, Dad?" I call after him.

"To lie down," he says without looking back at me. "I need to process what just happened here."

I set my eyes on May May. "I don't know about you, but I could use some caffeine. Can you spare a few minutes for coffee?"

"After what just happened here, I'll stay as long as you need me," she says, and we walk arm in arm to the kitchen.

My siblings and I would never have survived our childhoods without May May. When she wasn't homeschooling her own children or tending her small farm, she made sure we had food and clothing and school supplies, doing whatever she could to make our miserable lives less miserable.

I study her as I prepare the coffee maker to brew. She has sunspots on her face, but her green eyes are clear and bright.

Mama's death has been hard on her. She wears the sadness in the lines etched in her face.

We take our coffees out to the rockers on the veranda. As we settle in, I notice Will's boat is missing from the lift at the end of the dock. I hate the idea of him being out in his boat alone when he's so upset. Although, truth be told, he didn't seem all that upset.

"What *did* just happen to us, May May? What was Mama thinking?"

May May gives her head a solemn shake. "Lordy, child. I'm not sure. I know how much your Mama wanted your family to heal, to bring all you children back together again. I guess this has something to do with that."

I stare at her as if she's lost her mind. "But she did the exact opposite by leaving me everything and my siblings nothing."

"She didn't leave you everything, sweet girl. She left you a rundown old house. She provided for your father in the trust, which will pass to you four when he dies. Your mama may have been a mess, but she had a method behind her madness. She made her choices with careful consideration. There's a meaning behind each of her gifts."

My head pivots toward her. "So Mama talked to you about her estate?"

"No. But I could tell something was weighing heavily on her mind. Especially these last few years."

I drum my fingers on the chair's arm. "Leaving the house to me makes sense. I'm the architect, and I have the means to fix it up."

"True, but Will is the builder. He also has the means to fix it up."

"But Will doesn't love the house like I do. In fact, there's no place he'd rather *not* be."

We sit for a moment in silence, each of us lost in our thoughts. "I can't start renovating while Dad's living here anyway. I certainly can't kick him out, and he's too frail to withstand the inconvenience of remodeling." I shift in my chair, uncrossing and recrossing my legs. "Will you read her journals?"

"Mm-hmm." May May takes a sip of coffee. "Eventually. When I'm ready. My emotions are still too raw from her death."

"Will you tell me if you find something that makes sense of all this?"

"Perhaps. Depending on what it is. I believe Eileen intended for you to solve this mystery yourselves."

I hear the rumble of an outboard motor and turn to see Will's boat approaching the dock. He parks the boat, raises the lift, and heads back toward the house. When he passes the veranda, he lifts a hand in a wave, but he doesn't speak to us.

"You should talk to your siblings," May May says. "If the three of you put your heads together, you might figure out what your Mama was trying to tell you."

"Ha. The three of us haven't had a cordial discussion about anything since . . ." I furrow my brow. "We've never had one, now that I think about it. At least not during our adult lives. I feel bad for Carrie though. She was hoping to get some of Mama's jewelry. I should give her a few pieces. Maybe even half of it."

May May's head jerks toward me. "I advise you not to make any sudden decisions, Ashton. Not until you've thought things through."

My shoulders slump. "That's good advice. My head is still spinning."

May May pushes herself out of the rocker. "I need to get back to the farm."

I stand slowly with her. "And I need to get to work."

We deposit our coffee cups in the dishwasher as we pass through the house. When we reach the circular driveway, May May says, "I'm here for you, sweetheart. I know this comes as a shock to you."

"My emotions are all over the place. I'm furious at Mama. She knew her will would start a war with our family. Why would she do that to us?"

"Maybe that's what she wanted. You three kids have no relationship. Being at war with one another might force you to talk, which is the first step toward a peace treaty."

CHAPTER **FOUR**

I sit at my office desk for hours, staring out at the swing bridge named after my ancestor—my too-many-greats-to-count grandfather Orville Merriweather. Following Orville had come a long line of upstanding citizens who'd proudly served our town as mayors and state legislators. We even produced a US senator somewhere along the line. But the distinguished list of family members had come to an abrupt halt with my mother. The family had grown smaller over the decades, and Mama had been the only daughter of an only son, bringing the Merriweather lineage to an end. While my mother had been the last to bear the Merriweather name, she'd been the first to tarnish the family's reputation by being a drunk.

Mama's death saddens me, but losing her has released me from the burden of her addiction I've carried all my life. And now she's given me an additional burden to bear. One of guilt from having inherited our family's home. I agree with May May that Mama is sending a message. But none of this makes sense, and I have more questions than answers.

I finally give up on trying to work and return to Marsh Point for the second time today. I arrive to find a yellow taxicab parked in front of the house and the driver, a young man with tatted arms and a full beard, helping my father load his suitcases into the trunk. Dad has shed his frumpy house clothes, and he's wearing a navy sport coat and gray flannel pants. I haven't seen him dressed up since my mother's funeral.

I screech to a halt in the gravel and jump out of the car. "What's going on, Dad? Where are you going?"

"To whisper with the trees," he mumbles.

I don't realize at first that he's talking about the retirement community. "Right. Whispering Oaks. But why? Yesterday you refused to consider moving to Whispering Oaks."

He raises his cane, jabbing it heavenward. "Because your mother has spoken from the grave. The house belongs to you now."

"But I'm not kicking you out. I have no idea what I'll even do with the house. You can stay here as long as you'd like."

"You certainly can't do anything with it while I'm living here. Your mother has ordered me out of the house, and I'm going," he says and taps his way to the taxi's back door, swinging it open.

"Wait, Dad!" I hurry after him, preventing him from getting in the car. "Have you spoken to the administrators? Do they know you're coming? Do they even have room for you?"

"Of course I've spoken to them, Ashton. They have a one-bedroom unit in independent living waiting for me."

"You realize you have to buy into independent living. They don't rent those units by the month."

"I understand. I know what I'm doing." The firm set of his jaw tells me there's no point in arguing with him. Dad usually did what Mama wanted. At least in the later years of their lives.

I expel a deep breath. "If you're sure this is what you want, I'll go with you to help you get settled. But shouldn't you take your car with you so you can get around?" I can't remember the last time I saw him drive. Maybe cruising through town in his beloved 1965 red Mercedes convertible will inspire him to get out more.

Dad brandishes his cane toward the carport. "Ha! That old heap belongs to you now. Besides, it has two flat tires." He falls into the back seat and hauls his legs in after him. He looks up at me with weary eyes. "You can come with me if you'd like. Since my luggage is already in the trunk, you can follow in your own car."

"Perfect! I'll see you there in a few minutes."

As I follow the taxi through town, I consider calling my siblings to inform them of this development. But after what happened this morning with Mom's will, I doubt either of them wants to hear from me. Knowing Carrie, she'll blame me for driving Dad out of his home. Maybe Dad should be the one to tell them.

I've never been to Whispering Oaks, and I'm impressed by the manicured grounds and attractive brick buildings. I find a parking place and hurry to the front entrance, where the taxi driver is unloading Dad's suitcases onto the curb.

"Where's the bellman?" Dad grumbles.

"This isn't a resort, Dad." I motion him to the pile of suitcases. "Stay with your stuff while I find someone to help us."

I enter the attractive main lobby, which features comfortable seating, a saltwater aquarium, and a large screen television. A pleasant-looking, middle-aged woman greets me from behind a marble reception desk. "May I help you?"

"I need to speak with someone in your sales department. My father is under the impression you have an apartment available in independent living."

"Just a minute, please." She picks up a phone, explains the situation to the person on the other end, and hangs up. "Our sales coordinator will be right with you."

A moment later, the sound of high heels on the tile floor precedes the appearance of a striking woman about my age with caramel skin and yellow-green eyes. "I'm Harriet Snyder, director of sales. How may I help you?"

I introduce myself and shake her outstretched hand. "My

father, Ernest Darby, called earlier. He says you're holding a unit for him."

"The name isn't familiar, and I'm the only one in our sales office today." Her eyes drift past me to the window where Dad is now sitting atop one of his suitcases. "Oh. I see he came prepared to move in. I'm afraid we don't work that way. Our process is much like buying a house. There are forms and pricing structures and applications to complete."

"I understand. But for personal reasons, Dad needs to move out of our house right away."

Harriet appears unimpressed. "Everyone has personal issues, Mrs. Nelms."

"I realize that, but my family is going through a difficult time." Tears well in my eyes, and I rub them away with my index fingers, preventing my mascara from running. "My mother, Eileen Merriweather Darby, died a month ago, and Dad's been down in the dumps ever since." Sometimes using my family's illustrious name opens doors. Based on Harriet's nod of recognition, this is one of those times.

"There are ways to expedite the process, assuming he doesn't have any serious medical conditions. I'll need to do an evaluation, of course." She squints as she looks more closely at him. "I see he's using a cane. Is he physically impaired?"

"Not at all. He's using the cane as a crutch, figuratively speaking. He's depressed. He needs companionship and exercise and new hobbies to occupy his time."

"Then he's come to the right place." Harriet turns to the receptionist. "Please have someone from maintenance collect Mr. Darby's luggage and take it to my office."

"Yes, ma'am," the receptionist says, and lifts the phone receiver to her ear.

I follow Harriet outside to the portico, where she introduces herself to my father. "As I explained to your daughter, we typically follow a lengthy process for admitting our residents. In your case, I can help speed things along." She coughs into her hand. "Will you be needing financing?"

Dad fishes his checkbook out of the inside pocket of his sport coat. "No, ma'am. I brought my checkbook. I can stroke you a check for the full amount today."

Harriet chuckles. "Let's see how far we get with the forms. We actually have two units available. One is on the second floor of the main building. We'll tour that unit first," she says and leads us single file through the lobby to a bank of elevators.

Disappointment falls across Dad's face when Harriet opens the door to the one-bedroom apartment. The sparse decor is far from what he's used to at home. The plaid fabric on the matching sofa and recliner have seen better days, and deep scratches mar the wooden surface of the coffee table.

"Can we bring in our own furniture?" I ask, circling the living room.

"Of course. The previous occupant left these things behind. If you decide on this unit, I'll have maintenance remove them for you."

I'm surprised to find a hospital bed in the adjacent bedroom. Dad and I exchange a look, and I can sense his irritation growing. "I would expect a hospital bed in healthcare but not independent living."

"Another leftover from the previous tenant." Harriet hurries us out the door. "I think you'll find the other unit more to your liking."

"Where is that unit located?" I ask on the way down in the elevator.

"Between the main building and our wellness center in one of our newer apartment clusters. Most of our indoor activities take place in our state-of-the-art wellness center."

"Good to know," I say as we pass back through the lobby.

Harriet ushers us to a golf cart parked under the portico. "It's only a short walk, but for the sake of time, we'll take the cart."

The second unit is a drastic improvement over the first with real hardwood floors, leather furniture, and a poster bed. An oversized paned-glass door slides open onto a brick terrace, and beyond the terrace is a small Japanese-style pond with large rocks and waterlilies.

Harriet says, "These units come furnished, but if you prefer to bring in your own items, we'll clear everything out for you."

I nudge Dad's elbow. "What do you think?"

"It's better than the other unit. I'll take it. How much do I owe you?" he says, waving his checkbook at Harriet.

"We'll go through all the expenses while you fill out the paperwork." Harriet starts toward the door. "I need to run back to my office for the forms. Make yourselves at home. I'll be back in a minute. In the meantime, I'll have maintenance bring over your belongings."

After she leaves, I open the sliding door and step out onto the terrace. "You'll like it out here, Dad," I call to him. "It's so peaceful. We'll get a lounge chair for you so you can have coffee in the mornings and nap here in the afternoons."

"I never napped on the porch at home. I don't know why I would start now." He locates the television remote and plops down in the leather chair. "Now this feels like home."

The maintenance man arrives with Dad's luggage, with Harriet right behind him. For the next hour, we fill out applications, go over pricing information and discuss the long list of rules. After doing a brief assessment of Dad's health, Harriet deems him suitable for independent living and leaves us to unpack.

Dad packed nothing but clothes in his suitcases, and I make a mental list of decorative items to make the apartment cozier. I open the refrigerator expecting to find an old bottle of ketchup or jar of olives, but there's not a single item inside. "I'll bring you some groceries tomorrow. Let me know if there's anything special you'd like."

Dad cuts his eyes at me. "Don't bother. I won't be cooking for myself. I'll be eating in the cafeteria."

I'm relieved he's planning to take advantage of the cafeteria. "Still, you might get hungry for a snack. Or you may want a cup of your sleepy time tea before you go to bed at night."

He responds with a grunt.

I glance at my watch. "Gosh. It's already five thirty. Why don't we grab dinner in the cafeteria before I head home?"

"Fine," Dad says, and taps his way over to the door.

Even though the walk to the main building is short, Dad is winded by the time we get there. The exercise will either do him good or deter him from getting his meals.

The dining room reminds me of the grill room at our country club with attractive seniors seated together at four-, six-, and eight-top tables. We locate an empty table alongside the wall of windows overlooking another man-made pond with more Japanese features —a wooden bridge, stone lanterns, and a small waterfall.

When we go to the buffet, Dad serves himself small portions of baked chicken, roasted potatoes, and broccoli while I load up my plate from the extensive offerings on the salad bar.

While we eat, several of Dad's old friends stop by the table to welcome him to Whispering Oaks. He appears uninterested in talking to them and is even borderline rude to his best lifelong friend, Lester Hoffman. "You won't last long in this place without your friends," I scold.

I get up from the table and hurry after Dr. Hoffman. "I'm sorry Dad was so rude. He's having a difficult time."

Dr. Hoffman pats my arm and speaks to me in the calm bedside manner he once used as our family physician. "We all go through an adjustment when we first come to Whispering Oaks. But there's so much to do here. I'll make certain he doesn't sit around and mope."

"Are you still playing golf?" I ask, thinking back to the late nineties when Dad and Dr. Hoffman were club champions for several years in a row.

"Three days a week." He smiles softly at me. "Don't you worry, Ashton. I'll have your father back out on the golf course in no time."

Relief washes over me. "That would be great. Thank you."

I return to our table, and while we finish eating, I blabber on about Dr. Hoffman and golf. Dad appears to be listening, although he says nothing in response.

After dinner, I accompany Dad back to his apartment and help him into his pajamas. He settles himself in the leather chair and clicks on the television.

Hesitant to leave him alone, I lower myself to the sofa. "What am I supposed to do with the house, Dad?"

He waves the TV remote at me. "Renovate it. Tear it down. Sell it. It's yours now. Do whatever you want with it."

"You're so sure about what Mama wanted for you. You must have some idea what she wanted me to do with the house."

"I don't have a clue, Ashton," he says in a definitive tone. "Her message to me was crystal clear. Move out of the house. She very much wanted me to get on with my life, and she knew I would need a push. But the meaning behind the rest of her gifts is beyond me."

"Do you think she left me the house because I'm the oldest?"

Dad shrugs. "Or the one who cares the most about Marsh Point. And the one who cared the most about her. On the other hand, Eileen always insisted on treating each of you equally. To leave Carrie and Will virtually nothing makes no sense. Despite all her problems, your mother never did anything without a reason. I fear the three of you will never discover what those reasons are."

I shiver as cold dread descends upon me. That is my biggest fear as well.

I rise slowly from the sofa and kiss the top of his head. "I'll bring you those groceries tomorrow. Text me if you think of anything else you need."

I let myself out, locking the door behind me. On the way to the parking lot, I stroll through a walking path lined with tropical greenery. I feel bad leaving Dad here, but in my heart, I know this is where he belongs.

CHAPTER
FIVE

Owen is waiting for me when I arrive home from Whispering Oaks. "Where on earth have you been all day?"

"Getting Dad settled at Whispering Oaks. Give me a minute, and I'll tell you about it." I peck him on the cheek and go down the hall to the walk-in closet in our bedroom. Punching in the combination, I open the small safe where Owen keeps our passports, birth certificates, and a stack of cash in case of emergencies.

I've been guarding my purse with the suede jewelry bag since this morning, and I'm relieved to store it in a safe place. But the suede bag is too big for the small safe, preventing me from closing the door.

Owen appears behind me in the doorway. "What's that?"

"Jewelry," I say, brushing past him as I leave the closet for the bedroom. I dump the contents onto our king-size bed. Velvet boxes in various shapes and sizes tumble out, along with other loose trinkets.

Owen's deep blue eyes are wide as he approaches the bed. "Whoa. Where'd you get all this? Did you find a pirate's treasure chest?"

"Ha ha. Believe it or not, this is my family's heirloom jewelry.

Mama left it to me." I give the bag a final shake and out falls a stack of index cards, yellowed with age and tied with a frayed pink satin ribbon. "These cards tell the history of each piece, which ancestor the piece belonged to and who gave it to that ancestor for what occasion."

"Cool!" Owen says, reaching for the box nearest him.

I lower myself to the edge of the bed as my mind slips back in time. I'm in a different bedroom with bouquets of pink roses on the wallpaper and pink shag carpet on the floor. My sisters and I sit in a row on the edge of Mama's mahogany rice bed while she tutors us on the history of the family jewels—rubies and sapphires and emeralds set in necklaces and bracelets and rings worn by generations of Merriweather women.

Owen's voice brings me back to the present. "Who did these belong to?" he asks about a choker made of three strands of gray Mikimoto pearls.

I flipped through the cards until I find the right one. "According to this, my grandfather gave it to my mother when she made her debut."

Owen snaps the pearl box shut and opens a ring box, gasping at the sight of the twenty-four-carat fancy intense pink diamond.

His reaction surprises me. He's never cared much about jewerly. "Isn't it gorgeous? Fancy intense pink diamonds are extremely rare and highly sought after." I don't have to look at the card to know the ring's history. "My grandfather bought it for my grandmother during a trip to Australia, where the Argyle diamond mine is located. The mine is now closed, but they produced a significant portion of the world's pink diamonds."

Owen removes the ring and holds it up to the light. "Is this the most valuable piece in the collection?"

"That, and this." I open a green velvet box and show him the stunning necklace—three strands of diamonds culminating in a sapphire pendant weighing over three hundred carats.

"That looks like something royalty would wear."

I finger the sapphire. "I know, right? Some of these pieces are of that caliber."

"How much is this stuff worth?"

I roll my eyes. Everything is always about money for my husband. "You can't put a value on these jewels, Owen."

I gather up all the boxes and carefully arrange them in the safe until everything fits.

Owen's breath is hot on the back of my neck as he watches me. "You're not seriously going to wear that gaudy stuff, are you? Why not sell the collection? You'd have to go through an auction house to get top dollar, but I bet the collection is worth millions."

"No way. The memories are as priceless as the jewels. I will give it to my sister before I sell it." I close the safe door and make certain it's locked. "This safe isn't ideal, but it'll have to do until I figure something else out."

"Where did your mom keep it at Marsh Point?"

I laugh. "In her top dresser drawer."

Owen checks to make sure the safe is locked. "It'll be fine here. Although you should probably get it appraised. We have homeowner's insurance if anything were to happen."

I expel a puff of air, blowing my bangs off my forehead. "What a day? I need a glass of wine."

Owen follows me into the kitchen. "Why did your dad move to Whispering Oaks? Didn't your mom leave Marsh Point to him?"

Removing the cork from the open bottle of red wine, I give myself a healthy pour and take a sip before answering him. "I still can't believe it, but she left Marsh Point to me."

Owen's jaw drops to the floor. "You mean, alone? You don't have to share with your siblings?"

"Nope. Just me. My brother and sisters received token gifts. I was the big lottery winner today. Aside from Dad, who inherited her stock portfolio."

Owen falls back against the kitchen counter. "Wow. You *did* just win the lottery. The real estate market is hot right now. You'll make a fortune when you sell it."

I freeze, with my glass pressed against my lips. *Sell Marsh Point? Has he lost his mind?* I lower the glass and set it on the counter. "Why on earth would I sell my family's home?"

"Why would you keep it? We're certainly not moving there."

His unwavering tone makes my blood boil. I made the mistake of letting him talk me into selling my beloved beach house. I will not make the same mistake twice. "Because the property has belonged to my family for over a century. And because I'd rather live in a beautiful old home on the Catawba Sound than in a condo on the golf course."

"*Old* is the operative word here. Marsh Point is in shambles. There isn't a single modern convenience in that house, not even the Internet."

"We have Internet. But I agree the place needs remodeling. Good thing I'm an architect, and my brother is a builder."

Owen retrieves a beer from the refrigerator. "Speaking of your brother, how's he handling getting cut out of the will?"

"He didn't get cut out completely. Mom left him his boat slip on the dock." I open the french door and step out onto the terrace. Owen is right on my heels. I can't remember the last time he paid me this much attention.

"Sell the house, Ashton. Save yourself the headache of renovating. You could double, maybe even triple, your money by investing it in the market."

"I will carefully consider *all* my options, Owen." I don't tell him that selling the house isn't one of them. "I admit it hardly seems fair for me to get the house and the jewelry while my siblings got nothing."

"You're right. It's not fair to them. All the more reason to sell it and divvy up the proceeds," he says in an eager tone.

"Enough, Owen. I will come up with the right solution for my siblings and me."

"You're tired. We'll talk more about this later." He gives my arm a squeeze. "Have you eaten anything? I could make us some dinner."

I soften toward him. Why am I being so difficult when he's only trying to help? "I ate with Dad at Whispering Oaks. I need some time alone to think about everything that happened today."

"Of course you do. I'll give you some space. If you don't mind, I'll grab a bite with Rich at the club."

"I don't mind at all. Enjoy yourself," I say, stretching out on the chaise lounge. "I'll probably be right here when you get back."

Owen disappears inside, and I'm silently cursing at him for leaving the door open when he reappears with the bottle of wine. "Here. You might need this."

I take the bottle from him. "Thanks, sweetheart."

Owen may not be the perfect husband, but he has his moments. Plus, he's a financial genius. Will and I made a fortune developing Mariner's Point, and Owen invested the money in the stock market. I haven't seen a statement lately, but from what he tells me, that money has grown considerably.

He's right though. I stand to make millions by selling the house and investing the proceeds. Problem is, I don't feel like the house is mine to sell. Maybe once this new reality has sunk in, that will change. But for now, whatever decision I make must be in the best interest of both my family and the property.

I close my eyes and daydream about the changes I'll make to Marsh Point. Replacing the siding. Upgrading all the systems. Updating all the baths and kitchen. Windows overlooking the new pool and terrace. Properly renovating means taking the interior walls down to the studs. I'll have to cash in on some of my investments for the construction. Owen will pitch a fit over paying capital gains taxes. But I've been saving the money for a rainy day, and that day has come.

The house has too many maintenance issues to postpone the

renovations. First thing in the morning, I'll start work on the plans.

After another glass of wine, I doze off and sleep past ten o'clock. I'm rinsing out my wineglass in the sink when I notice Owen's car parked in the small driveway out front. I turn out all the lights and go down the hall. When I enter our bedroom, I hear a noise inside our darkened closet.

I call out, "Owen? Is that you?"

He emerges from the closet with his pajamas in hand. "I was looking for these."

"Why didn't you tell me you were home? Were you going to let me sleep on the patio all night?"

"Of course not. But you were so peaceful. I was letting you sleep a few more minutes while I got ready for bed."

Owen is speaking to me in a loving tone, but he has guilt written all over his face. What was he really doing in the closet?

CHAPTER
SIX

When I wake with a start before dawn on Tuesday morning, the events of the previous day come spiraling back. Marsh Point now belongs to me. Dad has moved to Whispering Oaks. And I need to get the family jewels out of our safe immediately.

I tiptoe around the room as I dress for work and empty the contents of the safe into the cream-colored velvet bag. Arriving at the office before my staff, I take advantage of the peace to focus on my to-do list. I return emails and address several issues with client projects before turning my attention to Marsh Point.

I have three options to explore. Renovate the house and live in it. Renovate and then sell. Or sell as is. I'm still not keen on the idea of putting the house on the market, but in order to make the right decision, I must consider all the options.

After years of contemplating the restoration, putting my ideas on paper comes easily. I have an idea of how much the project will cost. If what Owen tells me about my investments is true, I can easily afford to remodel. Although I need to see the statement of my brokerage account to be sure.

I eat a protein bar for lunch at my desk and work straight

through until my alarm sounds at two o'clock. While my rudimentary blueprints are printing, I spend a few minutes with my administrative assistant before heading out to Marsh Point to meet with Sadie, my friend whose husband is taking her to Italy for her fiftieth. Sadie is our town's top real estate agent. There is no one else I would trust with selling or buying a house.

When I arrive, Sadie is leaning against her sleek Range Rover in the driveway, twirling one of her blonde curls as she talks on her cell phone. She's professionally stylish in a chic khaki sheath dress and stylish leopard-skin wedges.

Noticing me, Sadie ends the call, slips the phone into her purse, and walks over to my car to greet me.

"Thanks for meeting me on such short notice," I say, unfolding myself from my convertible.

"Of course. Your email surprised me though. Are you seriously considering selling Marsh Point?"

"There's a slim chance." I raise my hand to show a tiny space between my pointer finger and thumb. "I mainly want to pick your brain about the possibility. I know I can count on you to give me honest feedback."

Sadie flashes a smile. "You know me. I will always give it to you straight."

I laugh. Sadie has always been brutally honest about everything. In high school, we knew better than to let her in on our secrets for fear she might rat us out to our parents.

"Come on in." I unlock the front door and step out of the way for her to enter.

The grand sweeping staircase immediately captures Sadie's attention. "Whoa. I haven't been in this house in ages. I'd forgotten how beautiful the place is."

"Beautiful but needs a lot of work." As we walk through the house together, I tell her about the upgrades I will make if I proceed with construction.

My brief tour lands us on the veranda outside the primary bedroom on the second floor.

Sadie stands at the railing, staring out across the marsh. "Hands down, you have the best view in town. Why would you ever think about selling?"

I join her at the railing. "I hope it doesn't come to that, but I have to consider all my options. *If* I decide to put it on the market, am I better off listing it as is or should I renovate first?"

"Good question. The market is insane right now, Ashton. People are moving here from the north in droves. They have deep pockets, and they will fight over a property like this. Most people, especially the younger generation, don't want the hassle of renovating. I can't assure you'll get your money back, but I feel confident you will, many times over."

"To what degree do I renovate? Are we talking Botox or a major facelift?"

Sadie giggles at my analogy. "That's up to you. If it were my house, I would proceed as though I was planning to live here myself. With a property of this magnitude, potential buyers will expect top-quality everything." Pushing off the railing, she walks over to the house and rips off a piece of peeling paint. "Bare minimum, I would paint."

"Bare minimum, I will replace the termite-infested siding with HardiePlank."

"Even better." Sadie turns back toward me. "Look at it this way. The time spent renovating will delay your decision about putting it on the market."

"Good point. Although my plans are borderline lavish. Not the same remodeling I would do for a potential buyer."

Sadie shrugs. "Then you'll have to find a happy medium, I guess. I hope you'll keep me in mind if you decide to put it on the market."

"Absolutely!"

As we retrace our steps back through the house, we talk about a potential listing price. The staggering amount shocks me. I didn't realize property values had skyrocketed so. Even if I shared the proceeds with my siblings, there would be enough money to affect all our lives.

After seeing Sadie to her car, I load up a cooler and shopping bags with food from the kitchen and drive out to Whispering Oaks. I'm discouraged to find Dad the same as I left him last night, wearing his pajamas and watching television in the leather chair in the darkened sitting room.

I peek in the bedroom at the neatly made bed. "Dad, please tell me you didn't sleep in that chair."

"Yep." He strokes the chair's arms. "She's mighty comfortable. More so than my bed at home."

I go over to the window and open the sheer curtains, letting in the afternoon sun. "Have you eaten anything today?"

"Nope. But dinner's soon."

"Dinner is still hours away."

I go to the kitchen to unload his groceries and return with a banana. "Here. Eat this." I trade him the banana for the remote and turn off the television. "When you finish, I want you to get dressed, and we're going to take a walk before dinner."

Dad grumbles, but he doesn't argue.

Stuffing the banana in his mouth, he rises from his chair and disappears into his bedroom. When he comes out a few minutes later, he's wearing the same gray flannel pants and white dress shirt he wore yesterday.

"You have a stain on your shirt," I say, pointing to the brown spot. "Let's find you some clean clothes."

Leading him back into the bedroom, I locate a pressed pair of khaki pants and a plaid button-down shirt. "You can't hide at Whispering Oaks like you did at home, and you need to be presentable when you see your friends."

"Why can't I hide? No one's going to make me see people if I don't want to."

My frustration is mounting. I was sure moving him to the retirement community would inspire him to reconnect with old friends, maybe even make some new ones.

As we stroll around the small pond outside his apartment, I say, "Dad, you need to take better care of yourself. If you don't, I'll have to hire a home nurse to stay with you."

"I don't need a babysitter, Ashton. I can take care of myself just fine."

"Then stop acting like an invalid. There's nothing physically wrong with you. The burden of nursing mom is gone. Enjoy life for a change."

He doesn't respond, but his pinched face lets me know I hit a nerve.

When we arrive back at his apartment, I suggest, "Why don't we go check out the wellness center? According to Harriet, that's where most of the activities take place. You might even find a poker game," I say with a mischievous grin. In his younger days, Dad belonged to a poker group that met on the first Tuesday of every month.

He shakes his head. "I'm tired. I need to rest before dinner."

I decide not to push him. *Baby steps.* "Do you want me to stay for dinner?" I have two important stops to make before going home, but if it means making sure Dad eats, I'll take the time to go to the cafeteria with him.

"No, sweetheart. You run along. I'll be fine," he says, eager to get rid of me.

I'm reluctant to leave him, but I need to hurry in order to make it to the bank before they close. "Okay. I'll check in with you later." I wag my finger at him. "And I expect to hear all about what you ate for dinner and who sat at your table."

He rubs his soft belly. "Don't worry. I'm getting hungry. I promise I'll eat."

Pecking his cheek goodbye, I racewalk back to my car and drive as fast as I dare back to town.

Delbert Lewis has managed the downtown branch of Palmetto Bank for as long as I can remember. He helped me open my first savings account when I was a young child. When I enter the bank's lobby, he emerges from his corner office to greet me. "Ashton, how lovely to see you."

I take his outstretched hand. "You're looking as young and fit as ever," I say to the seventy-year-old man. "I thought you would've retired by now."

His blue eyes twinkle beneath bushy gray eyebrows. "Next year. The missus and I are planning an around-the-world sailing trip."

"Good for you! You deserve a grand adventure after decades of exemplary service to your clients."

His eyes cloud over. "I've enjoyed every minute. Are you here to see the teller? Or can I help you with something?"

"I'd like to rent a safe deposit box. Do you have any available?"

"We have plenty. In all sizes. I'll show you," he says and leads me through the lobby and into the vault to a room lined with safe deposit boxes. "Do you have an idea what size you'll need?"

I set my purse on the table in the center of the room and remove the velvet bag. "I need one big enough for this."

He lifts the bag and quickly sets it back down. "Mercy. Do you have solid gold bars in there?" He chuckles. "I'm only joking. You don't have to answer that."

I laugh. "I don't mind. It's Mom's jewelry collection, actually." I remove the velvet boxes and stack them on the table. "There. That should help us determine how much room I need."

"Indeed." Mr. Lewis opens and closes several drawers before settling on the right size. "This should work. Would you like some privacy?"

"That's not necessary. I'm just going to stack everything inside."

"In that case, I'll help you."

Together, we organize the velvet boxes in the drawer. I leave the loose pieces of jewelry in the suede bag, tucking the bag inside the drawer with the boxes.

Mr. Lewis locks the box and hands me the key. "Now I just need you to fill out some paperwork, and you'll be on your way."

I follow him back to his office, sitting down opposite him at his desk. He locates the form and slides the paper and a pen across the desk to me.

"Your husband is certainly a busy man these days," Mr. Lewis says casually, as though making polite conversation.

My ears perk up. "Oh really? How so?"

The banker appears flustered. "He's been moving a lot of money around. Perhaps I shouldn't have said anything."

No, he definitely should not have. But he's piqued my curiosity. "Do you keep such close tabs on all your clients, Mr. Lewis?"

"Only the ones with large wire transfers."

My skin prickles. *Why would Owen be making wire transfers?*

I lower my head as I complete the form. "As you can see, I'm renting the safe deposit box in my name only," I say, sliding the form back across the desk to him. "I'd like for you to draw the fee from my personal account. I don't want my husband to know about it, and under no circumstance is he to have access."

"Yes, ma'am. I understand completely."

I feel Mr. Lewis's eyes boring a hole in my back as I exit his office. I have a sneaking suspicion he just let slip something my husband does not want me to know. An uneasy feeling settles over me as I leave the bank. To whom would Owen be wiring money? And why?

CHAPTER **SEVEN**

My brother lives across the golf course from me on a street lined with cookie-cutter, pastel-colored lowcountry-style houses. I designed the homes, and Will built them. They are charming as far as new construction is concerned. But like me, Will prefers old homes. Why he doesn't live in the historic section of town is beyond me.

I bang on the knocker, and my sister-in-law's muffled voice sounds from within. "Come in! The door's open."

I enter the house and followed the voices down the hall to the kitchen where Tracy is tending a boiling pot on the stove while her two- and four-year-old daughters run circles around her. When they notice me standing in the doorway, Caroline and Sophia rush over to their mother, placing their bodies between Tracy and the stove. It saddens me I'm a stranger to them.

Tracy smiles at me. "Hey, Ashton. This is a pleasant surprise."

"I can see you have your hands full. I'll come back another time," I say, backing out of the room.

"No! Please, stay! I haven't seen you in ages." She's always so perky, the cheerleader type. "Besides, I have something for you, a late birthday gift." She dumps the pot of steaming noodles in a colander in the sink. "Do you have time for a glass of wine?"

My heart warms. Tracy is more stranger than sister-in-law, but she's the only one in my family who remembered my birthday. "But your dinner's ready," I say, nodding at the noodles.

"The girls have already eaten. Will and I will eat later. Will!" she calls out to her husband. "It's time for the girls' bath."

The squeak of Will's running shoes on hardwood floors precedes my brother's appearance in the kitchen. His face falls when he sees me. "Ashton. What're you doing here?"

"I need to talk to you about a potential project," I say, removing the cardboard tube containing the construction plans from my tote bag.

"You can talk about your project later. Ashton and I are going to have a glass a wine while you give the girls a bath. Come on, girls! Go with Daddy," Tracy says, giving her daughters a gentle push toward their father.

"Yay! Bath time!" the girls cry out in unison. Taking their father by the hand, they lead Will out of the kitchen.

From the hallway, one of the girl's voices rings out. "Can we have lots of bubbles tonight, Daddy?"

"I suppose so," Will responds with little enthusiasm.

I chuckle. "I'm impressed. Will doesn't strike me as a hands-on type of dad."

"He's a work in progress. Getting him to spend time with them is a challenge. He's uneasy around them, like he's afraid he'll break them. You'd think he'd feel comfortable around girls having had three older sisters."

"Remember, he was ten years younger than me, and six years younger than Savannah. Besides, he's such a man's man. Do you think you'll have more children?"

"Will is ready to try for number three. He refuses to give up hope of having a son. I don't know if I have the energy for another child. Will forgets I have a full-time job. He doesn't view owning a lady's boutique as real work." Tracy removes a bottle of salmon-colored wine from the refrigerator. "Is rosé okay?"

"Sure. Whatever you have open."

Tracy fills two stemless glasses, handing one to me. "Let's go outside to the porch." She grabs a gift-wrapped package in the shape of a book off the island and leads me outside to the rockers on their screened porch. "Here! This is for you."

I take the gift from her. "I'm flattered, Tracy. You didn't have to do this." But I'm glad she did. This is the only birthday present I received.

"I thought of you when I saw it. Open it! You'll understand."

Setting my wineglass on the chair's arm, I carefully remove the Scotch tape from the package. Beneath the colorful paper is a coffee-table book featuring my favorite architect. Robert Mills was a South Carolinian famous for designing buildings and homes in the pre-Civil War South, as well as the Washington Monument.

"I hope you like it. I thought of you when I saw it in the used bookstore. I know how much you admire Mills's work."

I hug the book to my chest. "I love it. Thank you." I don't tell her I have a copy signed by the author on the shelves in my office.

She blushes. "You're welcome. Did you do anything special for your fiftieth?"

I place the book in my lap and lift my wineglass. "I did, actually. Hattie threw an elaborate party for me," I say, a grin tugging at my lips as I sip my wine.

It takes Tracy a minute to understand my joke. "Oh! The wedding. Ha ha. That was nice of Hattie. Bummer, I couldn't go. My babysitter canceled at the last minute."

"I was wondering where you were. I saw Will from afar, but I didn't get a chance to speak to him."

Tracy glances at the door. "Speaking of Will, there's something I want to talk to you about before he comes back. I'm sure you're aware he keeps his emotions locked inside. I'm trying to get him to open up about the past, but it isn't easy when the subject of your family is strictly off-limits. He seems so lost and unhappy." She looks away from me into the small backyard. "And angry. I sense something bad happened to him when he was young. It would really help if I knew what it was."

I hesitate as I consider how to respond. "I'm sorry, Tracy. It's not my place to tell you about that. Mom's alcoholism made our lives difficult. Has he seen a therapist?"

Tracy shakes her pretty blonde head. "I've suggested it, but he refuses."

Will clears his throat from the doorway. "Tracy, the girls are ready for their bedtime story now."

I wonder how long my brother had been standing there and how much he'd heard.

Tracy gets to her feet. "Duty calls. Thanks for stopping by."

I run my hand over the book's cover. "Thank you for the gift. It was incredibly thoughtful of you."

Tracy kisses her husband's lips before leaving the porch.

Will leaves the doorway, but instead of taking his wife's vacated seat, he leans against the porch railing. "This must be some project if it can't wait until tomorrow," he says with a note of irritation.

"The project can wait, if you'd rather set up a meeting for tomorrow. I mainly stopped by to tell you Dad has moved to Whispering Oaks. I thought you'd want to know."

"Really? When?"

"Yesterday afternoon. When I went back to Marsh Point to check on him, he was loading his belongings into a taxi. I went with him to Whispering Oaks and helped him get settled. He has a nice one-bedroom apartment overlooking a small pond. I'm worried about him though. He seems to have lost his will to live. I gave him a gentle nudge today. I told him we would have to hire a nurse if he didn't take better care of himself."

"Text me his apartment number, and I'll stop by to see him tomorrow," Will says, his face and tone impassive. My brother is a man of few words and little emotion. What Tracy says is true. *He seems so lost and unhappy. And angry.* He's been like that as long as I can remember. At least most of his adult life. I miss the chubby little boy who so loved to play with his construction trucks in the sandbox.

"Well, while you're here, we might as well discuss your project."

"That would be great." I slide the plans out of the tube and hand them to him. "I'm considering renovating Marsh Point."

"You didn't waste any time," he says, lowering himself to the chair next to me as he unrolls the plans.

"I'm an architect. I've been pondering this makeover for years." I lean in close as we look at the plans together. "The house has excellent bones, good flow, and expansive rooms. We'll take it down to the studs and replace all the systems. We'll work within the existing floor plan. I see no reason to blow out any walls except this outside kitchen wall here." I run my finger along the line representing the wall on the plan. "Which I'll replace with floor-to-ceiling windows."

Will looks up at me. "You're putting in a pool?"

"A small one. And a patio off the kitchen. But probably not right away. When the time comes, I'll use the Pittman brothers for those projects," I say about the local patio and pool contractors we typically work with.

"What about the guesthouse?" Will asks about the ancient two-story structure at the edge of the property on the other side of where the pool will be.

"I'll worry about that down the road." I sit back in my chair. "I know you're probably swamped. Any chance you can fit me in?" This will be a large project for Will. There's zero chance he'll turn it down.

"I'm finishing up a couple of projects. We'll make it work if you decide to move forward."

"Are you sure you want to do this? I know how uncomfortable

that old house makes you," I say in a lighthearted tone so as not to offend him.

"I'm a professional, Ashton. I can handle it." Will rolls up the plans and slides them back into the tube.

"Maybe the process will be therapeutic in helping you face the past."

"Why would I face the past when I spend every day of my life running from it?" Standing abruptly, Will drops the cardboard tube on the small dining table before leaving the porch.

I'm not sure whether he's dismissing me, or he expects me to follow him. Grabbing my tote bag, I step outside to the brick patio. "I guess I'll be going. Thanks for agreeing to do the restoration."

"Sure. Give me a couple of days to get some pricing together." Will turns on the spigot and begins watering their colorful container annuals. "So what does Owen think about moving to Marsh Point?"

"He's not thrilled. You know how much he loves living on the golf course." I finger the petals of a pink Knock Out rose. "I haven't decided yet, but I may sell Marsh Point. I met with Sadie earlier today. She advised me to fix up the house in order to bring a higher price. I'll get the work done and then decide. The dock goes with the house though. I'll have to buy you out."

"That's no big deal. I can easily keep the boat at the marina." He pinches off a dead rose bloom. "But why would you sell it? I thought you loved Marsh Point," he says as he adjusts his stream of water.

"I do. But the property belongs to our family. I don't know what Mom was thinking when she left it to me."

"She *wasn't* thinking. The booze pickled her brain." He moves the hose to the next container. "Fair warning. Carrie is threatening to contest the will. She tried to enlist my support, but I want no part of her scheme."

"Whoa. I knew Carrie was angry, but contesting the will seems extreme. I'm surprised you're not upset too."

"That house has nothing but bad memories for me."

"All the more reason for me to sell it and divide the proceeds four ways."

"Four ways? What will you do with Savannah's money? Stuff it in a bottle, toss it off the dock, and hope she gets it?"

"Funny. I'll invest it for her until she comes home."

Will gives me a long hard stare. "You're delusional, Ashton." He turns his back on me and enters the house.

"Wait up, Will," I say, following him inside to the center hallway. "You can't say something like that and walk away. Why am I delusional? Because I refuse to give up on our sister?"

"Savannah is never coming back. You need to accept that."

"You're wrong. I believe in my heart she will one day," I say, slapping my hand on my chest.

His penetrating blue eyes make me squirm. "You don't get it, because you were Mom's favorite. Her pet. You don't know what the rest of us went through."

"What *you* went through? How dare you say that to me? I gave up everything to take care of you three."

Sadness fills his face in a rare display of emotion. "You did when we were little. And then you went away and left us alone in that house of horrors."

"But Dad was back in the picture by then."

"What a joke. Dad couldn't control her. He was an enabler. He did every single thing she asked of him, no matter whether it was right or wrong. If you'd stayed, our lives would've been so much better."

I'm at a loss for what to say, and when I finally open my mouth to defend myself, my voice is too tight to speak. I have no excuse for abandoning my siblings.

CHAPTER **EIGHT**

I've driven by my sister's sweet, little yellow house dozens of times, but she's never invited me inside. I have no right to complain, though, since I've never invited her to my house either. The Darbys don't celebrate major holidays together like most families. Truth be told, I can't remember the last time we even shared a meal together, Mom's funeral reception notwithstanding.

Parking on the curb behind Carrie's old-model Volvo station wagon, I retrieve a cardboard box from my trunk and stroll up the uneven brick sidewalk. I admire her potted pink geraniums as I approach the wide front porch. I push the doorbell button, but when it doesn't ring inside, I clang the shiny brass knocker.

My sister comes to the door, her face registering surprise when she sees me. From somewhere within the house, a voice calls out, "Mom! Who is it?"

I assume the voice belongs to my niece. Sarah is a rising high school senior, but like my other nieces, Will's daughters, I barely know her. I had a pleasant conversation with her at my mother's funeral, but I doubt she'd recognize me if we passed on the street.

"Nobody, sweetheart. Just someone selling magazine subscriptions," Carrie yells over her shoulder before stepping out onto the porch, pulling the door shut behind her.

She's dressed for an afternoon at the country club in a Lily Pulitzer skirt and white sleeveless blouse with perfect makeup and honey hair pulled back in a ponytail. Does she belong to the club? I'm ashamed to say, I don't even know.

"A magazine salesperson? Really, Carrie? No one has come to my door selling magazine subscriptions since before the pandemic. Does anyone even read magazines anymore?"

Carrie gives me a death glare. "Why are you here, Ashton?"

Why *am* I here? I've asked myself that question a dozen times. To test the waters maybe. To see how upset she really is about our mother's will.

"I brought you the silver service." I hold up the cardboard box. "Everything is inside—coffeepot, teapot, creamer, and sugar bowl —all carefully wrapped in silver cloth."

"Just put it there." She points to an out-of-the-way spot on the gray-painted porch floor.

I gently set down the box and straighten, smoothing the fabric on my khaki work skirt. "Did you know Dad's moved to Whispering Oaks?"

My sister's face remains blank, but I can tell this is news to her.

"I'll text you his apartment number. I'm sure he would appreciate a visit."

"Why are you really here, Ashton? Are you hoping I'll forgive you for tearing our family apart?"

My head rears back. "What? No! How can you blame me? I didn't write Mom's will, Carrie."

"You may not have written it, but I'm pretty sure you coerced her into leaving you the house and the rest of us nothing. You always were her little lapdog, always cozying up to her and pushing the rest of us to the side."

I think about what Will called me yesterday. *Mom's pet*. Is this what my siblings think of me? What they call me behind my back?

A spark of anger quickly becomes a flame. "I never aspired to be her favorite, Carrie. But I was a dutiful daughter. Which is more than I can say for you. How often did you visit Mama when she was ill?"

Carrie refuses to meet my gaze. "I visited her."

"Are you sure? Because I was there every single day, and I never once saw you."

"She didn't need us. She had round-the-clock nurses taking care of her. Besides, she was in la-la land. She didn't know what was going on. But when we were young, you and Mama were always locked away in her room together. What were you two doing up there, playing dress-up?"

"I was cleaning up her vomit and force-feeding her Saltine crackers. I was protecting *you* from the unpleasantness of her addiction."

"Right. And just like that, you were gone," Carrie says, snapping her fingers. "You left a hole in our lives the size of a crater. You got away, but the rest of us were stuck dealing with her puke and drunken outrages."

My anger is now a full-on blaze. I need to leave before I say something I might regret. "There's no reasoning with you," I say and start down the sidewalk.

Carrie's voice chases me to my car. "I'm contesting the will. I've already consulted an attorney. She'll be in touch soon."

I start my engine and speed off. Tears blur my vision as I drive through town, and by the time I pass through the cemetery gates, I'm ugly crying. Parking the car, I walk the short distance to our family's gravesite. A wrought-iron fence surrounds the sprawling plot that houses the graves of my ancestors dating back generations. An imposing headstone bears the Merriweather name. My mother's fresh grave is to the right of her father. The sight of her death date on the recently installed footstone brings me to my knees.

"I'm sorry, Mama," I sob. "I didn't mean to abandon y'all. But

I had to get away, to start my life. I never would've left if I'd known things would be so bad. Carrie and Savannah were older. I figured they could take care of Will."

A voice startles me. "Your sisters weren't as strong as you."

I look up to find May May standing over me with a bouquet of pink zinnias.

"The first of the season," she says, nodding toward the flowers. Kneeling down beside me, she places the bouquet on the mound of fresh grass under which my mother's decomposing body lies in a mahogany casket.

"They're beautiful," I say, wiping snot from my nose with the back of my hand.

May May sits down on her bottom and pulls me close. "Talk to me, sweet girl. What happened today that upset you so?"

I tell her about my confrontation with Carrie. "It's all my fault. Things would've been different if I'd stayed. Carrie would've gone to college like she always dreamed of. Will would not have gotten in trouble, and Savannah would not have run away."

"That's hogwash, Ashton! You may have been the glue that held your family together for all those years, but you are not a miracle worker. Savannah made her own mess. Kids make poor decisions, which lead to stupid mistakes. Even kids with perfect parents get into trouble."

"Do you think I could've gotten Mama to quit drinking if I'd stayed?"

"Nope. She tried. She couldn't do it. She didn't love herself enough."

"You mean, she didn't love *us* enough," I mutter.

"That's not true. She loved you children more than life itself." May May strokes my hair. "You were just a child, and your parents burdened you with their responsibilities and problems. We all made dreadful mistakes back then, mistakes we would take back if we could live our lives over."

"Seriously, May May? I've never known *you* to make a mistake."

"You've always put me on a pedestal. But I don't deserve your adoration. I'm human, just like everyone else. Your mama was sick. We can legitimately blame her illness for her mistakes, but your father has no excuse."

"Why are you always so hard on Dad?" I ask, having often wondered what had happened to cause the rift between her and my father.

May May hesitates, and I think she's going to confide in me, but then she says, "That's a story for another time." She kisses the top of my head. "You did the right thing in going off to college. If you want a scapegoat, blame me. I'm the one who insisted you apply to the schools with the best architectural programs."

I rest my head on her shoulder. "Because you were the only one with my best intentions at heart. But no one intended for me to stay in Boston after I got my degrees."

"You found a new life for yourself. That's what young people do."

I think back to those miserable years. "Some life. I yearned for warmer winters and our charming southern ways. I stayed away, because I knew if I returned, Mama's addiction would suck the life out of me."

"Which it did."

"Not really. By the time I finally returned, her drinking had mellowed. I had ten good years here before her health declined."

May May and I help each other up and brush each other off.

She fishes a tissue out of her fanny pack. "Feeling better?"

I blow my nose. "A little. I'm still so confused about why Mama left me the house. After what just happened with Carrie, I don't feel obligated to give her a dime. But I have to be fair to my siblings. Otherwise I won't be able to sleep at night. And the only way to do that is to sell Marsh Point and divide the proceeds among the four of us."

Her eyes widen. "No, Ashton! You can't sell it. That's not what your mama wanted."

"How do you know? Did she say that in her journals?"

She shakes her head. "I've had neither the time nor the right frame of mind to read them. Even so, I don't think your mama intended for you to sell the house. She desperately wanted to keep Marsh Point in the family. She couldn't very well leave one house to four children, so she gave it to you, because she knew you'd make things right."

"But how?" I ask in a bewildered tone.

"I don't know. That's for you to figure out. You can start by fixing it up."

"I've drawn up my plans, and Will is working up his proposal."

"Good! That's a start." Her smile fades. "I don't envy you having to go through the contents of that house. No telling what you might find."

"Maybe some answers to my many questions."

"Maybe." May May kisses her fingertips and touches them to Mama's footstone. "Sleep well, my old friend." Taking me by the hand, we turn back toward our cars.

"Carrie is threatening to contest the will."

"Let her. No judge in this county would go against Eileen Merriweather's last wishes. Especially if restoration construction on Marsh Point is already underway."

"That's a valid point." When we reach our cars, I turn toward her, drawing her in for a hug. "I'm glad I ran into you, May May. I always feel better after talking to you."

"Any time, sweet girl," she says, rubbing my back. "Your mama loved you very much. I know you'll make her proud."

I feel pounds lighter as I drive out of the cemetery behind May May's beat-up red pickup truck. I don't have all the answers, but at least I have some direction. I'll sink as much money into Marsh Point as I can afford. A facelift will bring new life to the old home.

CHAPTER NINE

I'm usually accurate in predicting what a project might cost, but I'm blown away by Will's numbers when I receive his proposal late on Friday afternoon. I'm at the desk in our home office going over the spreadsheet when I hear the front door close. Seconds later, Owen appears in the doorway, dressed for golf with the armpits of his blue-striped polo darkened with sweat.

"What're you doing?" he asks, entering the office and peering down at the spreadsheet.

I close the file so he can't see the exorbitant numbers. "Going over Will's proposal for the Marsh Point renovation project."

"When did you decide to renovate?"

I'm not in the mood for an argument, so I don't tell him the whole truth. "Sadie suggested making some improvements before putting it on the market." I get up from my chair and go around to his side of the desk. "I need to sell some stock. Quite a lot, actually. I don't know the value of my portfolio because I haven't received a report in months. Can you print one for me?"

Owen presses his lips thin. "I moved your brokerage account to another platform. I must have forgotten to have the statements sent to you. You realize you'll have to pay capital gains."

"So I'll pay the taxes. I never intended for the investments to be long term." I gesture at the desktop computer we share. "Can you print a report from the account now?"

"I'll do it later. I'm in a hurry. I need to shower. I'm meeting Rich for a beer at the clubhouse."

When he starts out of the office, I grab his arm, holding him back. "Wait a minute. This is important. I need to know how much money I have."

"It's not as easy as pressing the print button, Ashton. I have to run the report, which will take some time. I'll do it first thing in the morning." He jerks his arm free and kisses my cheek. "Gotta run. Don't count on me for dinner."

Don't count on me for dinner? That's something a teenager says to his mother, not a husband to his wife. Another Friday night has rolled around, and Owen has made plans that don't include me.

I sit back down at the computer and search the browser's history for trading and brokerage platforms. There is not a single trace of financial activity on this computer. He must conduct his trading from his work computer or his phone.

I wait until Owen leaves the house before I tear into his file drawers. The only statements I find are copies of household bills. Why would Owen keep personal financial documents in his office at work? I remember what Delbert Lewis said about the wire transfers. Is my husband hiding something from me? Has Owen done something with my money?

Sensing the onset of a panic attack, I inhale and exhale slowly until my breath steadies, and I feel calmer. I'm being ridiculous, letting my imagination get the best of me. Owen may not be the perfect husband, but he prides himself on his sterling reputation as the CFO of Darby Custom Homes. He wouldn't do something so underhanded as stealing from his wife.

Leaving the office, I go to the kitchen and pour myself a glass of wine. I lean against the counter, considering my options for spending Friday night alone. I could order a pizza and watch a movie. I *should* go to Whispering Oaks to visit Dad, but I've been there every night this week, and seeing him so downtrodden breaks my heart. I could call Hattie and cash in on my birthday dinner at The Nest. But I haven't heard from her all week, and I imagine she's exhausted from the wedding. I envision myself lounging in the daybed on the veranda at Marsh Point. An infusion of salt air is just what I need right now.

Pouring the wine down the drain, I change into comfortable clothes and flee the confines of the condo.

The Marsh Point house is stifling and musty from being locked up all week with no air-conditioning. There's a gentle breeze blowing off the sound, and I open all the front and back doors to let it flow through the center hallway.

I call Will as I wander around the house, contemplating the work ahead. "I received your proposal, and your numbers are insane."

He sighs. "I've been waiting for your call. Inflation has driven the cost of materials and labor up so high, I can hardly believe it myself. I ran the numbers multiple times. I even reduced the percentage of my fee. That's the best I can do, Ashton. I totally understand if you need to get another estimate."

I pause at the open window in Mama's bedroom. "I trust you, Will. I know you're being fair to me. And I don't expect you to work for free. I'll pay you the normal percentage. But if this inflation keeps up, you and I might both be looking for new careers."

"Tell me about it," he says with a chuckle. "But there's good news. If you decide to proceed, I can start demo a week from Monday."

I watch a sport fishing boat speed across the sound, returning from a day out in the ocean. "I'll need to make some changes. I'm just not sure to what extent. Give me the weekend to think about it, and we'll talk more on Monday."

"Sounds good. Have a nice weekend, Ashton," he says, and we hang up.

I stare at the phone in my hand. *Have a nice weekend, Ashton.* That's the nicest thing my brother has said to me in years.

I square my shoulders. So I have a week to clear out the house. I turn my back on the window and face Mama's bedroom. Dad took most of his belongings with him to Whispering Oaks, but going through Mama's things will take time. Carrie cleaned out her room years ago when she married Tom. Will took his prized possessions when he went off to college, but he left behind remnants from his childhood—mostly sports related like baseball trophies, lacrosse sticks, and his football helmet from his high school team. Savannah's room remains untouched from the day she disappeared. I'll save her things for when she comes back because, despite what Will thinks, I know in my heart she'll one day come home.

I continue my assessment downstairs, where priceless antiques fill the common areas. I will keep the elegant chests and side tables and writing desks, but the clunkier Victorian pieces will have to go. I'll need to figure out something to do with the knickknacks cluttering every surface in the living room. While the porcelain figurines, heavy brass candlesticks, and Mama's collection of antique tortoiseshell objects are valuable, I don't want them on display in my home.

In the dining room, dust outlines the space where Carrie's silver service once sat on the sideboard. Mama would have a hissy fit if she saw her tarnished candelabra. I have neither the time nor the inclination to polish silver. I'll offer them to my sister if I ever decide to speak to her again.

Moving on to the kitchen, I open and close cabinet doors. There are china patterns for every occasion and cookware that was outdated a decade ago. Going through all this stuff is a daunting task. Maybe I'll have an estate sale if no one else in the family wants it.

Outside on the veranda, I stretch out on the daybed swing and watch the sun begin its descent over the sound. Despite the many awful things that happened to me in this house, there's no place on earth where I feel more at peace. Marsh Point is my place, just as it was my mama's. My Merriweather roots grow deep here. I could never sell it to a stranger, and I need to stop worrying about my siblings. The property now belongs to me, and I will never leave.

I FALL SOUND asleep on the daybed, and sometime during the night, I drag myself upstairs to my old room. The first rays of sunlight streaming through the open windows wake me the following morning. Propping myself up on pillows, I look around my childhood bedroom. There are no traces of the girl who once occupied this space. I've spent many nights here in the past few years, during the times I was sure Mama's life was ending. My clothes—pajamas and underwear and weekend loungewear–fill the chest of drawers. A spare electric toothbrush sits on the counter beside the sink, my favorite shampoo is in the shower, and some basic makeup products occupy the vanity drawers. I even bought a new white matelassé coverlet to replace the threadbare patchwork quilt.

I prefer my room to my parents' across the hall. Both rooms occupy a back corner of the house, but mine has a better view of the sound. When we remodel, I'll convert this room into a second primary suite. I'll reconfigure the remaining three bedrooms, my siblings' old rooms, and corresponding baths to make the best use of the space. I don't have any children, and I doubt I'll be having many guests. But one day, I'd love for my entire family to share the holidays under the same roof again.

Throwing my legs over the side of the bed, I stand and stretch and wander over to the windows. The sun sparkles diamonds off the sound's calm blue waters, the promise of a beautiful summer Saturday. Unfortunately, I will be working inside all day.

After dressing in cutoffs and a worn MIT T-shirt, I brush my teeth and spray my pixie hair with dry shampoo to give it some lift. I make coffee in a to-go cup before hurrying off to Coastal Hardware. I'm waiting in line with other Saturday do-it-yourselfers when they open at eight. After loading up on packing supplies—boxes and packing paper and tape—I stop in at Fancy Pantry for a few grocery items before returning to Marsh Point.

I set to work in the family room, snapping several pics of the bookcases to ensure I return the items to the proper shelves after the renovations. I discover a treasure trove of memorabilia. Personalized and signed copies of novels written by famous southern authors like Pat Conroy and William Faulkner. Leather-bound diplomas and certificates marking my ancestors' greatest achievements. Letters written from US senators and presidents like FDR, JFK, and Ronald Reagan. Some of the family photo albums date back to the 1800s.

My parents' wedding album holds me captive for more than an hour. My mother, an incredibly striking woman, was regal in her delicate lace gown. In nearly every photograph, my father is staring at her with a love-struck gaze. Mama appears sober. When had her drinking problems started? When she was in school at Hollins College? Or was it later in their marriage, after her children were born? Had the four of us driven our mother off the deep end?

I take short breaks throughout the day for snacks and refreshing glasses of sweet tea. By the time I head up to bed around ten o'clock, the contents of the family room are neatly packed in labeled boxes and stacked in the hallway near the front door. All the photographs I've seen and the letters I've read have given me a newfound respect for my family. But I'm disappointed not to have unearthed any long-held secrets, any clues why Mama left the house to me and not my siblings.

CHAPTER TEN

I put in a full day on Sunday. The packing goes smoother and faster in the living and dining rooms where there isn't as much memorabilia to distract me. But I still have a long way to go, and I'll need to take some time off from work this week in order to finish by next Sunday. As I sort through the contents of each room, the reality that Marsh Point belongs to me sinks in a little further. I'm enjoying my time here, and I want to take advantage of the house as much as possible before demolition begins.

Late in the afternoon, I load up on groceries from Fancy Pantry and head over to the condo for some clothes. When I arrive, Owen is lying on the sofa with the draperies drawn, watching one of the *The Godfather* movies on TV.

"Why are you sitting in the dark?" I ask, flipping the switch that turns on a pair of white porcelain table lamps.

"Hey!" he says, shielding his eyes. "Turn off the light. I've got a headache."

I move closer to him. His eyes are bloodshot, and he smells like a whiskey distillery. "Mm-hmm. You're hungover. What'd you do last night?"

Owen scrambles to sit up. "I went out with some guys." He

reaches over and turns off the table lamp. "Why do you care? You weren't here. Where have you been anyway?"

"At Marsh Point. I have to clear everything out ahead of the renovations. I'll be staying there this week. I came home to get some clothes. Did you print the statement for my brokerage account?"

"No. Sorry. I forgot that the account password is at work. I'll do it first thing in the morning."

My eyes narrow as I glare at him. "Why are you stalling, Owen? Are you hiding something?"

"Of course not. What would I be hiding?" He stands to face me. "I make trades during business hours when I'm at work. For extra security, I created a long password with a bunch of numbers, letters, and symbols. I do that for all our accounts. I have them in a file in a locked drawer of my desk."

I don't know whether to believe him, but his excuse sounds legitimate. "Is all my money invested?"

"Yep. Every last cent."

I jab his chest with my pink-tipped finger. "Email me the statement as soon as you get to work tomorrow." I turn my back on him. "I'm going to pack."

He follows me into the bedroom. "Wait a minute. Why do you have to sleep at Marsh Point?"

"So I can work in the mornings before work and at night when I come home." I open my rolling suitcase on the bed and toss in underwear, shorts, and T-shirts. I throw in several pairs of shoes and zip up the suitcase. I grab my cosmetic bag from the bathroom, a handful of hanging clothes from the closet, and exit the bedroom, with Owen trailing behind me.

When I reach the front door, I say to him over my shoulder, "Don't forget to send me that statement. I want it first thing in the morning, before you even have coffee."

But when I still haven't heard from him by noon on Monday, my worry meter ticks up several notches. I push back from my desk. That scoundrel is definitely hiding something. And I aim to find out what it is.

I leave my office and drive to the outskirts of town. As I'm approaching the Darby Custom Homes building, I spot Owen's silver Lexus sedan pulling out of the parking lot, presumably on his way to The Nest, where he eats lunch nearly every day. I yearn to give him a piece of my mind, and I consider going after him, but I realize his absence benefits me.

I park my car and enter the building, smiling and waving at Sam, the receptionist, as I pass through the lobby. No one is in the hallway, and I duck into Owen's office without being seen. Dropping my purse on the desk, I sit down in my husband's chair and begin opening drawers. None are locked, and only the bottom right contains files. I flip through the files, but I don't find any information regarding my brokerage account.

"Looking for something?"

My brother's voice startles me, and I slam the drawer shut. "I locked myself out of the condo, and I'm pretty sure Owen keeps a spare key here. But I can't find it."

Will raises an eyebrow. "Why are you looking in his file drawer? I would think he'd keep a spare key in the top middle drawer." His gaze drops to my open purse on the desk. "Your keys are in there." He slides the purse toward me.

Feigning surprise, I bring my hands to my cheeks. "Stupid me! I have way too much on my mind these days." I'm sure Will doesn't believe me, but I'm relieved when he doesn't question me further.

"Since you're here, you saved me a phone call. What did you decide to do about the renovations?"

"Full steam ahead. As laid out in the plans."

Will punches the air. "Excellent news. I promise we'll try to save money wherever we can. How's the cleaning out coming?"

"Good. I've ordered two PODS. They should arrive later in the week. I'll need to hire some muscle to help me move the furniture. Do you think any of your workers might be interested?"

"Probably. I'll send you Maurice's contact information, and he can ask around." Maurice has been a project foreman for Darby Custom Homes for over thirty years.

"That'd be great." I sling my purse over my shoulder and come from behind the desk. "You have some stuff left in your room at Marsh Point. Do you want to go through it?"

"Nope. Throw it all away. I don't want any mementos from my childhood. Which reminds me. I need to ask you about something." He glances around the room, and even though we're alone, he says, "Let's go outside where no one can hear us."

"Okay. You can walk me to my car."

Neither of us speaks as we go back down the hall and out the front of the building.

"When you were at the house the other day, did Tracy ask you about . . . you know . . . Bert." Will grimaces as though it pains him to say the name.

"She said she thought something bad had happened to you when you were young, but I told her it wasn't my place to talk about it. She's your wife, Will. I can't believe you've never told her."

We reach my car, and he leans against the front fender. "I try not to think about it. Tracy has a way of harping on things. If I told her, she'd insist I see a therapist."

My jaw goes slack. "You mean you never have? I can't believe Mom and Dad didn't make you."

"They tried, but I refused. All I wanted to do was forget about the accident. I couldn't very well do that if I was discussing it ad nauseam with a shrink."

"How's that working out for you? Have you forgotten about it?"

"Pretty much." His left eye twitches, a sure sign he's lying. "Until Tracy started interrogating me about my childhood."

"Keeping secrets from you wife is never a good idea, little bro," I say tapping the tips of my fingers against his cheek.

I get in my car and drive straight to The Nest. I push open the ancient wooden door and enter the old tavern, where the air is dense with the pungent scent of stale beer. The flooring is well-worn, grooved hardwood, and age-yellow photographs, old fishing nets, and taxidermy sea turtles adorn the walls. Owen sits alone at the bar, which runs the length of the room, its mahogany surface dulled by countless beer mugs and whiskey bottles.

I slide onto the seat next to my husband. "We need to talk."

He looks up from his Caesar salad. "Ashton! What a pleasant surprise."

I glare at him. "This isn't a social visit."

The waitress, a beautiful blonde with a curvaceous figure, places a menu in front of me. "Can I get you something to drink?"

"Sweet tea, please. In a to-go cup. I'm not eating." I hand her back the menu and watch her sashay away, her sexy hips swaying. "I'll bet she makes a lot of tips."

"I'm sure she does. But not for her looks. Cindy works hard. What're you doing here if you didn't come for lunch?"

"I stopped by your office and had a look around. Your desk drawers aren't locked. But I don't need to tell you this, since it's your desk. What are you hiding from me, Owen? Did you spend all my money?"

He barks out a laugh. "I couldn't spend that much money in a lifetime."

"Then why won't you show me the account statement?"

He lets out a loud sigh. "I've spent an enormous amount of time researching the stocks in your portfolio. It's performing extremely well, and I don't recommend you sell a single stock." He wads up his napkin and places it on his empty plate. "Look, you'll receive your first bill from Darby Homes sometime around the middle of July. It'll mostly be for demolition, which, between your salary and mine, we can easily afford. If we make some changes in our budget, we might even be able to pay for all the renovations without dipping into your investments."

The waitress delivers my tea, and I sip it as I consider this approach. I don't want him spending a dime of *his* money on *my* house. My firm is working on several large projects that will generate large fees for me in the coming months. I can always get a bridge loan from the bank. "Okay, fine. We'll take it as it comes. But if I get in a jam, I'm selling some stock. And I still want to see the account statement as soon as possible."

"That's fair." He runs a finger down my cheek. "I miss you. Why don't you come home tonight? I don't remember the last time we spent any quality time together."

"That's because you're always playing golf." I slip off the bar stool onto my feet. "Besides, I have too much work to do at Marsh Point."

When I start toward the door, he calls after me, "If I help you pay for the renovations, I want my money back plus ten percent when you sell the property."

I keep walking, pretending I don't hear him. Now is not the time to tell him I won't be selling the house.

CHAPTER **ELEVEN**

I work upstairs late at night when the air circulated by ceiling and window fans is cooler. Carrie left nothing behind when she moved out, not even one of the romance novels she reads obsessively. But I spend hours in Savannah's room, meticulously sorting through her belongings and packing them neatly in boxes. Notebooks of the songs she wrote fill the bottom drawer of her nightstand. Savannah was a gifted guitarist with a voice like an angel. As I read the lyrics, I travel back in time to the many concerts she held. Using the veranda as her stage, she performed to her audience—my siblings and me—on the ground in front of her. I've closely followed the country music industry, hoping she would become famous. She may have changed her name, but she could never hide her stunningly beautiful face.

Under the stack of song notebooks, I find a pamphlet from a local abortion clinic. I've often wondered if she ever considered terminating the pregnancy. One question answered. So many mysteries about Savannah left unresolved.

At the bottom of Will's desk drawer are newspaper clippings about the accident. I study the photograph of my brother and parents leaving the courthouse. Will's expression is evidence of his tortured emotions. Regardless of what he says, there's no way he could ever forget what happened. Why didn't my parents insist he go for counseling?

The only thing I find of interest in my parents' bedroom are empty liquor and wine bottles. Even as my mother lay dying, she continued to drink the poison.

By Friday afternoon, the house is packed up, and I've stored all the boxes in one container. Maurice and his crew will come first thing in the morning to move the furniture. I dread seeing this week end. I've enjoyed my solitude. I haven't missed my husband at all, and I'm not sure what that says about my marriage. Maybe that's normal after fifteen years of living with the same person.

I take a cold shower, slip on a sleeveless dress, and drive out to Whispering Oaks. My phone pings with a text as I'm pulling into the retirement community. I wait until I'm safely parked in the lot before I read the message from Hattie.

I've finally recovered from the wedding. Can we meet at The Nest tomorrow night for your belated birthday dinner?

I hate to miss the sunset on my last night at Marsh Point. I remind myself my separation from my beloved home is only temporary. Once the renovations are complete, I'll have the rest of my life to watch the sunset. And my best friend has been so preoccupied with planning her daughter's wedding, I have spent no quality time with her in months.

I text her back. *That'd be great. Can't wait to see you.*

I've been procrastinating visiting Dad all week, and I'm shocked at the state of his apartment and his appearance. Empty food containers litter every surface of the kitchen. The refrigerator is empty, the sink is piled high with dishes, and the garbage can is overflowing. Dad is still wearing the same pajamas, and when I bend over to kiss the top of his head, the stench of body odor assaults my nose.

"Where have you been?" he grumbles. "You just locked me away in this hellhole and haven't been to visit me for a week."

"Hold on a second, Dad. You made the decision to come here. And I haven't been ignoring you. I've been busy clearing out Marsh Point. I'm going to renovate the house, and when I'm finished, if you're still unhappy here, you can move back into the house with me."

"And live with your obnoxious husband? No thanks."

I scrunch up my face. Since when does Dad think Owen is obnoxious? I don't tell him Owen might not be living at Marsh Point with me.

I stand in front of him, blocking his view of the television. "Have you been eating in the dining hall?"

"Nope," he says, his face set in stubborn defiance.

"Have you even been out of this apartment?"

"Nope. I don't have anywhere to go, and no way of getting there if I did."

I make a mental note to get his car fixed. I gesture at the kitchen. "There's nothing in your refrigerator. What have you been eating?"

He stares blankly at me, as though he doesn't remember.

"Has Will or Carrie been to see you?"

He shakes his head. "They never came to see me at Marsh Point. I don't expect them to start now."

"I'm going to clean up the kitchen while you shower and dress. Then I'm driving you to the grocery store." Ignoring his complaints, I turn off the television and help him up from the chair. I take hold of his arm, and as I'm slowly walking him to the bedroom, I'm aware of how feeble he's become.

He enters the bathroom and I say through the closed door, "Don't forget to shave."

I remain outside the bathroom until I hear the shower running. Returning to the kitchen, I locate a trash bag and fill it with the empty food containers. I'm starting on the dishes when the doorbell rings.

Lester Hoffman is wearing tennis whites with a racquet case

slung over his shoulder. He's fit with a healthy glow from the sun. I want this same glow for my father.

"Ashton," he says, appearing relieved to see me. "Is your father okay? I've stopped by many times every day this week, and he's not here or he's not answering the door."

"He's avoiding you. He seems content to wither up and die." Lester doesn't ask, but I feel compelled to explain why I haven't been here. "I'm ashamed to say I haven't been to see him in several days. We're preparing to renovate the Marsh Point house, and I've been packing up the contents."

"You don't owe me an explanation, Ashton. I understand. You have a busy life. It's not your job to babysit your father."

"Someone clearly needs to. He's in the shower now, but I don't know when he last changed his clothes. When I got here, he was wearing the same pajamas I last saw him in. He wasn't doing well at home either. He's been out of sorts since Mama died. Maybe he needs to be in assisted living."

"Unfortunately, that's not an immediate option," Lester says. "There's a long waiting list for assisted living."

"Then I'll have to hire caregivers."

A smile curves the corners of his lips. "That might be the push Ernest needs to get him out of this slump."

I frown. "How so?"

"I hired a certified nurse assistant to help me when I broke my hip. Al was wonderful, and I was grateful for his services, but having someone with me all the time nearly drove me crazy. I know your father. Ernest will not appreciate someone watching him sleep."

I chuckle. "You're right. And you may be onto something. I've already threatened to hire nurses once. This time, I won't give Dad a choice. I'll arrange for round-the-clock care. Knowing my stubborn father, he'll do whatever it takes to get rid of them, including rejoining the world around him."

Lester gives my arm a squeeze. "Let me know how I can help. I'll keep trying to engage with him."

"That would be great."

When I go back inside, Dad is standing in the living room, looking around as though confused by his surroundings. He didn't shave, but at least he's wearing street clothes—khaki pants with a stain on the thigh and a wrinkled plaid short-sleeved shirt. Not much of an improvement, but baby steps.

"Why do I have to go to the store? Can't I give you my list?" he whines on the short walk to my car.

"You're perfectly capable of driving yourself to the store and doing your own shopping. But for whatever reason, you're acting like an old man."

"Humph. I am an old man."

I humph back at him. "Seventy-eight is not old in my book."

Dad moves like a creeping turtle, and shopping takes four times as long as it should. It's dinnertime when we finally return to his apartment.

"Do you want to go to dinner with Lester?" I ask Dad as I store items in his refrigerator.

"Lester will sit with his other friends," Dad says, like a child on the first day of school, terrified he won't have anyone to sit with in the cafeteria.

"They are your friends too, Dad."

"Not really. Not anymore. I'll just eat something here," he says, tearing into a box of Grape Nuts cereal.

"You need to eat a hot meal, not a bowl of cereal." I take the cereal box from him and place it in the pantry. "I'll go to dinner with you." I'd planned to order a pizza and enjoy my last sunset on the veranda. I'll skip the pizza, but I'll make sure I'm home in time to watch the sunset.

Ninety minutes later, on the drive back to Marsh Point, I call Gwen Flowers, the woman in charge of the home health care agency that provided nursing assistants for Mama. Gwen and I grew close during the years they supplied us with 24-hour care. I explain the situation, and she promises to line someone up for Dad within a few days. I smile to myself, thinking about Dad's reaction. He'll be madder than a wet hen. My smile quickly fades. If this doesn't snap him out of his funk, I'm afraid nothing will.

CHAPTER TWELVE

Maurice and his crew of five put in a full day's work on Saturday. I bring in made-to-order sandwiches from Custom Crust for lunch and make sure they stay hydrated in the sweltering heat. By five o'clock, they've stored all the furniture, accessories, and household items in the containers. All the leftovers wait in the empty bay of the carport to be transported to either charity or the dump.

"What're you gonna do with your daddy's car, Miss Ashton?" Maurice asks, running a hand over the hood of Dad's vintage convertible. "It's a shame to neglect such a beautiful machine."

I look up at Maurice, a mountain of a man with dark chocolate skin and hazel eyes. "I'd like to fix it up. I certainly don't want to sell it. I refuse to believe Dad's driving days are over."

"My brother-in-law owns a garage that specializes in antique cars. He'd be happy to take care of the repairs. She probably just needs a tune-up and some air in the tires." Maurice crouches down beside the car to inspect the tires. "Although I see some signs of dry-rotting."

I clasp my hands together. "Perfect! But don't mention this to Dad. I want to surprise him. Maybe we can inspire him to drive again. Please have your brother-in-law make any repairs necessary. Make sure he polishes her up nice and shiny."

Maurice gives me an appreciative nod. "I'll get right on it."

I pay the crew handsomely and see them off in the driveway. Excitement flickers inside me as I wander through the empty rooms. With all the furnishings gone, the house is a blank canvas for me to create my new home. I envision a warm neutral palette, with furnishings and walls in soft beige hues and accents in shades of blue—the colors of the sky and water.

My open suitcase lies on the floor of my vacant bedroom. The knit dress I plan to wear to dinner with Hattie is the only garment remaining in my closet. I've already loaded the rest of my hanging clothes in the trunk of my car for my return to my life with Owen tomorrow. I will sleep tonight on the daybed on the porch and pack up my toiletries in the morning.

I shower and dress and head to town. When I arrive at The Nest, I spot Hattie seated at our favorite booth in the far corner. As I force my way through the crowded tavern, I stop to speak to several friends.

Hattie stands to greet me. She's the essence of summer in a Lily Pulitzer sundress with her strawberry-blonde hair piled atop her head in a messy bun. She engulfs me in a warm embrace. "Happy belated fiftieth!"

I mumble a thank you. It seems silly to be celebrating two weeks after my birthday. I slide into the booth and examine the tuna nachos and margarita waiting for me on the table. "This looks delicious, and I'm starving."

Hattie lifts her glass. "Cheers! To the next half century."

"I'm not sure I want to see a hundred," I say, laughing as I clink her glass.

Hattie sips her frozen cocktail and sets down her glass. "Please tell me Owen remembered your birthday."

I nod. "He cooked me a fantastic meal and bought me a gorgeous bouquet," I say, embellishing Owen's birthday dinner.

"Your fiftieth is right around the corner. Do you have big plans?"

"Are you joking? I just spent my birthday budget on Melissa's wedding." Mischief sparkles in her blue eyes. "Although I have a hunch, Allen has a surprise up his sleeve. I accidentally saw an email confirmation from Zero George in Charleston for my birthday weekend."

I fold my hands together on the table. "By *accidentally*, do you mean you were snooping around in his email?"

She gives a flippant wave of her hand. "Maybe. After all, we share the same desktop computer at home. But enough about me. I've been so absorbed in planning the wedding these past few months. Tonight is all about you. Tell me everything that's going on in your life."

"A lot has happened, actually. Mama left me Marsh Point in her will."

Hattie lets out a squeal. "That's the best news ever, Ash! I know how much you love that place."

A warm glow settles over me. "I do love it. More than I ever realized. I've been staying there this week, packing everything up to get ready for construction. Will is starting the renovations on Monday. We're taking it down to the studs."

"Wow! You have been a busy girl."

"You don't know the half of it. On top of everything else, Dad moved himself into independent living at Whispering Oaks. Unfortunately, he's not doing so great, and I'm really worried about him."

"That's understandable after all he's been through. Poor Ernest. Give him some time. He'll come around."

"I hope you're right," I say, loading up a fried wonton chip with ahi tuna and avocado.

"How does Owen feel about living at Marsh Point? Will he be able to give up his precious golf course condo?"

I pop the chip into my mouth. "He refuses to live at Marsh

Point. He thinks I'm fixing it up to sell it."

Hattie narrows her blue eyes at me. "So, things aren't any better between you two?"

"Things are status quo. I admit I haven't missed him this week."

"Apparently, he hasn't missed you either. You should know that rumors about him are circulating around town."

My blood runs cold. "What sort of rumors?"

"That he's been here every night this week with Rick," Hattie says, tapping the lacquered wooden table with her manicured fingernail. "Drinking in excess and hitting on women."

Hattie's gaze makes me squirm, and I stare down at my frosty drink.

"I meant what I said at the wedding. You should totally divorce him. I've never understood what you see in him."

I run a thumb around the salty rim of my glass. "You make divorce sound so simple. Part of me still loves him."

"He's your husband, Ash. Part of you will always love him. That doesn't mean you should stay married to him."

The waitress makes a timely appearance, saving me from having to respond. As we always do on our birthdays, we forget about our diets for one night and order cheeseburgers and fries.

"You know what you need?" Hattie says once the waitress has gone.

With a chuckle, I say, "I'm afraid to ask."

"You need a romantic getaway. Take Owen somewhere special for a long weekend. If you don't rekindle your passion on your trip, you'll know your marriage is truly over."

I consider her suggestion as I pick at the nachos. "That's not a bad idea. Although we'd have to go to a place that doesn't have golf."

"Lucky for you, our nation's most romantic city is right up the road. There's so much to do in Charleston. If things don't go well, you can easily get in your car and drive home."

"That's true." The thought of spending the weekend with my husband no longer appeals to me. My week alone at Marsh Point has given me a taste of single life, and I rather like my freedom. Based on the rumors Hattie mentioned, so does Owen.

Hattie jabs a wonton chip at me. "And you can use your romantic getaway to tell Owen you plan to move to Marsh Point when the renovations are finished."

"That would put an abrupt ending to our romantic getaway."

Hattie slurps down the rest of her margarita. "What if he refuses to live at Marsh Point?"

I shrug. "Maybe we'll keep the condo and split time between the two." As the words leave my mouth, I realize I would never be happy living part-time at the condo. I dread having to return there tomorrow.

"Who's paying for these renovations? I hope you're using your money."

My mouth falls open. "Hattie! Way to be nosy!" I would be offended if anyone else asked me this question. But Hattie is the keeper of my secrets. Most of them anyway. My husband refusing to show me the statement on my brokerage account is one secret I won't tell my best friend.

"I'm not being nosy. I'm being a concerned best friend. Since your marriage is on the rocks, I'd hate for you to get into a messy financial situation."

A lump develops in my throat, and my voice is tight when I say, "Isn't divorce always financially messy?"

Earth, Wind & Fire's "September" blasts out from the jukebox, and Hattie's butt comes off the bench seat. "I love this song! I'm feeling a rowdy vibe in The Nest tonight. Should we order a bottle of bubbly?"

I'm suddenly homesick for Marsh Point. I've grown accustomed to my solitude. I massage my temples. "I feel a headache coming on. I'll probably go home after we eat."

Hattie settles back down in her seat. "Oh, honey. I'm sorry."

She reaches for my hand. "You have so much on your plate right now. How can I help?"

I manage a smile. "You always help. Just by being my friend."

The waitress arrives with our burgers, and while we eat, I tell her about the changes I'm planning at Marsh Point. Hattie insists on picking up the tab, but as we're leaving the tavern, she joins a table of friends for one more drink.

On the way home, I turn off the radio and drive in silence with the top down and wind whipping through my hair. I'm a block away when I catch the first whiff of marsh. I enter the kitchen through the backdoor. The room with its green Formica countertops and yellowed-from-age cabinets looks even more pathetic with all the homey touches gone. Only a few bottled waters, a Miller Lite beer, and a half-eaten container of chicken salad remain in the refrigerator. Grabbing a water, I go outside to the veranda and stretch out on the daybed. As dusk falls over the sound, I replay my conversation with Hattie. *I meant what I said at the wedding. You should totally divorce him. I've never understood what you see in him.*

I think back to the night Owen and I met. We were both staying in the same hotel in Atlanta. He was attending a financial planning convention, and I was consulting with a potential client about a renovation project in Buckhead. We struck up a conversation at the bar over dinner. Owen was everything I needed at that point in my life. I'd just moved back to Water's Edge from Boston. All my friends were married, and I was beginning to worry I'd become an old maid. Owen, who was looking to change careers, was the ideal candidate to take over when Dad retired as CFO from Darby Custom Homes. We had a lot in common back in those days. We were both outgoing and hardworking, and loved spending time on the water. And Owen was the only guy I ever dated who didn't want children.

CHAPTER THIRTEEN

I delay my departure from Marsh Point as long as possible on Sunday. I put on my bikini, which I'm entirely too old to be wearing, and sunbathe on the dock until the sun gets too hot. I eat the last of the chicken salad for lunch and wash it down with the Miller Lite beer. The beer makes me sleepy, and I doze for hours on the daybed. Late afternoon, when I can no longer put off the inevitable, I shower and dress and drive home to the condo.

Owen greets me at the door with a peck on the cheek. "I was hoping you'd come home today. I bought a dozen steamed crabs for our dinner."

He knows me well. Steamed crabs are the way to my heart. "That sounds nice. I'd like to unpack first though."

"Sure thing!" His gaze slips past me to my convertible. "Is there anything else in the car?"

"No, this is it," I say about the suitcase at my side and tote bag slung over my shoulder.

"Then I'll get everything ready for crab picking while you unpack."

I roll my suitcase down the hallway to our room, which is in complete disarray, with the shades drawn, bed unmade, and the laundry hamper overflowing with Owen's dirty clothes. I roll my eyes. He's not eager to see me. He was hoping I'd come home today to clean up his mess.

I spend the next thirty minutes unpacking, changing the bed linens, and starting a load of laundry. When I return to the kitchen, Owen is seated at the newspaper-covered table on the patio with a bottle of chilled wine and a pile of steamed crabs.

A deep longing for Marsh Point hits me as I sit down across from him. I grew up picking crabs with my family. We used to sit at the picnic table on the lawn with the view of the sound in the background. We had no need for newspaper. When we finished eating, we sprayed down the table with the hose and dumped the crab shells in the water. Sitting on our hot patio isn't the same, but I warn myself not to complain. Owen probably went to a lot of trouble to get the crabs.

"These look yummy," I say, eyeing the crabs.

"They are. I sampled a claw while I was waiting for you." He fills a glass with wine and hands it to me.

I sip the wine and set down the glass. "Where did you get them?"

"Rich's friend gave him a bushel. Since he couldn't eat all of them himself, he gave some to me."

I should've guessed. My husband wasn't trying to impress me after all.

Owen sucks on a crab finger. "So, did you get it out of your system?"

"Did I get what out of my system?" I ask as I peel off the crab's shell.

"Marsh Point. Did you get enough time there?"

"No, Owen, I did not. I will never get enough of Marsh Point. Did *you* get enough partying while I was gone? Rumor has it you and Rich were tearing up the town every night."

He drops his head. "So? I went out a few times. I was lonely here without you."

I soften. Why am I being so hard on him? "What do you think about us going away for a long weekend?"

His face lights up. "Sure! Let's go to Kiawah."

"Kiawah could be fun. I've been dying to stay at the Sanctuary. But you have to promise not to play golf." I crack a crab claw and stick the juicy meat in my mouth.

"Are you joking? Of course I'm going to play golf. You can spend the day in the spa."

"The point is for us to be together. There are plenty of other things we can do, like playing tennis and riding bicycles."

He reaches for another crab. "Let's wait until the fall when the rates go down."

I let the subject drop for now. I'm not especially keen about spending the weekend with him anyway.

Owen breaks a crab's body in half and smashes the shell with his palm. As he picks at the meat, he says, "I spoke to Will about your renovation project. I made sure he understands the urgency to finish by the end of October. If you put it on the market right away, you could potentially have the deal done by year's end."

My anger flares. "Stay out of my business, Owen."

He looks up from his crab. "What? I'm only trying to help."

My appetite vanishes, and I set down my crab cracker. I can no longer continue this charade. "Finishing in four months would be great. I could get settled before the holidays. I've decided not to sell Marsh Point."

His head snaps back as though someone punched him. "Why on earth would you keep it?"

"Because I love everything about the place. Because Marsh Point is in my blood, and I can't bring myself to part with it."

"But we already live here," he says, tapping the table with his cracker.

"Then we'll use Marsh Point as a second home. We can spend weekends and holidays there."

Owen tears off a sheet of paper towel and wipes his hands. "But that house is a maintenance nightmare."

"Not for long. Everything will be new when we finish with the construction."

"The yard, with acres of grass to cut and hedges galore to trim, will cost a fortune to maintain."

"Don't worry about it. I'll pay the lawn service." I look away from him at the wilting flowers in my containers. Besides making a mess of the house, he neglected to water my plants while I was gone. When we were first married, we divvied up the chores fifty-fifty. But along the way, he stopped doing his share, and I took up the slack.

"Seriously, Ashton. Why do we need an antebellum mansion when we don't have any children? It's not like we're going to be hosting out-of-town guests. My parents are dead, my siblings live on the West Coast, and everyone in your family has their own houses here in town."

"Because Marsh Point is my *home,* Owen. More than this condo will ever be. Mama would roll over in her grave if I sold it to a stranger. She left me Marsh Point to assure it stays in the family." As the words spew from my lips, I've never felt more certain about anything in my life. Mama must have realized that Carrie couldn't afford the upkeep and Will detests the place. Given the opportunity, those two would sell the property and not think twice about it.

"Where is all this animosity coming from, Ashton? You are so uptight these days."

"It's coming from here." I slap my chest. "Years of pent-up anger at myself for letting you control my life. I'm sick and tired of you making all the decisions in our marriage. I let you convince me to sell my beloved beach house and move into this condo. But I enjoy being outdoors, and there's nowhere for me to go except this tiny patio." I sweep an arm at the small, enclosed space. "I feel confined here. I can't breathe. I'm suffocating."

He bangs his fist on the table. "God! Listen to yourself! You sound like a spoiled brat. We have a perfectly lovely home here, but you're whining like a child who has to give away her Barbie dream house. Act like a responsible adult, Ashton. Sell the house and invest the money."

I set my steely gaze on him. "You want me to give you *more* money to invest in the stock market when you refused to show me the account balance for the stocks I already own?"

Owen tosses up his hands. "Suit yourself. But I refuse to spend one night at Marsh Point."

"Fine. I may move there permanently."

He raises an eyebrow. "Are you asking me for a separation?"

I stand abruptly, kicking my chair out of the way. "You don't control me, Owen. I don't need your permission to leave you."

His shoulders slump. "Come on, babe. Don't be like this." He rises out of his chair. "Let's both calm down and talk this through rationally."

"I'm done talking. Give me my money." My hand shoots out, palm up, as though I'm asking for a wad of cash instead of my stock portfolio.

His face beams red as he grabs the edges of the newspaper. In one fell swoop, he snatches the newspaper off the table and sends crab shells and gills and gross yellow crab mustard flying toward me.

His behavior stuns me, and I emit a manic-sounding laugh. "Way to go, Owen!" I say, clapping my hands. "Now who's acting like a child?"

My response infuriates him more, and he stomps off the patio into the kitchen. A minute later, I hear his car engine start and the squeal of rubber meeting pavement as he peels off down the road.

I stare down at the particles of crab goo stuck to my skin and clothes. I don't dare move for fear of transporting the mess all over the house. I brush off as much as possible and tiptoe inside for the broom and a plastic trash bag. After cleaning up the patio, I take a long, hot shower, pouring liquid soap all over my body and scrubbing until my skin is raw. But I can still smell crab as I'm toweling off afterward.

It's not until I get into bed in my pajamas that I allow myself to think about what just happened. Owen and I crossed several lines here tonight. For the first time, we dared use the word *separation*. And when I asked for my money, he assaulted me with crab goo. I have no idea where we go from here. Should I leave? I could stay in the guesthouse at Marsh Point. I decide against it. I'm not ready for such a drastic move. Leaving would be the nail in the coffin of my marriage, and I might never see my money again.

CHAPTER **FOURTEEN**

The faint sound of a phone alarm wakes me on Monday morning. Throwing my legs over the side of the bed, I follow the beeping noise down the hall to the living room, where my husband is sleeping curled in a ball on the sofa. I don't know where he went after our fight or what time he came home.

To avoid another confrontation, I turn off his alarm and leave him sleeping. I quickly get ready for work and slip out of the condo. I don't relax until I'm among friendly faces at my office. My life with Owen has officially become hostile.

I've no sooner settled in at my desk when I receive a call from Gwen at the home health care agency. "Happy Monday, Ashton!"

Gwen's cheerful voice evokes a smile despite the rough start of my week. "Good morning, Gwen. I trust you had a pleasant weekend."

"Very relaxing, thanks. It took some doing, but I've found just the right person to take care of your father. The timing is ideal. Clyde has been working for a patient recovering from abdominal surgery. That patient no longer needs him, which means Clyde can start with your father tomorrow morning."

"That's wonderful news, Gwen. Thank you."

"I've watched Ernest decline during these last few years. I believe he's fine physically. He just needs someone to perk up his spirits. And Clyde is just the man. He's a good listener and a Christian. He's a good-hearted soul, but he can be tough when warranted."

"He sounds ideal. Do you want me present for the initial meeting?"

"That would be best. Let's meet tomorrow at nine o'clock in the visitor's parking lot at Whispering Oaks. We'll make a game plan before we see your father."

"Perfect. I'll see you then."

After we hang up, I place a call to the estate attorney, arranging for my mother's trust to pay for Dad's care. Twenty-four-hour care will eat through the millions Mama left him in no time. And he might live another fifteen or twenty years.

After spending much of the day catching up on the work I missed last week, I drive out to Marsh Point to check on the demolition project. I'm pleasantly surprised to find the crew has torn out all the plaster walls, revealing thick wooden studs and antiquated wiring and plumbing.

I run into Maurice in the driveway on my way out. "I'm impressed. I had no idea you'd accomplish so much in one day."

Maurice chuckles. "My crew loves destroying stuff with their sledgehammers. Progress will go slower from here on out though. Jackhammering them tile bathrooms will take some time and a lot of effort."

"I imagine so. Keep up the good work," I say, slapping his muscular shoulder.

"By the way, I had your daddy's car towed to my brother-in-law's garage. I gave Jed your contact information. He'll get in touch soon about the cost of the repairs."

I glance over at the carport. I hadn't noticed Dad's car was missing. "I appreciate that, Maurice. I'll be on the lookout for a call from Jed."

I cross the lawn to the guesthouse—a two-story structure built in the mid-1800s from tabby, which is concrete made from lime, water, sand, and crushed oyster shells. While everything about the interior is outdated, a thorough cleaning would render it habitable. A breakfast bar separates the galley kitchen from the large room used for both living and dining. Three modest bedrooms, one with its own bath, occupy the upstairs. The appliances are still functional, and the ancient air conditioner still blows cold air.

On my way out, I sit for a few minutes in a rocker on the small front porch. The view isn't half bad. I could easily live here until the renovations in the main house are complete.

After our fight last night, the possibility of a legal separation is on the table. But I wouldn't dare make such a bold move without consulting a divorce attorney first. I know of several in town, but only one whose reputation precedes him. I need to get to Cedric Morton before Owen does.

I search Google for his contact information and click on the number. When I explain my reason for calling to the receptionist, she informs me Cedric is out of the country until the end of the month, and his first available appointment isn't until the second week in July. I consider calling someone else but make the split-second decision to stick with Cedric. Disappointed, I consider moving out of the condo anyway. But with Owen in control of my money, I decide to stick it out a little longer.

I rest my head against the back of the chair and close my eyes. The workmen have now gone for the day, taking with them their loud banging, and the only sound I hear is an outboard motor somewhere in the distance. I doze off, and I'm awakened a few minutes later by a bumblebee buzzing near a clump of lantana in the overgrown flower bed at the base of the porch.

Abandoning the rocker, I walk back to my car, tearing myself away from the magnetic hold the property has on me and returning to my dismal reality. After stopping by the Fancy Pantry for a few groceries, I arrive home to find Owen's sedan parked in our driveway.

As I enter the house with the grocery bags, I pass Owen in the foyer on his way out, but we don't speak. I'm unloading my groceries in the kitchen when I hear voices outside in front of the condo. Through the front window, I spot Owen and Carrie having an animated conversation in the driveway. I can't decipher their muffled voices, but I assume they are talking about me. When they part a minute later, Owen takes off in his sedan, and Carrie heads toward the front door. Seconds later, the doorbell rings.

"Carrie, what a pleasant surprise," I say, as though I hadn't seen her in the driveway with Owen. I open the door wider, motioning her inside. "Come in."

"This isn't a social visit, Ashton. We can talk out here."

"Fine." I join her on the small stoop, leaving the front door open. "What's up?"

"You! You're destroying all our lives."

I can't help but smile at her absurd accusation. "Oh? How so?"

"I drove out to Marsh Point earlier! I can't believe you're tearing down our family's home. Then I went to see Dad, to get him to talk some sense into you about the house, and he claims you've been neglecting him."

I glance around at the neighbors who are making discreet glances our way. "Please, keep your voice down. We have neighbors."

When Carrie brushes past me into the foyer, I enter the house and close the door behind me. "For your information, I'm renovating Marsh Point, not tearing it down. As you're aware, the place is in rapid decline. What were you doing out there anyway?"

"I was looking for you. I need to talk to you about Mom's estate. I think we should settle out of court."

"There's nothing to settle, Carrie. Mom's intentions were clear, and her estate was straightforward."

"Not necessarily. My attorney says I have a good chance of winning my lawsuit. In which case, you would lose Marsh Point. But if what Owen says is true, if you're planning to use the house as a second home, there may be a way for us to work something out."

Carrie wouldn't be here if her attorney thought she had a chance of winning her will contest. "Using the house as a second home is one option I'm considering, although I'm leaning toward living there permanently."

Carrie presses her hands against her temples as though coming down with a headache. "This is all so unfair. I don't know what Mama was thinking."

"I agree. But by law, we have to abide by her wishes."

"That's easy for you to say when you got everything, and we got nothing." She reaches for the doorknob. "You leave me no choice but to contest the will."

"Do what you think is right."

She lets out a humph as she swings the door open.

I grab hold of her arm, preventing her from leaving. "As for Dad, I am most definitely not neglecting him. He's in a bad way, and he needs help. Starting in the morning, he'll have a caregiver staying with him."

She jerks her arm free of my grip. "You mean around the clock?"

"Probably just a few hours a day to start with. I'll know more after I meet with Gwen in the morning. We're meeting at nine. You're welcome to join us."

"Sorry. I have a doctor's appointment at nine. Who's paying this caregiver?"

"His estate. I've already spoken to Mom's attorney about it."

"Great! These caregivers will blow right through the money Mom left Dad. You're determined to see me die poor, aren't you?"

"Dad needs someone with him to make sure he eats and bathes and participates in social opportunities available to him at Whispering Oaks. Will and I both have careers. If you'd like to take over the responsibility—"

"Are you saying taking care of two teenagers isn't demanding?" Carrie says, her fists balled at her sides.

"Not at all. But those teenagers are in school all day. You could spend a few of your free hours with Dad."

"Fine! Hire the caregivers. Spend every dime of Mama's money, if it makes you happy." Carrie goes into the living room and peeks out the french door at the patio. "Why would you ever leave this condo? And why are you ditching your husband? You're one of those people who is never happy. You don't know how lucky you are. Owen is successful and social and attractive."

I'm stunned speechless. *Ditching my husband?* "What exactly did Owen tell you?"

"That you're acting like a spoiled princess. That you're threatening to leave him." Carrie passes back through the foyer on the way to the door. "It's a good thing you never had children. You would've made a lousy parent. You're way too self-absorbed." She storms out of the house, sucking all the air in the room out with her.

My sister's comment cuts me to the core because, for once in her life, she's spot-on. I would've made a lousy mother.

Feeling the walls close in on me, I go outside to the patio and stretch out on the chaise lounge, tucking my feet beneath me. I have a perfectly nice life here. Who am I to want more? Owen's words from last night rush back to me. *You're whining like a child who has to give away her Barbie dream house.* Nothing is clear to me anymore. Maybe I should share Marsh Point with my siblings. Maybe I should try harder to make my marriage work.

I fall into a deep sleep, and when Owen arrives home later, he shakes me awake. "I assume you don't want to sleep out here."

I slowly sit up. "I think we should see a marriage counselor, Owen."

"I refuse to see a shrink." He nudges me over and sits down

beside me. "But I think we can work out our problems if we communicate better. Let's start by going on a date tomorrow night."

"I like that idea," I say, smiling softly at him.

"Good. I'll make a reservation for us at the Mariner's Club."

Our neighborhood clubhouse is more suitable for a family with young children, not a romantic evening for a married couple trying to work out their differences. But I don't argue. I need to learn to keep my opinions to myself.

"Let's go to bed," Owen says, helping me to my feet.

My mind races as he tucks me under his arm and walks me to our bedroom. I hope he doesn't expect sex. It's been so long, and things are so awkward between us, I'm not sure I can perform. I take my time in the bathroom, and when I emerge, I'm relieved to find him fast asleep. At least he appears to be. I study him closer as I crawl in beside him. His eyelids are fluttering, a sign that he's faking. So he doesn't want to have sex with me either. I suspect our marriage is too far gone, but I'm willing to give it one last chance.

CHAPTER **FIFTEEN**

Gwen draws me in for a warm embrace. I relish the moment, the softness of her plump body bringing back memories of all the times she dried my tears and whispered encouraging words during my family's darkest hour. She'd played such a vital role in my life for so many years. I didn't realize what a dear friend she'd become until she was gone.

"Oh, Gwen. I don't know how I've survived these past few weeks without you."

"I've missed you too, sweetheart." She gives me a tight squeeze before turning me loose and introducing me to Clyde.

The warmth in his golden-brown eyes immediately sets me at ease. I extend my hand to him. "I hope you brought your patience with you today. You've got your work cut out for you with my father."

He chuckles as he shakes my hand. "I never shy away from a challenge."

"Clyde and I talked about scheduling on the way over," Gwen explains. "We think it best to start out with a few hours a day, so as not to overwhelm your daddy. We can make adjustments once we've assessed his needs."

Clyde chimes in, "If I'm here from ten until six, I can help him with his grooming in the mornings, take him out to run errands or take part in activities during the afternoon hours, and make sure he eats dinner in the cafeteria before I leave in the evenings."

"This sounds ideal. I assume you're familiar with Whispering Oaks."

He grins, revealing perfectly straight white teeth. "Yes, ma'am. This is a popular place. Most of my clients live here."

I gesture toward the wellness center. "There's so much to do here. I want Dad to take advantage of all they offer."

Clyde gives an enthusiastic nod. "I'll make sure of it. No more sitting around feeling sorry for himself. However, if it turns out there's something more serious going on with him, we'll get him the proper treatment he needs."

Relief washes over me as my gaze drifts skyward. "Clyde, you're a gift from God. Or Mama. Maybe both," I say, and we all three laugh.

We leave the parking lot and walk toward Dad's apartment.

"A word of caution though," I say in a more serious tone. "Dad's pretty feeble. He hasn't gotten much exercise lately. And he insists on using his cane, even though I don't think he needs it."

"I understand, and I promise to take it slow. They have a weight room in the wellness center. I'll have him pumping iron in no time."

"Good luck with that," I say under my breath.

I knock on Dad's door, and when he doesn't answer, I let us in with my key. Dad, as usual, is lounging in his chair, wearing his pajamas while watching the news.

"Dad, I brought some visitors to see you," I say, powering off the television.

His face lights up when he sees Gwen, but when Clyde enters the room behind her, anger slides behind his smile. "Who are you?" Dad demands, but Clyde's blue scrubs give him away. "I don't need a nurse. Especially not a man nurse."

I motion for Clyde to move closer. "This is Clyde, Dad. If you don't need a nurse, you'll need to prove it to him."

"The sooner you rejoin the real world, Mr. Darby, the sooner you can get rid of me," Clyde says, digging a thumb into his broad chest.

Dad stares daggers at Clyde. "I don't have to prove anything to anybody when I'm paying the bills. And I'm getting rid of you right now. You're fired."

I plant my hands on my hips. "You're not responsible for this bill, Dad. Mom's trust is paying Clyde. Which means you don't have the authority to fire him."

Gwen's fingers graze my arm. "We should give these two a chance to get acquainted."

"Behave yourself," I say, kissing the top of Dad's bald head and following Gwen out of the apartment.

I chew on a fingernail as I walk with Gwen back to the parking lot. "I hope we're doing the right thing."

"Trust me on this, Ashton. Clyde is a miracle worker. If anyone can get through to your daddy, Clyde can."

"I hope you're right," I say and give her a hug in parting.

I spend the rest of the day in my office detailing kitchen plans in advance of my client meeting tomorrow. I'm late leaving work, and I text Owen to tell him I'll meet him at the Mariner's Club. I arrive to find him seated at the bar with a bleached-blonde bombshell. Everything about her appears enhanced—boobs, lips, cheeks. To my surprise, I experience neither anger nor jealousy at the sight of the woman batting her fake eyelashes at my husband. I give the hostess my name, and she shows me to a table in the corner.

"Can we sit outside?" I ask about the seating area on the screened porch, away from my husband and the beautiful stranger.

The young hostess looks at me as though I'm crazy. "Are you sure? It's like *so* hot out there."

"I'll take my chances," I say, and burst through the door onto the porch before she can argue.

With ceiling fans circulating the air, the temperature on the porch is pleasant. The table overlooks the pool where parents with young children are drinking fruity cocktails while their offspring splash in the water. The atmosphere beats the stark dining room with its tan carpet and walls. And if Owen and I get into an argument, the children's loud voices will drown out our angry ones.

Our waitress is taking my drink order when Owen finally makes it to the table. "Jack Daniels and water," he says rudely to the waitress as he sits down opposite me.

I look up at her. "And I'll have a glass of the house pinot grigio."

I wait for her to leave before I ask my husband, "Who's your little friend?"

He furrows his brow, pretending he doesn't know who I'm talking about. "Oh, you mean Harmony? She's not my little friend. She's just an acquaintance."

I snicker. "Harmony? What kinda name is that?"

"A pen name. She's a romance author. She's new in town. She's renting the condo at the opposite end of the street from us."

"Water's Edge is off the beaten path. How did she end up here?" I ask as I arrange my eating utensils on the table and spread my napkin in my lap.

"She moves around a lot, apparently. She likes to find remote settings for her characters."

"For an acquaintance, you sure know a lot about her."

A flush creeps up his neck. "We keep bumping in to each other. She's one of those people who likes to talk about herself."

"I bet she does." My husband is a looker. A romance author with sex on the brain would easily find him attractive.

The waitress delivers our drinks, and we sip for a minute in awkward silence.

"So what's new in your life?" Owen asks finally.

"Well, let's see." I settle back in my chair, crossing my legs.

"Dad's being difficult. He's not taking care of himself, and I've had to hire Gwen's agency to provide additional support."

Owen gives me a look over the rim of his glass. "And who's paying for that?"

"Mom's trust."

"That's brilliant, Ashton. Assuming he lives to ninety, twelve years of around-the-clock care will blow right through your inheritance."

"I'm more concerned about my father's well-being than the money. Besides, I'm pretty sure there's nothing physically wrong with him. I'm hoping his caregiver, Clyde, can get him back on his feet so he'll no longer need help." I take a sip of the crisp cool wine. "What's new in *your* world? Besides Harmony," I add in a barely audible voice.

"Rich and I are playing in the member-member golf tournament this weekend. There's a reception on Thursday and a dinner Saturday night if you wanna come."

"Maybe. We'll see." Why should I go with him to his events when he refused to attend Melissa's wedding with me?

As though reading my mind, he asks, "How's Hattie?"

"She's fine. She took me out for my birthday last weekend."

We go back and forth, asking each other about our lives like strangers who haven't seen each other in a while. When the waitress appears with a basket of pretzel rolls, Owen asks for another drink, and we both order the salmon salad for our entrees.

Owen's eyes follow the waitress's shapely backside as she leaves the table. "Carrie was upset when she stopped by yesterday evening."

"I'm aware. And you didn't help matters by fanning her flame."

He appears surprised. "What do you mean?"

I take a roll from the breadbasket. "You told her I was threatening to leave you."

"Truth hurts." Owen rattles his ice cubes before draining the last of his whisky from his glass.

"I'm here, aren't I? Why'd you tell her I'm acting like a spoiled princess?"

"If the shoe fits. I hope you set your sister straight. She thinks Marsh Point belongs to all three of you. You inherited Marsh Point. You don't have to share it with your siblings."

I refrain from rolling my eyes. He's not concerned about me sharing the house. He doesn't want me to share the money when I sell it. "For the duration of this dinner, I'm declaring the subject of Marsh Point off-limits."

"Why? The purpose of this dinner was to talk about our marriage. Marsh Point is the source of all our problems."

"The problem isn't the property itself. The problem is you not understanding how much Marsh Point means to me."

His face reddens. "That's not true! I know you love the place, Ash, but it's not practical for us to keep it. Your money pit will be an enormous burden on us. Not only will the maintenance be a constant drain on our bank accounts, we'll be married to home improvement projects. We won't be able to pick up on the weekends and go places."

"We're talking about a house, Owen, not a child. We have nothing tying us down now, but we haven't been on a trip in years. I can't even get you to go to Kiawah for a long weekend."

He sets down his glass and folds his hands on the table. In a calm voice, he asks, "Do you want a divorce, Ashton?"

My breath hitches. I'm unprepared for his frankness. "I'm not sure, honestly. We have issues we need to work on. Maybe—"

"What issues? Aside from our disagreement over Marsh Point. I admit we're not the same people we were when we got married. We've both changed. But in good ways."

"You think throwing crab goo on your wife is a good thing? By the way, I'm still waiting for an apology."

Owen hangs his head. "I'm sorry, honey. I admit that was

uncalled for. But you made me angry."

"Because you made me angry first," I say in a voice loud enough to make one of the young mothers at the pool look our way. I lower my voice. "Don't you sense this disconnect between us?"

Owen reaches for my hand. "All marriages have their difficulties. But you and I make a good team."

"A *team*?" I scoff. "When have we ever worked together on anything? We don't have children. We've never even planned an event together. Not even a small dinner party for our closest friends."

"That's not true. We developed Mariner's Point."

"Correction. Will and I developed Mariner's Point. You merely controlled the money. As usual," I add in a snide voice.

The waitress brings our salads, and we eat in silence. When the waitress asks if we want dessert, before I can respond, Owen asks for another drink and the check.

After he signs the check, he takes his drink with him and walks me back through the dining room to the main entrance. "You go ahead home. I'm going to finish my drink here. I'll be there shortly."

As he's kissing my cheek, I sneak a glance at the bar. Harmony has gone, but several of his single golfing buddies are watching a golf tournament on television.

I leave the restaurant feeling more desolate than I did after my mother died. During the short drive home, I realize the absence of intimacy in our relationship may be contributing to our problems. Could something as simple as having sex break through this tense barrier between us?

I change into a sexy nightgown and crawl into bed with my kindle. But when I turn out the light an hour later, Owen still hasn't gotten home. As the minutes tick by on my alarm clock, I envision Harmony fulfilling her kinky sexual fantasies with my husband.

CHAPTER
SIXTEEN

The uber-contemporary beach house I designed for Cliff and Cory Matheson may very well be my crowning glory. Which comes as a great surprise to me, considering I typically prefer more traditional architecture. But in order to accomplish their objectives, I had to step outside the box. While the project initially intimidated me, I'm pleased with the way it's taking shape.

But I can't take all the credit. Mother Nature contributed dramatically. The Mathesons, for whom money is no object, purchased the unspoiled hundred acres at the north end of Sandy Island. Built in the shape of a U, the ten-thousand-square-foot house has sleek lines with open spaces and glass walls that take advantage of the sweeping views of the ocean and sound from every room. Nestled within the embrace of the home's three wings is a serene Japanese garden, and on the lush stretch of lawn that merges into pristine sandy beaches, an infinity pool adds a touch of elegance.

The Mathesons, whose primary residence is in Connecticut, haven't visited the construction project in months. Their bright eyes and broad smiles indicate how pleased they are with their retirement home in progress.

The couple wears the scent of old money like expensive perfume. They are dressed casually but stylishly—Cliff in five-pocket pants and a black polo that outlines his fit torso and Cory in a black linen sheath with heavy gold jewelry adorning her neck and arms.

Cory throws her arms around me. "It's simply fabulous, Ashton. You've outdone yourself. You've made our dream home become a reality."

Cliff nods agreement. "Truly outstanding. I'd originally planned to work a few more years before retiring, but this place will be difficult to resist once we're finished."

Proud of my accomplishment, I hold my chin high. "I'm so glad you're happy." I spread the kitchen plans out on two sawhorses. "You get a gold star for discovering Regal Woodworks. The cabinet company is turning out to be a true gem. I've been working closely with their team, and your kitchen is coming along nicely. There are, however, a few things I'd like to go over with you before I meet with the project manager next week."

We spend the next thirty minutes discussing the kitchen plans. When Cory's phone rings, she excuses herself and steps outside to take the call. When she returns a few minutes later, her face is pale, and her pale eyes are brimming with tears.

Cliff looks up from the kitchen plans. "What's wrong, darling? You're as white as a sheet."

"That was Abbey who called. She had a checkup with her doctor earlier," Cory says, dabbing at her eyes with a tissue.

"Forgive my wife," Cliff says to me. "Our daughter is expecting a baby. A little girl. Our first grandchild."

Cory inhales an unsteady breath as she draws herself to her full height. "Abbey isn't due for another two weeks, but the doctor doesn't think she'll make it through the weekend." She tugs on her husband's shirt. "We need to get on the road to Raleigh right away."

The wrinkles in Cliff's forehead deepen. "But what about Palmetto Resort?"

Cory retrieves her purse from the floor by the front door where she left it. "We'll have to cancel. I refuse to miss the birth of my first grandchild."

"I don't want to miss it either, darling, but the reservation is nonrefundable if canceled inside the seventy-two-hour window." Cliff looks over at me. "Are you free this weekend? How would you and your husband like an expense-paid weekend to Palmetto Resort?"

"That's a marvelous idea," Cory chimes in. "Consider it a bonus for a job well done."

My eyes pop. "Are you serious?"

Cory squeezes my arm. "Yes! You've earned it, Ashton. You and your husband will have a splendid time."

"In that case, I accept. I've been dying to visit the Palmetto Resort. Thank you so much."

"You're most welcome." Cliff places a hand on his wife's lower back. "Let's go, sweetheart."

I hurry behind them out of the house. "Good luck with everything. Let me know when the baby is born. Does she have a name yet?"

Cory beams. "Amelia."

I repeat the name. "That's lovely."

Helping his wife into the front seat, Cliff says to me, "I'll call the resort on the way to Raleigh and make the arrangements. They'll transfer our itinerary to your name and email you the deets."

"That'd be great." I thank them again and wave as they head off in their Cayenne.

I wait until the sports car disappears out of sight before letting out a squeal. I can hardly believe my luck. During their peak season, standard rooms at Palmetto Resort run more than a thousand dollars a night. And I'm pretty sure the Mathesons weren't planning to stay in a standard room.

I drive back to town on a cloud. Not only am I thrilled about the free weekend, I'm grateful the Mathesons are pleased with the house. I'm too excited to return to the office. The workday is nearly over anyway. On a whim, I park in front of Tracy's Threads. I can't remember the last time I treated myself to a new outfit, and I can't think of a better opportunity to splurge.

My sister-in-law is the only one in the women's boutique. Tracy hurries out from behind the counter to greet me. "Hey, Ashton! Welcome to Tracy's Threads. Are you shopping or visiting?"

"Both," I say because I've been meaning to follow up with her after she gave me the thoughtful birthday gift. "How are things with Will?"

"About the same. Let's shop first. Then we can talk. Are you looking for anything specific?"

"A client just gave me an expense-paid weekend at Palmetto Resort," I say and explain about the Mathesons' reason for canceling their trip. "I'm looking for something special to wear to dinner, at least one night maybe both."

Tracy taps her chin as she assesses my body. "Everything will look good on you with your figure." She goes to a rack of dresses and removes an off-the-shoulder, ruffled midi dress in a striking emerald-green color. "What about something like this?"

"Beautiful, but it looks more like you than me."

Tracy turns toward the full-length mirror and admires her reflection. "It does look like me, doesn't it? It's one of my all-time favorites. But I don't have anywhere to wear it."

"Are you kidding? You can wear that to lots of places. Even to church."

"You're right. I should buy it." She hangs the green dress behind the counter and returns to the rack, flipping through more garments.

I reach for a knit maxi dress in a vibrant orange swirly pattern. This is nice."

"You have excellent taste. It's Trina Turk, and it's your size. What about this one?" She shows me a white linen wraparound dress, featuring a V neckline and ruffled hem.

I nod, smiling. "Gorgeous. I'll try them both."

She ushers me into a fitting room, and while I'm changing into the white dress, she brings in an armful of more clothes for me to try on.

I can't decide between the dresses, so I buy them both along with a one-piece swimsuit, a lacy white cover-up, a pair of white shorts, and three cute tops.

I laugh as I hand her my credit card. "So much for my free vacation. I just spent what it would've cost me to stay at Palmetto Resort for one night."

Tracy wags her finger at me. "But you'll be wearing your new threads long after you return home."

"Very true. I can't remember the last time I bought anything new."

Tracy processes the charge and hands me back the card. "Do you have time to grab a gelato? I have something I want to talk to you about."

I glance at the wall clock above her head. "I do. But the sign on your door says you close at five, and it's only four thirty."

She dismisses my concern with a flick of her hand. "I can close a few minutes early. It's been a slow day anyway. No one will notice."

"In that case, I'd love some gelato."

While Tracy is locking up the shop, I place my packages in the trunk of my car, and we walk a block south to Velvet Spoon.

I whisper to her as we wait in line. "I'm surprised at the number of people eating gelato so close to dinnertime."

"Right? No one follows rules anymore," she says with a giggle.

We both order single scoops in cups—Tracy the butter pecan

and me the strawberry—and take our treats to a table on the back patio.

"Have you told Owen about the free weekend yet?" Tracy asks.

I shake my head. "He probably won't go with me. He's playing in a golf tournament this weekend. But I won't let that stop me."

"Are you and Owen having problems?" Tracy raises a hand. "I'm being nosy. You don't have to answer that."

"I don't mind. The truth is, I inadvertently neglected my marriage when Mama was sick. I was so focused on taking care of her, I failed to notice that Owen and I were growing apart. And now the rift is so large, I don't know how to repair it."

"Do you think you'll get a divorce?" Tracy asks with head lowered, her gaze on her ice cream.

"I honestly don't know. Divorce is complicated, even when you don't have children," I say and shovel a spoonful of the creamy treat in my mouth.

"My husband will fire him if you do. Will can't stand Owen." She looks up from her cup. "I'm being unfair. It's not that he doesn't like Owen. I don't think Will trusts him."

I furrow my brow. "Really? Will has never said anything to me about that."

"He wouldn't as long as Owen is your husband." Tracy pushes her half-eaten treat away. "You never know what goes on in a marriage."

The sadness in my sister-in-law's face tugs at my heartstrings. "I'm a good listener if you want to talk. I promise, nothing you say will leave this table."

"Will hasn't been the same since your mom died. Even though they weren't close, her death has been really hard on him. He has such a short fuse, snapping at everyone about every little thing. He's like a rumbling volcano on the verge of erupting."

I abandon my gelato. She has my full attention now. "If you're worried about your safety, you should go visit your parents in Savannah for a while."

She shakes her head. "It's not like that. I'm not worried he'll hurt me or the girls. I just don't know how to get through to him. Was he ever close to your father?"

I think back to our childhood. "Not that I remember. Dad and Will have always worked well together. But my brother doesn't let anyone get close. I'd assumed you, being his wife, were different."

"I've been trying to get him to open up about the past, but I pushed him too far, and now he's shut me out completely. He won't even tell me what he wants for dinner."

"I'm sorry, Tracy. Is there anything I can do?" I ask, even though I've already tried talking to my brother.

"No. But thanks for asking. I just need to be patient, and hope he comes around soon."

I'm afraid Tracy is in for a very long wait. My brother needs a therapist to help him come to terms with the past. And that's not likely to happen in Will's lifetime.

CHAPTER SEVENTEEN

As I predicted, Owen refuses to go with me to Palmetto Resort for the weekend. What starts out as a disagreement about the weekend turns into a dreadful argument about Marsh Point. He storms out of the condo, and for the first time, he stays out all night.

I'm in my office midmorning on Thursday, finalizing the Matheson's kitchen plans, when May May pops in unannounced.

She stops short a few feet inside the doorway. "I can see you're busy. I should've called first. I'll come back another time," she says, stepping backward toward the hall.

"Wait! Don't go!" I come around from behind my desk. As I move closer, I can see the dark circles under her eyes and a deep crease between her brows. "What's wrong, May May? You don't look well."

"I . . . uh . . ." She wrings her hands together. "I'm not sure, honestly. I was on the way to the grocery store and here I am. You've been on my mind a lot lately, sweet girl." She pats my cheek. "I just needed to set my eyes on you, to make sure you're okay."

May May has always had a sixth sense about us Darby children. She has a habit of showing up at the exact moments we need her the most. "I'm fine," I say, even though I'm far from it. "How are you?"

"I could use some coffee. If you can spare the time, I'll treat you to a coffee from Corner Cup, and we can take a stroll along the water."

I hesitate. I want to wrap up some loose ends so I can leave for my trip early in the morning. But May May is full of helpful advice, and I could definitely use some words of wisdom about my marriage. "I always have time for you, May May. But I insist on buying," I say, grabbing my purse.

As we're leaving my office, I receive a call from Gwen. "I just spoke with Clyde. He's having a terrible time with your father this morning. He wants us to come. He needs our help."

"Oh goodness. I'm on my way."

May May looks at me with concern etched in her face. "What's wrong, sweetheart?"

"Dad is giving his caregiver a hard time. Clyde needs me at Whispering Oaks. Can I take a rain check on coffee?"

"Forget the coffee. I'm coming with you," she says, and we hurry out of the building together.

On the drive to the retirement community, I explain to May May about Dad not taking care of himself and me having to bring in a caregiver. "I don't think there's anything physically wrong with him. He's just in a slump."

"Ernest has been in a slump for years. He needs to stop wallowing in self-pity and get on with his life." May May says this with such vehemence my head jerks toward her. But she's turned away from me and is staring out the window, her expression a million miles away.

We arrive at Whispering Oaks to find Dad and Clyde facing off in front of his apartment. Dad is wearing his pajamas, his feet bare and hair disheveled. With fists balled at his sides, he stands with feet apart and chest stuck out as though ready to take on his caregiver. Opposite him, Clyde appears calm with arms crossed over his chest and a smile tugging at his lips.

"What on earth is going on?" I ask as we approach them.

Dad jabs a finger at Clyde. "Get this man out of my life. I didn't ask for his help, and he's cramping my style."

I bite down on my lip to keep from smiling. "What style, Dad? You mean the man who used to cruise around town in his flashy antique Benz convertible, wearing his seersucker suits, red-striped bow ties, and Panama hats? When you show us that man again, we'll let Clyde go. Until then, you're stuck with him."

Dad turns on me with face beaming red. "How dare you try to control my life? Just leave me be. I don't need anyone's help, most especially yours. I have nothing left to live for. I've lost my wife and my home. I just want to die."

May May slaps Dad hard across the cheek. "Hush your mouth, Ernest Darby!"

Clyde tenses, ready to protect his charge from the angry woman with the gray braid.

Placing a hand on Clyde's arm, I whisper, "Don't worry. May May is an old friend. She knows how to handle him."

Dad's face crumbles. "You don't understand, May. My life is over."

May May takes him in her arms. "You have plenty to live for, Ernest," she says, stroking his back as he sobs.

I've seen my father shed a few tears, but I've never seen him ugly cry. Not even when my mother died. And I'm grateful when May May says, "Come on, let's you and me go inside and have a chat." With an arm around his waist, she walks him into the apartment and closes the door.

Gwen appears from the tunnel of the foliage-lined path. "What'd I miss?"

Clyde strokes his chin, bewildered. "I'm not sure what just happened here."

I laugh. "May May just happened."

Gwen shakes her head. "Oh, Lord. May May is a tough bird. She's liable to give Ernest a piece of her mind."

Clyde's golden-brown eyes travel to the apartment's red door, and I can tell he's considering going in. "She's not gonna rough him up, is she?"

I laugh. "Not at all. If anyone can talk some sense into him, May May can. I should've asked her to visit him sooner. What set him off this morning?"

"It wasn't one particular thing. Like he said, he resents my presence. His frustration has been building all week. I figured he'd blow his top soon enough. Patients like Ernest always do. Once they get it out of their systems, they usually improve. Kinda like hitting rock bottom for an addict."

"Has he shown any progress at all these last few days?" I ask, my gaze now on the red door.

"We certainly haven't been sitting around, twiddling our thumbs. I've been making him take short walks several times a day, and we've been over to the wellness center a lot. But he complains about everything and refuses to engage with the other residents." Admiration creeps across Clyde's face. "Did he really used to own an antique Benz?"

"Still does. She's a beauty. Bright red with whitewall tires. I'm having the car fixed up for him as a surprise."

"You don't say." Clyde's deep baritone voice is rich like molasses when he laughs. "I can see the two of us cruising around town in such a fine machine. Instead of *Driving Miss Daisy,* I'll be driving Mr. Ernest."

I laugh out loud. "That would be a sight. I'll let you know when the car is ready. Maybe it will perk him up."

"I would certainly hope so," Clyde says.

Gwen fans her flushed face. "It's as hot as the devil's kitchen today," she says, and the three of us move to the shade of an oak tree while we wait.

Thirty minutes pass before May May emerges with my fully

clothed father. They come to stand in front of us, and May May nudges Dad. "Ernest has something he'd like to say."

"I apologize for being difficult. I've been going through a hard time." He casts a shy smile at May May, and she nods at him to continue. "If I promise to do better, can we reduce Clyde's hours?" He looks over at the caregiver. "Nothing against you personally, Clyde. I just don't enjoy being watched over like an infant."

"Then stop acting like one." I give my father a hug and then hold him at arm's length. "I love you, Dad. I only want what's best for you. But you have to want that for yourself."

His chin quivers as he nods his head.

"We all know you can take care of yourself. Once we see dramatic improvement, we'll talk about reducing Clyde's hours."

He nods again, but he doesn't speak, as though too choked up for words.

"Then we have a deal."

I leave Dad in Clyde's capable hands and return to the parking lot with May May. "Once again, you worked your magic. What did you say to him?"

"Mostly, I guilted him for wallowing in self-pity. And for wasting the precious time he has left." May May stops walking when we reach the car. "But hold your breath until you see the results. Your father and I have been through a lot together over the years, and I've never seen him this down."

Her words weigh heavily on me as we head back toward town. "I desperately need that coffee now. Do you still have time?"

"You bet." May May removes a tissue from her pocket and blows her nose. "I lied earlier when I said I didn't have a specific purpose for visiting you. I've started reading your mama's journals, and they've upset me deeply."

I glance over at her. "Anything you can share with me?"

She shakes her head. "Not yet. Maybe later. Probably never. Eileen was my best friend, but I never understood the extent to which she wrestled with her demons. I don't normally believe in ghosts, but I have this eerie feeling your mama is sending me vibes from the grave."

I return my gaze to the road. "I know what you mean. I feel the same way about Marsh Point."

"I surprised myself by showing up at your office this morning. I suspect Eileen had something to do with that. She wanted me to be a part of the showdown with your father."

"The other day at the cemetery, when I asked why you are so hard on Dad, you said that was a story for another time. Are you ready to tell me the story now?"

May May stares down as she wrings her hands together in her lap. "Our relationship is complicated, sweetheart. We were both devoted to your mother, but she didn't make it easy for us. There were times I wasn't sure their marriage would survive."

I tighten my grip on the steering wheel. "Like when Dad lived in the guesthouse. I think I was around eight at the time."

"That sounds about right. You were just a vulnerable child. Your mother's alcoholism had reared its ugly head. Her drunken displays and angry tirades put an end to their active social life. Except for me, none of their friends could tolerate her. I'm surprised you kids turned out normal after the things you experienced in that house."

"I wouldn't exactly call any of us normal." I locate a parking spot in front of the coffee shop and turn off the engine. "What made Dad move back into the house?"

"The fire was a wake-up call. I assume you remember it," she says, fingering a strand of hair off my face.

"How could I forget nearly burning down my family's home?"

May May withdraws her hand. "You were cooking bacon for your starving sisters. Something Ernest should have been doing. For the sake of his children, he knew he had to give his marriage another chance. Nine months later, Will was born."

I furrow my brow as I try to recall another memory. "He left a second time, a longer time. When was that? And where was he staying? I don't think he was in the guesthouse."

"You'll have to ask your father about that," she says and gets out of the car before I can press her for more answers.

Corner Cup is named for its location at the corner of our town's busiest thoroughfares—Main Street and Second Avenue. May May and I order cold brews with cream and take them down to the waterfront.

"Owen and I are going through a rough patch. He's pressuring me to sell Marsh Point. If he forces me to choose between him and Marsh Point, Owen won't win."

"Oh, honey," May May says, resting a hand on my arm. "Have things gotten that bad?"

My eyes fill with tears. "Things have been bad for a while. But the argument over Marsh Point has taken our fights to a new level. He'll never live there with me. And I don't want to live anywhere else. What should I do, May May? Should I divorce him?"

"Only you have the answer, sweet girl." She touches the tip of her finger to the space between my breasts. "Right here in your heart. Although you may have to do a little digging to find it. Marriage is a long journey, and both parties must be equally committed to make it through the tough times."

I stare down at my coffee. "I'm not sure I love him anymore." Saying the words takes my breath away, and I gasp. "I can't believe I just admitted that."

"That doesn't mean your marriage has to be over. Unless you really want it to be. In matters of the heart, I certainly don't have all the answers. But I know this much." She tilts my chin up. "You, Ashton Merriweather Darby, are a special woman with a beautiful soul. If Owen isn't treating you like a queen, then you need to find someone who will."

CHAPTER **EIGHTEEN**

I arrive home from work to an empty condo on Thursday evening, but I can tell Owen has been here at some point during the day. He left his damp towel on my side of the bed and a dirty coffee tumbler in the sink. I remember him mentioning a kick-off event for the member-member golf tournament tonight. Maybe he won't come home until after I'm asleep. If I'm really lucky, he won't come home at all.

I spend a ridiculous amount of time accessorizing my wardrobe for my trip to Palmetto Resort. Mama's Mikimoto pearl choker would look stunning with the white dress, and the diamond tennis bracelet would be fun to wear with all my outfits. I make a mental note to stop by the bank and retrieve the two items from my safe deposit box on my way out of town in the morning.

By eight o'clock, my suitcase is packed and I'm ready for my trip. But I'm too excited to sleep, and it's way too early for bed. I pour a glass of wine and take it outside to the patio. I've just settled onto the chaise lounge when I receive a text from Hattie.

Get down to The Nest asap. There's something here you've gotta see.

I let out a heavy sigh as I drop the phone onto the lounge chair beside me. A sick feeling in my gut tells me this *something* has to do with Owen. Leaning my head back, I close my eyes and try to block all thoughts of my husband from my mind. I don't want to be bothered by Owen tonight. I want a peaceful night's rest before my much-anticipated weekend away.

The chair vibrates with another text, and I snatch up the phone. It's Hattie again.

This is serious, Ashton. Get here fast.

Hattie isn't one prone to hysterics. If she says it's serious, she means it. I thumb off my response. *Fine. I'm on my way.*

Scrambling to my feet, I return the untouched wine to the refrigerator and grab my purse on the way out the door.

The parking lot at The Nest is crowded, and inside is standing room only, but right away I spot Owen seated at the bar. Harmony is standing next to him, her body leaning against his, their heads pressed together, a gesture that hints at their intimate relationship.

My blood boils as I tunnel my way through the mob of people toward them. Holding up my phone, I snap several pics of Owen fingering a lock of bleached-blonde hair off her cheek and Harmony pressing her inflated lips to his.

Rich, who is sitting next to Owen, notices me first. He barks out a laugh and sends an elbow crashing into Owen's side. "Dude! Your wife's here," he says in a voice loud enough to get the attention of those around us.

Owen's brow hits his hairline. "Ashton! What're you doing here?"

"Taking photographs of you and your little bimbo," I say, waving my phone at him. "You make a lovely couple."

The crowd has quieted, and Harmony's voice is shrill. "Hey! Who are you calling a bimbo?"

"If the shoe fits." I glance down at her hot pink platform heels. "Oh, look. You're even wearing bimbo shoes."

Harmony lets out a loud huff. "How dare you!"

"How dare you?" I jab my finger at her. "You're the one

sleeping with my husband." I toss up my hands. "You know what? You can have him. He's not worth the trouble." I wave my phone at Owen. "I'll be sure to show these to my divorce attorney."

Spinning on my heels, I hold my head high as I push through the astonished crowd to the exit. I wait until I'm in my car before letting out a piercing scream and bursting into sobs. Mine aren't tears of sadness. They are tears of humiliation. My husband had the gall to make out with his girlfriend in front of the entire town.

I park in front of the condo, but I can't bring myself to get out of the car. I never wanted to live here, never wanted to sell my beach house. But I let him talk me into moving to Mariner's Point, like I let him talk me into so many other things over the years. Because, like Hattie said at the wedding, I've never had the courage to stand up to him.

I suddenly know what I have to do, what I should've done a long time ago. There is only one place where I belong. And this condo with Owen Nelms is not it.

I shake off the self-pity and let anger take control of my mind. I won't spend another second of my life in this place. I turn the car around in the driveway, backing in until the rear bumper is practically touching the front steps. Inside the condo, I fill every duffel bag and suitcase I can find with my belongings and toss them into the trunk alongside my suitcase for the weekend.

As I speed away, a sense of relief like I've never experienced before overcomes me. I've left him. After years of uncertainty, I've finally made the decision that I know, deep down in my core, is right for me.

Arriving at Marsh Point, I park my car in the carport and let myself into the guesthouse. Too keyed up to sleep, I strip linens from the beds and stuff them in the washing machine, along with an armload of musty towels.

When my phone vibrates in my back pocket, I expect to see Owen's name on the screen, but I'm relieved to see Hattie's the one calling. "I know you're worried," I blurt. "But I'm fine. Or I will be fine. I need some time to process what just happened."

"Are you at the condo? Do you want me to come over?"

"I just moved out of the condo. I'll be staying in the guest-house at Marsh Point, but don't tell anyone. I don't want Owen to know where I am. I'll talk to you soon, Hattie." I end the call before she can argue and power off the phone.

I vacuum and dust and spray lemon-scented air freshener in all the rooms. I scrub toilets and showers and wipe down every surface in the kitchen. When the guesthouse is spotless, I make several trips out to my car for my belongings and spend an hour arranging my clothes in the closet and drawers.

It's nearly one in the morning by the time I change into my pajamas and slip between the crisp sheets. When I turn off the bedside table lamp, the soft glow from the full moon fills the room, and I get up again to close the blind. I stand at the window looking out at the moon's rays glistening off the sound. I think back to a lazy summer afternoon I spent with Mama a couple of years ago. It was one of her rare, good days, and we'd sipped sweet tea and talked on the veranda for hours. While I never told Mama about my marital problems, I think she suspected. She said to me, "No matter what happens, sweetheart, Marsh Point will always be your home."

I wonder if she ever said the same to Carrie or Will? Had she already planned to leave Marsh Point to me in her will? But why me? I stare up at the starry sky. "Why, Mama?"

My mother lived at Marsh Point for most of her life, minus her years in college and the brief time after she and Dad were first married when they rented a small house a few blocks away. Mama was an only child. There was never any question she would one day inherit the property. When my grandparents decided to travel around the world, they turned the house over to Mama, and she and my father moved in. What would Mama's life have been like if not for her refuge? Would she have gotten sober if forced to live in the real world? I stop myself from traveling down the path of *what-ifs*. Marsh Point was Mama's safe haven, where she drank herself to death, hidden from the prying eyes of the people who judged her. Whether this is what Mama intended, Marsh Point has now become my safe haven as well.

CHAPTER NINETEEN

Tendrils of hope spiral through my body when I open my eyes on Friday morning. I recognize my surroundings right away, despite never having spent a single night in the guesthouse. Rolling onto my side, I stare out the window at the first rays of dawn casting the sky and sound in a golden glow. At long last, I'm home to stay.

I'm on my way to becoming a single woman. While the idea terrifies me, I'd rather be alone than with a man I don't trust. I nestle beneath the sheets as I plan the day ahead. After going over a few important matters with my staff at the office, I'll stop by the bank for my jewelry before heading off to Palmetto Island. The drive will take an hour, plus or minus a few minutes depending on traffic. Assuming I'm not delayed by work or traffic, I should arrive at the resort way ahead of check-in. I'll leave my bag with the front desk staff, have lunch on the deck at the resort's casual restaurant, Carolina Breeze Bistro, and then sit by the pool until my room is ready. I'll pack an extra tote bag with my bathing suit, cover-up, and a Taylor Jenkins Reid novel I've been wanting to read.

Eager to start my mini vacation, I throw back the covers and sit up in bed. I need caffeine to burn off the haze of exhaustion from having stayed up late cleaning and unpacking. Downstairs in the kitchen, I find an old coffee maker but no coffee. I walk outside in my pajamas—the workers won't arrive for hours—and stroll across the front lawn and down to the end of the dock. The tide is high and the salty air fresh, and I spend a few minutes watching a lone pelican dive for fish.

Returning to the guesthouse, I take my time in getting ready, familiarizing myself with where things are in my new living quarters. It's nearly nine o'clock when I load my suitcase into my trunk and head off to work.

I'm shocked to find Owen waiting for me in my office. He jumps to his feet when I enter the room. "Ashton! Where have you been? I've been worried out of my mind."

I drop my purse on my desk with a thud. "As you can see, I'm perfectly fine. I'm no longer your problem to worry about."

He grabs my arm. "Come on, babe. Don't be like this. I'm sorry about last night. Despite what you think, nothing happened between Harmony and me. The only thing I'm guilty of is having too much to drink at the tournament's welcome party. I should've discouraged Harmony when she came onto me, but I was weak." He pulls me close, breathing hot air into my ear. "It's been so long since we've had sex, and I got carried away."

"So now all our marital problems are *my* fault?"

"I didn't say that. I take full responsibility for my share of the problems." He plants a trail of kisses down my neck. "But I'm not ready to give up on our marriage. If the invitation is still open, I'd like to go with you to Palmetto Resort. This weekend will give us a chance to reconnect."

Self-doubt threatens to penetrate my newly discovered confidence as I study his face. Is that sincerity in those dazzling blue eyes? And why his sudden interest in working things out? Whatever is going through his mind, I can't let myself fall victim to his trap yet again.

I wrench my arm free of his grasp and push him away. "You're too late. I'm going away alone this weekend, and as soon as my attorney returns from abroad, I'm filing for divorce." I don't tell him Cedric Morton won't be back from his trip for several more weeks.

Tears glisten in his eyes, and his voice is unsteady when he says, "I totally understand if you need to be alone this weekend, but will you at least have dinner with me when you get back on Sunday? Give me one more chance, babe. I promise I can make it up to you."

I move over to the window, and as I stare out at the Merriweather Bridge, I ask God to give me the strength to stand up to him.

Owen appears beside me. "I realize I've been a jerk these past few months, but I'm willing to do whatever it takes to make it up to you."

I shoot him a sideways glance. "Does that include cashing in my stock portfolio?"

His jaw tightens. "We can talk about it when we have dinner on Sunday." He places a hand on the small of my back. "Will you be coming home to the condo when you get back from your trip?"

I shiver beneath his touch. "Probably not."

He kisses my cheek. "Then I'll touch base with you Sunday afternoon."

"Fine." I'm willing to have dinner with him if it means getting my money back. "Now, please leave. I have work to do before I head out for the weekend."

I wait until Owen has left my office before summoning my assistant. I quickly go over the task list I need completed today and my schedule for early next week.

"Are you free on Monday afternoon?" Liza asks. "A potential client has requested a consultation about renovating their home in the historic section."

"I'm already booked on Monday. I have a meeting with the

project manager from Regal Woodworks about the Mathesons' kitchen. See if they can meet another time."

"Will do."

I gather my belongings and we exit the office together and part in the hallway. "Let me know if you need anything. I'll just be lounging by the pool this afternoon. Yay, me," I say, and do a little dance step before taking off down the hall.

Liza calls after me, "I wouldn't dare disturb you. Enjoy your time off."

Leaving my office, I drive straight to the bank where Delbert Lewis greets me in the lobby and escorts me to the vault. He waits patiently while I retrieve my metal drawer from its locked slot and then shows me into the same private room as before, closing the door behind him on his way out.

One at a time, I remove the velvet jewelry boxes until I locate the two rectangular cases with the diamond tennis bracelet and Mikimoto pearls. I set those aside and begin organizing everything back in the drawer. I realize the green velvet box containing the diamond necklace with sapphire pendant are missing.

My pulse racing, I dump the boxes out again and begin frantically opening them on the table. Sparkling gemstones stare back at me from their black velvet liners, but none of them are the diamond necklace. I can't think of anything else that's missing, but I can't rely on memory. I have to be certain. Untying the stack of index cards telling the jewelry's history, I match each piece with the coordinating card. When I'm finished, two index cards are left. One for the necklace and the other for the twenty-four-carat fancy intense pink diamond ring. The same two items I told Owen were worth the most.

My stomach knots into a heavy ball of dread, coiling and churning. I think back to the night I brought the jewelry home from Marsh Point after the reading of Mom's will. When I showed Owen the pieces, he said the jewelry was too gaudy for me to wear and suggested I sell it. I'd fallen asleep on the chaise lounge, and when I came inside from the patio hours later, Owen was emerging from the closet with his pajamas in his hand and guilt written all over his face.

I place everything back in the drawer, except for the pearls and tennis bracelet, and return the drawer to the slot. I race over to the condo and search my closet from top to bottom on the remote chance the missing jewelry dropped out of our safe when I was transporting it to the bank. Just as I suspected, I come up empty-handed. How could I have been so naïve? I've allowed this man to steal me blind. But no more.

On my way out of the condo, I slip off my gold wedding band and modest diamond engagement ring and leave them on the table by the front door.

CHAPTER **TWENTY**

I leave my troubles behind as I drive down the palmetto tree-lined entrance to the resort. The main building is a three-story, lowcountry-style building with deep porches offering sweeping views of the May River. I park under the portico in the brick-lined driveway and turn over my keys to a valet attendant. When I enter the lobby, I pause momentarily to take in the opulent furnishings—plush seating, grand chandeliers, marble floors, and an upscale bar.

I give my name to the front desk clerk, and she prints an itinerary for my stay that makes my mouth fall agape. Dinner reservations and spa treatments. A wine tasting and sunset cruise. My mind reels as I mentally add up the expenses.

At a loss for words, I lift my gaze from the itinerary to the desk agent. I'm considering canceling my reservation when the agent leans across the counter and says in a low voice, "The Mathesons are picking up the tab for everything. That must be some house you're designing for them."

Her words bring a smile to my face. I fold the itinerary and slip it into my purse. "They are excellent clients. They know what they want, which makes them easy to please."

After a leisurely lunch—grilled shrimp over mixed greens with a glass of crisp white wine—I change into my swimsuit and search the pool deck for a vacant lounge chair. I'm on the verge of giving up when a couple abandons two lounge chairs near the infinity edge of the pool.

I spread out my towel on the end chair, overlooking the May River, and make myself comfortable with my Taylor Jenkins Reid novel. I only read a couple of pages when the warm sun and wine buzz make me sleepy, and I doze off. When I awaken, an attractive redhead is occupying the chair beside me, reading my book's back-cover copy.

I clear my throat, and she looks up, startled. "Oh! I'm so sorry. Your book fell onto the pool deck while you were sleeping. I picked it up so it wouldn't get wet. Here." She hands me the book. "Looks good, by the way."

I smile as I take the book from her. "I just started it, but Reid is one of my new favorite authors. She wrote *Daisy Jones & The Six*. You may have seen the Amazon Prime series."

She sips the green concoction in her tulip-shaped glass as she considers my question. "I don't believe so. Then again, I don't watch much television."

"What brings you to Palmetto Resort?" I ask.

"I'm on my honeymoon." My face must register shock, because she quickly adds, "My second marriage. What about you? Are you here with your significant other?"

Unexpected tears fill my eyes. "I'm recently separated."

"Oh, honey. I'm so sorry. How recently?"

"As of this morning."

"Girlfriend, you need a drink!" Sitting straight up in her chair, she flags down a young woman wearing a blue polo bearing the resort's logo. "My friend here would like a drink."

The waitress hands me a cocktail menu. "What can I get you?"

I eye the redhead's drink. "What're you having?"

"A cucumber martini, and it's delicious."

I've never had a martini, but it sounds wicked. As the child of an addict, I carefully monitor my alcohol consumption, but vacations are meant for splurging. I scan the menu and order the only drink I recognize. "I'll have a blueberry mojito, please."

"And I'll have another martini," says the redhead, even though her glass is still half full.

"Coming right up." The waitress takes the menu and disappears.

The woman extends a hand to me. "I'm Susan Nicholson, by the way. From Richmond, Virginia."

I shake her hand. "And I'm Ashton Nelms. From Water's Edge."

Susan crinkles her nose. "I've never heard of Water's Edge. Where is it?"

"About an hour from here. It's a sleepy, out-of-the-way coastal town."

"Sounds charming." Susan rests back in her chair. "As for your separation, I know what you're going through. I'm divorced myself. I was married to my first husband for thirty years. You either grow together or you grow apart. That's what happened to us anyway. What about you?"

"The same, I guess." Although I'm beginning to wonder if Owen has always been a dirty rotten scoundrel, and I am too much of a fool to realize it.

The waitress returns and places our drinks on the small metal table between us. Susan drains the rest of her first martini and hands the waitress her empty glass.

Reaching for the second martini, Susan says, "My career saved me. I'm an interior designer. Do you work?"

I nod. "I'm an architect. And I know what you mean. I'm grateful for the distraction." I take a small sip of the blueberry mojito. The sugary lime juice and blueberries make for a refreshing mixture on a hot summer day. "If you don't mind me asking, when did you get divorced?"

"A couple of years ago." Susan removes a collapsible sun hat from her bag and fastens it to her head. "I don't know about you, but it took me forever to get up the nerve to leave my husband."

I nearly choke on my drink at her honesty. "Same. Why *is* it so hard to leave them?"

"Because no matter how unhappy you are, marriage is safe." Susan sets her drink on the table and slides down in her chair. "I had no intention of ever marrying again, but it's lonely on the other side. You'll find that out soon enough. Going to social functions by yourself sucks. There's no one to fetch you drinks from the bar, and no one to cling to during awkward moments."

Going to cocktail parties without Owen is the least of my concern. "Then it's a good thing I'm not very social. I don't mind being alone. In fact, I kind of enjoy it."

Susan peers at me over the top of her designer sunglasses. "I'm just saying, don't be afraid to look for love again when you're ready." She giggles. "Although I wasn't ready, but love found me anyway."

"How did you meet your new husband?"

"We met at a bar in New York. Never mind we both live in Richmond." Susan crosses one long creamy leg over the other. "We were both in the city on business, eating dinner alone at our hotel bar. We struck up a conversation. Turns out we have a long list of mutual friends." Her cheeks turn a dainty shade of pink. "We have a lot in common, actually."

"How wonderful for both of you. Where is your husband now?"

I expect her to say he's playing golf. But she surprises me when she tells me he's in their room making business calls. "He's in finance, a real workaholic. But I am too, so I can't complain." She grips my arm, her fingers digging into my skin. "You won't believe it. Being in love is *so* much better the second time around. It is for me anyway."

"I'm glad to hear there's hope for my future," I say, although I don't feel very hopeful at all.

Susan glances down at her phone. "This is Tom texting me now. He's finished with his work, and we're going for a bike ride before dinner."

"That sounds like fun."

She gulps down her martini, gathers up her multiple tubes of sunscreen, and throws those long legs over the side of her chair. "I enjoyed meeting you, Ashton. You've come to the right place to clear your head. Be sure to book yourself a spa treatment while you're here."

I smile up at her. "I'm spending tomorrow morning in the spa. Enjoy your evening. I hope I run into you again."

I watch Susan's slim figure skirt the pool and disappear inside the main building. Opening my book, I peer over the top of the binding as I study the other guests around me. Most are my age or older, although I spot a few who appear to be in their thirties. None of them are alone, and nearly all of them appear to be in love.

The idea of being in love on a romantic weekend seems so foreign to me. Finding love again is the last thing on my mind right now, but one day, when I'm ready, I'd like to have someone to share my golden years. I close my eyes and think about the man I would want for a second husband. Foremost, I want someone who understands and appreciates me. Someone who doesn't constantly need to have his ego fed. Someone who treats me like a queen. And someone who doesn't play golf.

A front desk clerk informing me my room is ready interrupts my musings. She hands me a small envelope containing my keycards. "You're on the third floor. The elevators are located just off the lobby behind the reception desk. Our bellman has already delivered your luggage to your room. You may go up whenever you're ready."

"Thank you," I say, fishing a generous tip out of my wallet.

Eager to see my room, I abandon my drink, pack my things into my tote bag, and find my way to the third floor. The waterfront room features a spa tub, king-size bed covered in luxurious Italian linens, and a private balcony with two lounge chairs and a small table.

After unpacking my suitcase, I soak in the spa tub for thirty minutes, wrap myself in a fluffy white towel, and stretch out on the balcony for a nap.

I sleep for two hours and wake feeling groggy. Because I'm not much of a wine enthusiast, I skip the tasting, and take my time getting ready for dinner. A cold shower invigorates me, and at seven o'clock sharp, I take the elevator downstairs to the premier restaurant for my dinner reservation.

Heavy paneling lines the walls of Lowcountry Lantern, while brass lanterns hang from the ceiling between exposed ceiling beams. Guests waiting for their tables crowd the bar. I'm the only single person in the dining room, and I stick out like a sore thumb, although I'm pretty sure no one else has even noticed me. I valued my solitude the week I spent by myself at Marsh Point. Why do I feel so alone here? Is it because I'm surrounded by couples so obviously in love? Is my soon-to-be-divorced status sinking in? Or is it because I'm making a huge mistake in leaving Owen?

CHAPTER TWENTY-ONE

My luxurious spa treatments on Saturday morning include a facial, massage, and seaweed body wrap. I'm so relaxed after being pampered for three hours, I have to return to my room for a nap. When I wake refreshed and famished around two o'clock, I purchase a bowl of fresh fruit from the hotel canteen in the lobby and head out to explore.

I take a long walk around the resort and then go for a bike ride in the neighboring residential section. With hours to kill before my sunset cruise, I head to the fitness center where a deep-water exercise class is about to begin. I hurry to my room to change into my swimsuit, and when I return, the instructor, Beverly, is leading her small group of women outside to the center's fitness pool. The workout is more fun than I imagined, and my muscles scream at me as I make my way back to the room an hour later.

I take extra time with my appearance, and when I stare at my reflection in the mirror, I almost don't recognize myself in the chic white dress with the Mikimoto pearls around my neck. I'm no longer the haggard woman trapped in an unhappy marriage. I've survived the first thirty-six hours of separation. I'm a fifty-year-old single woman, with the rest of my life ahead of me, ready to take on the world.

My spirits tank when I venture out to the dock and find four couples boarding the resort's pontoon boat for the sunset cruise. But the couples include me in their conversation as though we're old friends. The three couples who are on their second marriages offer encouraging words for surviving divorce and finding new love.

Feeling inspired, I enter Lowcountry Lantern with a newfound confidence and ask the hostess if I may have dinner at the bar.

"I'm not sure if there are seats available. Let me check." She stands on her tiptoes as she surveys the situation at the bar. "You're in luck. I see two seats at the other end."

As I follow the hostess through the restaurant, I notice Susan, my friend from the pool yesterday, sitting with her husband at a far-off table. I flash her a wave, and she wiggles her fingers in return.

I've ordered a red wine and I'm perusing the menu specials when an attractive man in a blue sport coat slides onto the chair beside me. "I hope you don't mind. I understand this is the singles corner. You and I appear to be the only ones flying solo at this resort." His clear green eyes fall to my naked ring finger. "I assume you're not married, but maybe I'm mistaken."

"Recently separated," I say, self-consciously covering my left hand.

"Your husband's a fool to let a pretty woman like you get away."

Normally, I would find his pickup line cheesy, but his tone sounds sincere, and I smile softly in response.

He signals the bartender for a Mount Gay rum and tonic, and when the drink arrives, he settles back in his chair. "Will your divorce be ugly?"

I find this an inappropriate thing to ask a stranger, and I tell myself he's just making conversation. No sense in being rude when we have to sit together. "It's too early to say. What about you? Are you divorced?"

"I never married, actually."

"Interesting. How does one stay single all their life?"

He shrugs. "I just never met my soul mate." Mischief sparks in those electric green eyes. "But I haven't given up trying." He sips his drink. "What brings you to Palmetto Resort?"

"The weekend is a gift from clients."

His eyes widen. "Wow! I want your job. What do you do?"

I laugh. "I'm an architect. It's not really a gift. Their first grandchild was born earlier than expected. Since they couldn't get their money back, they sent me in their place. Chalk it up to being in the right place at the right time. Lucky me," I say, holding up my glass.

He clinks his glass to mine. "You mean lucky *me*."

I roll my eyes. "Using corny lines won't help you land a wife."

He laughs. "I'll remember that . . ." He narrows his eyes. "I'm embarrassed to say, I don't even know your name."

"I'm Ashton Nelms. Soon to be Ashton Darby."

"And I'm Jake Loomis. Soon to be Jake Loomis."

The giggle that slips out from my lips sounds foreign to my ears. I sound like a schoolgirl with her first crush. The schoolgirl I never got to be. "You're incorrigible." I give his arm a playful punch.

When the bartender comes to take our order, Jake gestures at me. "Ladies first."

"I'll have the soft-shell crab special with a side house salad, please. And no nuts. I'm highly allergic." Out of habit, even though I never leave home without it, I check to make certain my EpiPen is in my clutch.

The bartender scribbles on his pad. "Yes, ma'am. Our house salad doesn't have nuts, but I'll let the kitchen know to be extra careful." He turns his attention to Jake. "And you, sir?"

"I'll have the soft shells as well. And please bring us a dozen raw oysters to start," Jake says, handing back the menu.

I raise an eyebrow. "*Us*. Does that mean you're planning to share? Because I have an insatiable appetite for raw oysters."

"In that case, you'd better order your own. I was only planning to give you one," he says, a smirk tugging at the corner of his lips.

"Pretty please," I say in a sugary sweet tone. I can't remember the last time I flirted with a man, but I'm having so much fun.

Jake lets out a sigh. "All right, then. I'll give you two. But only if you promise not to abandon me until after we eat. I can't bear the thought of sitting here alone."

"Deal!" I say, offering him a high five. "So, Jake Loomis, what do you do for a living?"

"I'm a wildlife photographer." His expression turns serious, and I can tell how much his work means to him.

I give him an appreciative nod. "I grew up on Catawba Sound. I consider myself the quintessential nature lover. Have you been published in *National Geographic*?"

"Many times. All the major wildlife magazines, actually. I've published several coffee table books as well."

My eyes grow wide. "I bet you've been on some amazing adventures."

He grins. "Spectacular. In my younger days, I traveled around a lot. Which is the main reason I never married. I'm slowing down now though. I just bought a small house in the residential section here at the resort."

I think about the large attractive homes I saw on my bike ride. He must do well in his career to afford one of those homes.

The bartender delivers our oysters, and while we eat them, Jake holds me spellbound with some of the harrowing escapades he experienced while traveling. Jake's relaxed manner sets me at ease, and his goofy sense of humor makes me laugh. We're never at a loss for words during our next courses—mixed green salads with sweet onion vinaigrette and soft-shell crabs lightly coated in batter and sautéed to perfection.

I have no intention of sleeping with him tonight, but I can't help but wonder if a relationship between us might be possible down the road. Maybe when I'm ready, we can go on a proper date. After all, he only lives an hour away from me. For now, having someone find me attractive and interesting is good for my ego.

The bartender clears our empty plates and presents us with dessert menus. "Can I tempt you two with dessert?"

I wave the menu away. "None for me. I'm stuffed. Dinner was delicious."

"I'm glad you enjoyed it." The bartender looks over at Jake. "And for you, sir?"

"I don't care for dessert, but I wouldn't mind another glass of wine." He finishes the pinot noir he'd had with dinner and hands the empty glass to the bartender. "What about you, Ashton? It's still early. We can sit by the pool for a while."

"I guess another glass won't hurt." I wait for the bartender to leave before whispering to Jake, "In the interest of full disclosure, I'm not sleeping with you."

He bursts out laughing. "Understood. I promise not to make a pass at you, no matter how much I'm tempted."

"Good! I'm holding you to it. No funny stuff." I slide off the stool to my feet. "I need to use the restroom first."

"Go ahead. I'll wait here for our wine."

There's a long line in the women's restroom, and when I finally emerge, Jake is standing outside the door with two glasses of wine.

He offers me a glass. "Ready to go out to the pool?"

I look down at the glass and back up at him. "I need to pay my bill first."

"No worries. I took care of it."

I take the glass from him. "That's awfully kind of you. But I'm still not sleeping with you."

He chuckles. "I get it."

We pass through the lobby and exit the back door to the empty pool. Kicking off our shoes, we sit on the edge with our feet dangling in the water.

I sip my wine and smack my lips together. "Is this the same wine I was drinking before? It tastes kind of bitter."

"Hmm. I watched the bartender pour it. Mine came from the same bottle." He takes a sip from his glass. "Tastes fine to me."

"Must be my taste buds." I drink another mouthful and set down my glass. I flutter kick my feet in the water. "The pool is so serene at night."

"We could skinny dip."

I smack his abs with the back of my hand. "I warned you. No sex. Keep it up, and I'm going back inside." I lean back on my hands and tilt my face to the sky. "I see the Big Dipper, and the Little Dipper. I bet you know all the stars, don't you?" When I look over at Jake, dizziness overcomes me. "Whoa. What was that?"

"What was what?" Jake's voice sounds muffled, like he's underwater.

My head spins, and when I try to speak, to ask for help, my tongue is heavy.

"Come on. Let's get you to your room."

I'm aware of Jake helping me to my feet. I don't want him to take me to my room, but I'm too weak to fight him. My legs are jelly, and I have no choice but to lean into him for support. He's dragging me into the hotel through a different entrance, and the hallway inside is one I've never seen before. He punches the elevator up button, and when the doors slide open, the floor slips out from beneath me, and I tumble into the abyss.

CHAPTER **TWENTY-TWO**

I wake with a start from the depth of darkness. My eyes dart about the small beige room from the long counter littered with medical supplies to the sliding glass door to the young black woman in a tan sheriff's uniform dozing in a straight-back chair at the end of my bed. Neatly stacked in the chair beside her are my white dress, clutch, sandals, and my pearl choker.

My mind races as I recall the events of the previous evening. I had dinner at the bar with that man. Jake. He was waiting for me when I came out of the restroom. We went outside to the pool for a nightcap. The wine tasted funny. Bitter. Did he slip something into my wine?

Peeling the blanket back, I see that I'm wearing a hospital gown. I swing my feet over the side of the bed, but I stand too quickly and a wave of dizziness overcomes me. I ease back down to the side of the bed and wait for my head to stop spinning.

"Mrs. Nelms! You're awake!" The uniform officer gets to her feet and looms over me. "How're you feeling?"

"Confused. How do you know my name? And why am I in the hospital?" I squint as I inspect her badge. "The Beaufort

County Sheriff's Department? What on earth is going on? Did I do something wrong?"

"Not at all. I'm Officer Richelle Wilks." She shows me her credentials. "I'm here to help. You came close to being the victim of date rape last night."

"Date rape? Oh my god."

She sits down on the bed beside me. "Your friend Susan Nicholson saw your dinner companion slip something in your wine when you left the bar. She followed him into the lobby, and when you emerged from the restroom, she watched him give you the wine and lead you outside. She reported it to the bartender, who called security. By the time they caught up with you, the man was dragging you into your room. You were out cold. Security called the rescue squad, and they drove you to a nearby regional hospital. And that's when I got involved."

I shake my head. "I don't understand. Did I overdose?"

"Not at all. The drug screening revealed traceable amounts of GHB in your system. GHB is also known as a club drug and is used frequently in these types of situations. The drug metabolizes rapidly. You should have no lingering effects."

The enormity of what almost happened sends a shiver through me. "I can't believe this."

"I realize it's a lot to comprehend." Officer Wilks gestures at the chair with my belongings. "If you'd like to get dressed, I'll drive you back to the resort, and we can talk more along the way."

"Okay," I mumble and slide off the bed to my feet.

The officer steps outside the examining room while I change out of the hospital gown into my clothes. When I emerge, she's waiting for me with two cups of coffee.

Taking a coffee from her, I follow the officer outside to her patrol car in the parking lot. "This is a day of firsts for me, Officer Wilks. I've never ridden in a cop car, and I'm not in the habit of picking up strange men in bars."

"No one is judging you, Mrs. Nelms." She starts the engine

and heads out of the emergency room parking lot. "Why don't you start at the beginning and tell me everything?"

I stare out the window as the night's events come back to me. "He sat down next to me, we struck up a conversation, and we ate dinner together. It all seemed harmless enough. I was very upfront with him. I told him I would not have sex with him."

"Men like him don't need permission. They take what they feel entitled to. According to hotel security, other women have filed similar complaints against this man. Unfortunately, none of them could remember enough about him to provide an accurate description. You got lucky."

"I don't feel very lucky," I say, taking a tentative sip of the steaming coffee.

"Don't beat yourself up. Jake Loomis is a con man, a true snake in the grass. His real name is Mark Brooks. He's married to a woman ten years his senior."

I let this sink in. He lied to me about his marital status. He probably lied to me about everything else, including being a wildlife photographer. "Where is he now?"

"Behind bars in the Beaufort County Jail."

This news only offers a slight sense of relief. "Will there be a trial?"

"There's a good chance." Officer Wilks makes a left-hand turn into the resort entrance. "Would you be willing to testify?"

"Of course! Whatever it takes to get that man off the streets, permanently."

"I'm glad to hear it." She pulls up in front of the resort and puts the car in park. "Here's my business card in case you think of anything else."

"Will do." I take the card and gather up my things.

"Do you need help to your room?"

"I'm fine. But thanks. And thanks for looking out for me. Spending the night in the hospital with me was beyond the call of duty, especially after you'd arrested the creep."

"I wanted to be there when you woke up. I figured you might not remember what happened, and you'd have a lot of questions. I didn't want you to be afraid." The officer squeezes my hand. "Susan told me you're recently separated. Don't dwell on this situation, Mrs. Nelms. You did nothing wrong, but the world is full of men like Mark Brooks. Just be more careful in the future."

"Don't worry. I will."

I make a beeline through the lobby and up to my room. I quickly freshen up, change into khaki shorts and a blue-striped shirt, and toss everything into my suitcase. After checking to make certain I haven't forgotten anything, I return to the lobby. When I stop by the reservation desk to check out, the agent hands me a printout of my charges.

"The Mathesons covered everything," she says with a wink.

I scan the itemized list, my eyes landing on a large charge from Lowcountry Lantern from last night. Jake told me he had picked up the tab. He must have charged dinner to my room when I went to the restroom. But how did he know my room number? I certainly never told him. Was he stalking me? The possibility makes my arm hairs stand on end.

When the valet attendant brings my car around, I exit the lobby and give him my suitcase to store in the trunk. I'm opening my car door when Susan appears.

"Ashton! I've been so worried. Are you okay?"

I close the door and turn to face her. "I am, thanks to you. You deserve the good citizen award. I'm so grateful to have met you."

"The pleasure was all mine." She hands me a business card. "Come see me in Richmond. I have nice men friends I can set you up with."

I moan. "I've sworn off men for a while."

Susan appears alarmed. "Don't do that! There are plenty of honorable single men out there. You just have to be picky."

"Trust me, I've learned my lesson. Maybe we can collaborate on a project together sometime." An idea comes to mind. "Actually, I know just the project. I'm renovating my family's historic home on Catawba Sound, and I haven't yet hired a designer. Are you interested?"

"You bet!" Susan points at the business card in my hand. "But check out my website first. If you like what you see, I'll come for a visit."

"Sounds like a plan." I give her a hug. "Thanks again for what you did. Most women I know would've shied away from getting involved."

"I have a feeling you would've done the same thing for me."

I'd like to think I would, although I'm not entirely sure.

I drive back to Water's Edge with my tail between my legs. Or in my case, with my body slumped over the steering wheel. I wanted my freedom, and my first weekend out on my own turned out to be a disaster. The thought of returning home to my beloved Marsh Point, my sanctuary, lifts my spirits. I don't even mind having to stay in the guesthouse until Will finishes the renovations. I may never leave the property again. I'll find a spot for a desk and work remotely as much as possible.

On the way into town, I stop by Publix and buy enough groceries to last a month. I'm unloading the bags from the car when I spot my old kayak on the rack at the back of the carport. After last night's fiasco, a strenuous workout on the water is just what I need.

Quickly putting away the groceries, I change into my swimsuit, lather up with sunscreen, and drag the kayak across the lawn to the water. Boats of all sizes and types are cruising around Catawba Sound. Staying out of the line of traffic, I paddle down the coast, past the Merriweather Bridge to the city marina. I'm coated in sweat by the time I get home, but I feel much less anxious.

I haul the boat out of the water and leave it on the end of the dock for easy access for future use. Instead of going to town for exercise classes, I'll spend my early morning hours kayaking on the water. Or maybe I'll splurge on a paddleboard. The full-body workouts are just what I need. I'll tone and strengthen my muscles, improve my balance, and get my heart rate up. If any man tries to rape me again, I'll be in top physical shape to defend myself.

Back at the guesthouse, I take a cold shower and dress in loungewear—linen drawstring Capri pants and a knit tank. I don't bother putting on a bra. I'm certainly not expecting company. Pouring a tall glass of sweet tea, I grab my novel and head over to the veranda at the main house. Settling onto the daybed swing, I tuck my feet beneath me and lose myself in the pages, the soft murmur of nature providing a tranquil backdrop to the late afternoon.

CHAPTER
TWENTY-THREE

I hear a car door slam, followed by my husband's voice calling out for me. I consider hiding, but with the inside walls torn out, he would easily see me. I could make a run for it. Will's boat is on the dock, but I don't know where he keeps the key. With no other choice, I remain on the daybed swing like a sitting duck until he finds me.

"There you are! I've been looking all over town for you," Owen says, looming over me. "I thought you were coming home. We have a date tonight."

I fold the corner of the page and close my book. "This *is* my home, Owen. And I never agreed to the date."

"I figured you'd blow me off. Which is why I brought the date to you. How was your trip to Palmetto Resort?"

"Lovely," I say in a sarcastic tone. "How was the golf tournament?"

His face lights up. "Outstanding. Believe it or not, Rich and I won."

"I believe it. You two have certainly practiced enough these past few months. Did Harmony help you celebrate?"

Owen lets out a sigh as he eases down to the swing. "I understand why you might think something's going on between Harmony and me, but I promise you we're not having an affair."

I glare at him. "Your promises mean nothing to me, Owen."

He runs a hand up my leg. "When did you stop trusting me, Ashton?"

I kick his hand away. "When you refused to give me back my money. When you stole my jewelry."

His eyes bug out. "What jewelry? I don't know what you're talking about."

"Two pieces of my mother's jewelry are missing, and I believe you took them."

He lowers his head, shaking it as though disappointed. "We've grown further apart than I thought. But I refuse to give up on us. I'm even willing to go to marriage counseling, if that's what it takes."

I once thought marriage counseling was the answer to our problems, but I no longer believe we can save our marriage. "Are you willing to give me access to my brokerage account?"

"Of course, Ashton. I was only trying to prevent you from making a mistake. But it's your money. You can do whatever you want to with it. I packed a picnic dinner with all your favorites from Fancy Pantry. Fried chicken, buttermilk biscuits, deviled eggs, and broccoli salad. Shall I get the bags out of the car?" His eyes travel to the glass-topped wicker table. "We can eat here on the porch."

The idea of my favorite foods makes my stomach rumble, and I realize I've eaten little all day.

"I even have a chilled bottle of sparkling rosé," he adds in a hopeful tone.

After what happened last night, I may never drink again. I certainly won't accept a beverage from a man I don't trust.

"Please, Ashton. The least you can do is hear me out. I have some ideas about ways we can save our marriage."

"All right, fine. I'm kind of hungry anyway."

"Excellent. You won't regret it." He stands and pulls me to my feet. His eyes travel downward to my nipples, visible through the flimsy fabric of my tank.

I fold my arms over my chest. "I need to run to the guesthouse to use the restroom."

"I'll go with you," he says, following me off the porch. "I've never been inside the guesthouse."

"Don't get your hopes up. It's nothing special." When we reach the guesthouse, I make a beeline for the stairs. "Have a look around. I'll be right down."

I freshen up in the bathroom, and as I'm putting on a bra under my tank, I hear Owen calling up to me. "I'll get the food out of the car and meet you back on the porch."

By the time I return to the porch, he has food containers spread out on the table, and he's spooning healthy portions of my favorite broccoli salad onto two paper plates. The salad is so popular with locals, Fancy Pantry sells two different versions, one with and one without nuts.

I take the seat next to him. "You're sure this is the salad without nuts?"

"Positive," he says and shows me the label indicating no nuts.

He opens the wine, but when he offers me a glass, I refuse. "No, thanks."

"Party too hard at Palmetto Resort?" he asks, a smirk tugging at his lips.

"Busted," I say and sink my teeth into a chicken thigh. Why not let him think I had a fabulous time at Palmetto Resort? Owen has always loved a party, and I'm always the first one to go home. Which has often been a sore subject in our marriage.

We eat in silence. I'm hungrier than I realized. I devour the chicken thigh and shovel mouthfuls of broccoli salad into my mouth. I'm dragging a biscuit through a puddle of honey when my neck begins to itch. My panic mounts when the itch spreads to my face and arms. I stare down at my skin where hives are blooming, red and angry, like a map charting an invasion of my body. I know what's happening. I had the same reaction when I first realized I was allergic to peanuts.

"I need my EpiPen," I explain to Owen. I push abruptly back from the table, knocking over the chair, and stumble down the steps and across the yard to the guesthouse. I locate my purse in the kitchen, and dump out the contents on the counter, but my EpiPen isn't there. I have a spare. Where is it? I can't think straight. Then I remember I left it in the medicine cabinet at the condo when I moved out.

My breathing becomes labored, each inhalation shorter and faster than the last. I need to get Owen to drive me to the hospital. As I bust through the door onto the porch, I come face to face with Maurice's broad chest. "Evening, Miss Ashton. I brought your daddy's car back. Jed followed me over in my truck."

I pound my fist on his chest, and he holds me at arm's length. "Are you okay?"

With my hand on my throat, I choke out, "I can't breathe. Nuts. Allergy. Hospital."

Scooping me into his beefy arms, he runs with me over to his truck and deposits me in the back seat. I curl into a ball. The hospital isn't far, but I'm not sure I'll make it. My airway constricts, slowly cutting off my oxygen supply, and my blood pressure drops, leaving me feeling faint and disoriented. I'm only barely aware of Maurice speeding through town. And for the second time in less than twenty-four hours, the world around me blurs and then everything goes dark.

I REGAIN consciousness in the emergency room. An oxygen mask covers my face. A tube connects the needle in my arm to bags with clear liquid suspended from an IV pole. And a monitor, somewhere behind my head, sounds the rhythmic beat of my heart.

An attractive young woman wearing a white coat over blue scrubs is standing beside my bed. "Welcome back. You gave us quite a scare. Your friend got you here just in time."

My eyes dart around the room, but instead of locating Maurice, they land on Owen standing over near the door.

"We're giving you antihistamines and steroids and fluids through the IV. You should be as good as new in a few hours."

I try to ask a question, but the oxygen mask muffles my words.

"Here. Let me help you with that," the doctor says, and replaces the mask with nasal cannulas.

"When can I go home?" I ask.

The doctor gives me a sympathetic smile. "I'd like to keep you overnight for observation. I don't have to admit you. I can treat you here in the emergency room. I should be able to release you first thing in the morning."

The doctor and nurse fuss over me a little longer before leaving the room.

I lock eyes with my husband. "Where were you? If Maurice hadn't been there, I would've died."

Owen takes a tentative step toward the bed. "I'm so sorry, Ashton. I was cleaning up the picnic. You know I hate needles. I didn't want to watch you jab yourself with the EpiPen. I assumed everything would be okay. When you didn't come back, I went to check on you and saw Maurice speeding off with you in the back seat." He sets my purse on the bed table. "I grabbed this. I figured you might need your insurance card. I don't understand what happened. Why didn't the EpiPen work?"

"Because it wasn't in my purse." I double-check my purse for the EpiPen. There's a chance I may have missed it. I was in such a state of panic. But it's not here. I look up at Owen. "You can go home now. I'll get May May to drive me home in the morning."

Instead of offering to stay with me in the hospital, he says, "If you're sure. I should get some sleep. I have to be at work first thing in the morning." He kisses my forehead and exits the room. Only an hour ago, he was intent on saving our marriage, and now he can't get out of here fast enough.

Fighting back tears, I close my eyes, but the emergency room is noisy, and sleep doesn't come easily. I replay the evening's events over and over in my mind. How did this happen? Did Fancy Pantry get the salad labels mixed up? And what happened to my EpiPen? I'm usually so careful with the device that could save my life in situations like these. I specifically remember it being in my clutch at dinner last night, but I don't recall seeing it when I switched purses before I left my hotel room this morning. Did it fall out when Jake was dragging me upstairs to my room? I shudder to think what might've happened if Maurice hadn't appeared when he did. I doubt I would've made it back to the veranda to get Owen.

I finally doze off around three in the morning. When I wake again, a different nurse is removing the IV from my arm. "The doctor is working on your discharge papers. You should be good to go soon."

"Thanks." I send a text to May May, asking her to come get me but not explaining why I'm in the hospital.

She responds immediately, no questions asked. *I'm on my way.*

I text back. *I'll meet you in front of the ER.*

Ten minutes later, May May's red truck is waiting on the curb when the orderly wheels me out of the hospital.

Lines of concern etch her face. "You scared the bejeezus out of me. Are you okay?"

"I will be. I accidentally ate some nuts and had an anaphylactic reaction."

"Bless your heart. How did this happen? You're always so careful about nuts."

When I tell her what happened, she listens with face tight and lips pressed thin. "You realize that EpiPen didn't just get up and walk away?"

My stomach knots. "What are you suggesting, May May?"

"Do you have a life insurance policy?"

"Yes . . . You don't think?" But I can tell by her grave expression that she thinks my husband tried to kill me.

She pulls into the driveway at Marsh Point and parks near the carport. Taking her truck out of gear, she turns toward me. "Just be careful, sweet girl. If you don't feel safe here, you can come stay with me at the farm for a few days."

I give her a reassuring smile. "I'll be fine, but thanks for the offer. Have you read any more of Mama's journals?"

"I've finished reading them, and now I'm processing them. I'm not ready to talk about them. I'll let you know when I am."

"That bad, huh?"

She gives her head a grave shake. "Not great."

I kiss the tips of my fingers and touch them to her cheek. "Thanks again for the ride."

I watch her truck leave the driveway before going inside and getting ready for work. As though it's any other day and I didn't almost get date-raped over the weekend. As though it's any other day and I didn't almost die a few short hours ago.

CHAPTER TWENTY-FOUR

As I'm heading out for work, I spot Maurice in front of the main house and call him over. When he reaches me, I throw my arms around his neck. "You saved my life. I don't know how I'll ever repay you."

He holds me tight. "You don't need to repay me, Miss Ashton. I'm just glad I came along when I did. You were out cold by the time we got you to the hospital. Your face was so pale and your lips blue. I thought for sure we'd lost you." He pushes me away to get a better look at my face. "How're you feeling today? You're as pretty as ever. If I didn't know better, I never would've guessed you almost died last night."

"Tell me about it. I feel surprisingly okay, considering what I just experienced. I'm gonna take it easy for a couple of days though. Do you have time to help me with a few things?"

He turns me loose and runs his big hand over his cropped gray head. "I believe so. I got a full crew today. What do you have in mind?"

I turn to face the guesthouse. "I want to set up a home office on the second-floor landing. You know, the area at the top of the stairs in front of the big window." I gesture at the window. "It'll be tight, but I think I can make it work. I'd like to use the desk from the family room if we can find it in the POD."

He gives his head an affirmative nod. "I know just where it is."

Lowering my voice, I draw my head closer to his. "Have you ever installed a home security system, Maurice?"

"Yes, ma'am. I put one in for my daughter last year."

We discuss the options available, and I give him my credit card. "Get whatever you need from Coastal Hardware. Do you mind swinging by my condo while you're out and picking up my drafting table?"

"I'd be happy to."

I remove the condo key from my key ring and hand it to him. "You should be able to manage it by yourself. I'd go with you, but I don't want to risk running into my husband."

Maurice's eyes fall to the ground, and he kicks at the dirt with his foot.

I place a hand on his forearm. "What is it, Maurice?"

Still staring at the ground, Maurice says, "I saw your husband's truck when I got here yesterday evening, but I was in such a rush to get help for you, I didn't have time to go looking for him. When he came to the hospital later, I asked him where he'd been, and why he didn't bring you to the hospital himself. He said it was none of my business. He ordered me to leave the hospital, and he warned me if I talked to anyone about what happened last night, I'd lose my job." He lifts his gaze. "I can't afford to lose my job, Miss Ashton."

"Nobody's firing you, Maurice. You worked for my family long before Owen came along."

"I ain't gonna lie, Miss Ashton. I never much cared for your husband. And now . . . well, I'm concerned for your safety."

"That's why we're putting in a security system," I say in a cheerful voice that doesn't match the dread I feel inside. I notice Dad's car in the carport. "Wow! Dad's car looks brand-new."

"Mm-hmm. Turned out nicely, if I say so myself."

We walk over to the carport, and I run my hand down the glistening red front fender. "Your brother-in-law did an amazing job."

Maurice's hazel eyes light up. "Jed put a shine on her, just like I asked him to."

I inspect the new whitewall tires. "Do you have an invoice for the work?"

"I left it on the front seat." He opens the front door and hands me the invoice. "Here ya go."

"Great." I fold the invoice into my purse. "I'll take care of it right away. Dad will be thrilled. Maybe this will inspire him to drive again."

"I hope so, Miss Ashton." He turns back toward the house. "Let me get my crew started before I head out to the hardware store."

"I'll be at my office. Call me if you need anything."

As I drive toward town, the events of the past twelve hours race through my mind. Why didn't Owen follow me to the guesthouse when he knew I was having a reaction to the nuts? While it's extreme to think he tried to kill me—stuff like that only happens in the movies—I can't dismiss the gnawing feeling in my gut that something is way off with Owen. If he tried to kill me last night, what's stopping him from trying again?

I PICK up my new EpiPen prescription from the pharmacy and continue on to my office, where I spend the morning packing up the things I'll need for work.

"What's all this?" Liza asks when she sees the cardboard boxes lined up beside the door.

"I'm going to work remotely from Marsh Point until further notice. Being on-site during construction will help make on-the-spot decisions easier."

Liza's face falls. "But I need you here. What will we do without you?"

I laugh. "You'll be fine. I'm only a phone call and a few miles away."

She straightens, her smile returning. "I don't blame you, actually. If I owned a gorgeous property like Marsh Point, I'd never want to leave either. I'm happy to drive out anytime. I can bring you coffee or lunch. Or if you have papers to sign, I can bring those too."

"I'll remember that. I don't know what I'd do without you," I say, patting her cheek.

Liza helps me load the boxes in my car, and I drive toward Sandy Island for my meeting with the cabinet maker about the Matheson project. I'm crossing the Merriweather Bridge when I notice darkening clouds. At the next stoplight, I pull out my phone and access the weather. A wicked-looking line of thunderstorms is moving toward us from the southwest. I'd like to get this meeting over with quickly, so I can make it home before the storm sets in.

A lone white pickup truck is parked in front of the Mathesons' house. The rest of the crew has presumably been transferred to another project. Entering the house, I find a man with sandy hair stroking his chin as he studies the blank walls in the kitchen. He turns to face me, and my breath hitches. Even though I haven't seen him since high school, I would know Sully Brown anywhere.

"Ashton? I don't believe it." He opens his arms, and I walk into them, the years falling away as we embrace. Growing up, Hattie and Sully were my closest friends, the only people I allowed into my dysfunctional world. Countless times, Sully had helped carry my drunken mother to bed and held me in his arms while I cried for my broken family.

I place my hands on his chest so I can see his face. "What're you doing here? What happened to Roberto?" I ask about the project manager I've been working with.

"He had an emergency on another project. I hope you don't mind me stepping in. I'm the company's owner, but I'm not nearly as talented as my staff."

"Hush!" I say, smacking his chest. "Regal Woodworks didn't get its sterling reputation on its own."

"I could say the same thing about you. Roberto mentioned I'd be meeting with the architect. I had no idea you were the genius behind Constructive Edge. This house is cutting edge."

"And very different from my other projects. Most of which, as you might imagine in Water's Edge, are historic restorations."

"Let me get a good look at you." Sully takes my hand and twirls me around. "You're positively stunning, Ashton. Age certainly agrees with you."

If only he knew what I'd been through in the past two days, I think.

"You're looking well yourself." Other than a few lines around his baby blues, he's hardly changed a bit. He still has a smattering of freckles across his cheeks, and his smile is as kind as ever.

An awkward silence settles over us. "I think we're in for a doozy of a thunderstorm," I say. "Let's go over the plans, so you can get back on the road to Charleston."

Sully waves away my concern. "I'm in no hurry. I can wait it out if necessary. We have some issues we need to iron out. And I can always stay with Mom and Dad."

"So your parents are still alive? How are they?"

"Doing very well. Thanks for asking. They've downsized from the big house on Tidal Trail to a charming bungalow on the sound. Near Marsh Point, actually."

"I'm glad to hear they're doing well."

I drop my purse on the floor and unroll the blueprints for the kitchen design. We are deep in discussion about the cabinets thirty minutes later when darkness overcomes the room and a boom of thunder echoes through the empty house. As we move to the living room windows, streaks of lightning cut across the dark sky.

"This is a seriously cool place to watch a storm," Sully says.

"I agree. It's breathtaking."

We drag two five-gallon buckets of joint compound over near the windows to sit on.

Sully says, "Since we're gonna be here a while, tell me about your life. Are you married? Do you have children?"

"I'm separated, and I never had children."

His face softens. "Because you'd already raised your family."

He means my siblings. He knows how much I sacrificed to take care of them. No one has ever understood me like Sully once understood me. He was the closest thing to a soul mate I've ever had. "What about you? Are you married?" I ask, my eyes falling to his bare ring finger.

"I got divorced a few years ago. My son will be a junior in college next year. Kendall's a great kid. I don't know how I got so lucky. He's planning to take over the business when I retire."

I raise an eyebrow. "A son in college? Wow! You must've gotten an early start."

He sets his blue eyes on me. "I married the first girl that came along who helped me forget about you."

I crinkle my nose. "What're you talking about?"

He chuckles. "I had an enormous crush on you back then. But you never gave me the time of day."

This does not surprise me. I always knew he wanted more than friendship. "I didn't have time for anything except my family. You know that, Sully."

"I do. How is your mama? Is she still alive?"

I shake my head. "She died in May." The dam that has been holding back my emotions for the past twenty-four hours breaks, and I burst into tears. "I'm sorry," I sob. "I'm a mess right now."

Sully pulls me to my feet and holds me close as I cry a torrent of tears like the rain pounding the windows outside. When I finally pull myself together, I tell him about my miserable marriage, missing jewelry and money, nearly getting date-raped, and the allergic reaction. He hands me a red bandanna, and I blow my nose.

"Some things never change, I guess. We haven't seen each other in over thirty years, and I'm already crying on your shoulder."

"And understandably so. You have more than your fair share of problems, Ashton. I realize this is none of my business, but do you have a life insurance policy?"

I turn my back on him, facing the window. "You're not the first person to ask me that today. Yes, I have life insurance. Do I think my husband tried to kill me? Maybe."

"You need a private investigator."

"I *have* a private investigator. He's been looking for Savannah for three decades."

"Then he's not a very good detective if he hasn't found her yet. I heard about what happened with Savannah. And you've heard nothing from her in all these years?"

"Not a word."

"Then you need to fire your investigator and hire my guy. After he straightens out your marital problems, you can put him on Savannah's case." Sully pulls out his phone. "Give me your number, and I'll forward you his contact information."

I call out my number, and seconds later, my phone pings with the text. I read the name on the contact card. "Carter Leach. Is he a client?"

"No. I used him to catch my wife with her lover."

My mouth forms an O. "I'm sorry, Sully. That must have been awful for you."

"No more awful than what you're going through."

I glance back down at my phone. "I'm tempted to call him now while I have the courage."

Sully waves his phone. "How about if I get him on the line, and we can talk to him on speaker?"

"That would be great," I say, bobbing my head.

Clicking on the number, Sully crosses the living room for

privacy, but I hear enough to know he's telling the private investigator about my toxic marriage. When he returns to my side, he puts his phone on speaker and introduces me to Carter.

"If I rearrange a few things on my schedule, I can drive down and meet with you late morning tomorrow," Carter offers.

Tomorrow seems so imminent, and I'm not sure I'm ready for such a big move. "My case isn't that urgent. We can wait until a more convenient time for you."

"Based on what Sully told me, I don't advise waiting," Carter says.

I look up at Sully, who gives me a nod of encouragement. "All right," I say with a sigh of resignation. "I'll see you tomorrow morning. I'll text you the address."

Sully ends the call and pulls me in for a half hug. "I've been in your shoes, Ashton. I know this isn't easy. But you can trust Carter to find out whatever it is your husband is hiding."

I lean into him. "How did I survive all these years without you?"

"Clearly not very well," he teases.

"Look! The sky is clearing." I point at the sliver of blue sky off to the south. "I think more bad weather is coming though. You should get on the road."

As he gathers his things, he asks, "Do you want me to come back tomorrow for your meeting with Carter?"

I hesitate. I would love to have him here, but some of what I have to tell Carter is too personal, too embarrassing. "Thanks. But I should probably meet with him alone."

We walk out of the house together, and as I watch him drive away, I experience the first glimmer of hope I've felt in as long as I can remember.

I'm still standing in the driveway a few minutes later when I receive a text from him. *Missing you already. Now that I've got you back in my life, I have no intention of letting you go.*

I thumb off my response. *Good! I need your friendship now*

more than ever.

CHAPTER
TWENTY-FIVE

Seeing Dad smile when I deliver his Mercedes boosts my spirits. I texted Clyde ahead of time, asking him to have Dad waiting out in front of his apartment. When I pull up with the top down and horn tooting, Dad presses his hands to his cheeks in delight.

"I don't believe it! She looks amazing!" He runs his hand over the hood. "Who's responsible for this?"

"Maurice's brother-in-law owns a garage. Jed replaced the tires, tuned up the engine, and gave her a good waxing. None of it was free, of course. I have the bill for you to pay." I remove the invoice from my bag and hand it to him.

Dad gives the invoice to Clyde. "Here! Put that inside for me." He scurries around to the driver's side. "Move over. I'm driving."

My hands grip the steering wheel. "No way, Dad. You haven't driven in years."

"Driving is like riding a bike. And my license is still valid." I glance over at Clyde. "What do you think?"

He shrugs. "Why not? Your father has been getting stronger every day. I think he's ready to drive."

"All right, then. But I'm riding with you." I open the driver's door and climb out of the low-slung car.

Dad has one leg in the car when he jumps back out. "Wait! I need my hat." He hurries into his apartment, walking faster than I've seen him move in years.

Rounding the car to the passenger side, I say to Clyde, "Look at him go. You've worked wonders. He's come a long way in a few days."

Clyde snickers. "He certainly has. His attitude has drastically improved."

I gesture at the car. "There's only room for two. Would you like to take my spot?"

"I would love nothing more. But it's time for me to go home. I'm taking my missus out for her birthday dinner. Besides, it'll do your father good to have some one-on-one time with you. He talks about you an awful lot, Miss Ashton."

A pang of guilt tightens my chest. "I'll try to visit him more often. I have a lot of personal stuff going on at the moment."

"I totally understand, and I wasn't judging you. It's obvious you do the best you can."

Dad emerges from the apartment with his Panama hat atop his head. He practically skips down the sidewalk to the car. "Get in!" he orders me. "Let's go."

"Yes, sir." I wink at Clyde as I slide into the car. "Enjoy your evening and wish your wife a happy birthday for us."

I've no sooner buckled my seat belt than Dad's foot hits the gas pedal and we speed off. "Slow down, Dad! You're gonna run over someone."

Dad eases off the gas pedal. "Where to?"

"Your call. You're in the driver's seat."

"Let's drive past the wellness center first. I want these old farts to see me."

We cruise slowly around the circular drive in front of the wellness center. When Dad blasts his horn at a group of men standing on the sidewalk out front, they whistle and cheer him on. One gentleman hollers, "Take me for a ride, Ernest."

"Another time," Dad calls back.

I play punch Dad's arm. "Go, Dad! You're the big man on campus."

His cheeks turn pink. "I'm making some new friends."

He drives past his apartment and the main building on our way out of the complex.

"Where are we going now?" I ask.

"I'm taking you home. I'm keeping my car with me. I'm feeling cooped up at Whispering Oaks. I need to go places."

I smile at his enthusiasm. Seeing Dad coming back to life warms my heart. "I'm staying at Marsh Point. Are you sure you're up for driving back through town alone? If you'll wait until tomorrow, Clyde and I can figure out how to get the car to you."

Dad cuts his eyes at me. "Don't be ridiculous, Ashton. I'm perfectly fine to drive myself a few miles. Why are you staying at Marsh Point?"

"Well . . ." I hesitate, not sure how much to tell him. "Let's just say Owen and I are taking a breather."

"The women at the old folks' home love to gossip, and rumor has it your husband is cheating on you."

"Tell those women to mind their own business." I look away, staring out the window. "Owen and I are having some problems, but it's nothing for you to worry about."

"If that rascal hurts you, he'll have to answer to me."

I bite down on my lip to keep from laughing. He sounds like my father from twenty years ago. Why spare this rare happy moment by talking about Owen? "We should probably order a cover for your car, since it'll be exposed to the elements in the parking lot at Whispering Oaks."

"That's an excellent idea," he says and increases speed.

The wind noise makes it impossible for us to talk. I wait until we stop at the first light in town to ask him about the women spreading gossip. "Are they your new friends?"

"Some of them. But they talk incessantly about frivolous things. There are more important matters to discuss, like current events and books and the stock market."

I laugh. "Most women, including me, find the stock market boring."

"That was probably a poor example, but you know what I mean." The light turns green, and he punches the gas.

"Slow down, Dad! If you get a speeding ticket, they might take your license away."

He immediately slows down, as though the thought never occurred to him. Entering the historic residential section, we drive through a tunnel of moss-draped branches. Dad inhales a deep breath of air. "I've missed the smell of the marsh."

"I hope you'll come and stay with me when the renovations are finished."

He gives a slight nod. "I'd like that."

Will and Maurice are standing in front of the main house at Marsh Point. They appear deep in discussion about something. When Will sees our father behind the wheel, a smile spreads across his face, and they walk toward the car.

"Looking good, Mr. Ernest," Maurice says with a chuckle. "I ain't seen you wear your Panama hat in decades."

Dad tips his hat to Maurice. "Had to brush off the dust, Maurice. Of the hat, I mean, not of me," he says, and we all share a laugh.

Dad glances at his watch. "Almost time for dinner. I need to get back to the old folks' home."

I get out of the car. "Don't forget to call me as soon as you get there."

"I'll try, but my memory ain't what it used to be. See you youngsters later," Dad says and peels out of the gravel driveway.

My brother's eyes follow the car. "Should he be driving alone?"

"Probably not. If he doesn't slow down, he's going to get a speeding ticket."

Maurice wipes the sweat from his face with a red bandanna. "Sure is hot today. I'm almost finished with your project, Miss Ashton. When you get a chance, I'll show you how everything works."

"Thanks, Maurice. I'll be there in a few minutes."

Will watches his foreman walk away. "What kind of project is he working on?"

"He's installing a security system in the guesthouse," I say, and brace myself for my brother's interrogation. We've never had a reason to even lock our doors at Marsh Point.

He's about to say something but then clamps his lips tight.

"What is it, Will? I can tell something's wrong."

He hangs his head. "I told Tracy about Bert. Now she's convinced I have an anger management problem. She keeps hounding me to seek therapy." He presses his palms against his temples. "Ugh. I can't take it anymore. She won't let up. She's like a gnat, constantly buzzing around my head."

I think back to my conversation with Tracy over gelato last week. *He has such a short fuse, snapping at everyone for the least little thing. He's like a rumbling volcano on the verge of erupting.*

"Then why not see a therapist? It'll get Tracy off your back, and it might do you some good."

He falls back against his truck. "It's a waste of time and money. You know me, Ashton. I've never been one to talk about my problems."

"Sometimes we have to do things we don't like for the sake of our marriage."

He glares at me. "You mean like when you let Owen convince you to sell your beach house? How'd that work out for you?"

I've never thought about it before, but selling the beach house was the beginning of the end of our marriage. I lean against the truck next to my brother. "I guess I'm not the best person to ask for marital advice."

"I've heard the rumors. Everyone in town knows Owen is sleeping with that Harmony woman. I've never trusted him." Will shoulder bumps me. "Say the word, and I'll fire him."

I run a hand down my face. "It may eventually come to that. I'm meeting with a private investigator in the morning. I'm hoping he can help me figure some things out."

"Whoa. A private investigator is big time. What's going on, Ashton?"

I'm too ashamed to tell him about my missing money. "Documented proof of his affair will help expedite a divorce."

"There's more you're not telling me. Are you worried Owen might hurt you? Is that why you're having Maurice install a security system?"

"Something like that." My throat swells, and I'm afraid I might cry.

Will pushes off the truck. "You're welcome to stay with us, although things are kinda tense around our house at the moment."

I give him a hug. "Thanks, bro. I appreciate the offer, but I'm fine here."

"Call me anytime, Ash, day or night." He runs his knuckles over the top of my head before getting in his truck and driving off.

I'm not sure what to make of what just transpired between us. He hasn't called me *Ash* since we were young, and he's never spoken to me with such sincerity. Is it because we both recognize the other is hurting? Maybe it's not too late for us to develop a brother-sister relationship after all.

CHAPTER
TWENTY-SIX

Carter Leach is not the Columbo type I imagined. He doesn't have bushy eyebrows, and he's not wearing a trench coat or jabbing a cigar stub at me. He's average-looking without a single defining feature. Even his hair is a nondescript shade of brown. Although I can see where his ordinary appearance might benefit him when surveilling suspects.

I make coffee, and we go out to the table on the guesthouse porch to talk.

Carter pauses for a minute to take in his surroundings. "This place is amazing. The view is stunning. What does your husband think of Marsh Point?"

His question strikes me as odd. Then I realize he's easing into the discussion about Owen. "He thinks I should sell the property and invest the money in the stock market," I say, and tell him everything about my marriage that comes to mind.

Carter takes extensive notes on his legal pad, only occasionally interrupting me to ask questions. Besides the rumor about my husband's mistress, I tell Carter about Owen's refusal to give me access to my portfolio, the jewelry I believe he stole, and my near fatal nut reaction, including the untimely disappearance of my EpiPen.

When I'm finished talking, I sit up straighter in my chair, feeling pounds lighter after unburdening myself. "Well? What do you think?"

Carter tosses his pen on the pad and sits back in his chair. "My gut tells me your husband is hiding more than your money and his mistress. Have you ever had a nut reaction like that before?"

"Only once. As a child, when we first discovered the allergy. Anaphylactic reactions are terrifying. I keep my EpiPen with me at all times."

He cocks an eyebrow at me. "Until the other night when it mysteriously disappeared at the exact moment you accidentally ate nuts? I don't think your EpiPen vanished on its own, Mrs. Nelms. Which makes me extremely concerned for your safety."

"Please, call me Ashton." I shift in my seat. "Should I report the incident to the police?"

Carter hesitates before responding. "If the police question him, your husband will know we're onto him. I'm on friendly terms with several officers and detectives on your local force. I'll reach out to them. It won't hurt to be on their radar."

"Whatever you think best." I gulp back fear. Getting the police involved makes the situation real. "At least I have my new security system installed," I say, gesturing at the security camera hanging from the eave of the porch.

Carter cranes his neck to see the camera behind him. "Mm-hmm," he says, seemingly unimpressed with the equipment. "I'm going to make your case a priority. We will find out whatever it is your husband is hiding."

The *we* part surprises me. I'd assumed he worked alone. "So you have a staff. Tell me about your process."

"I have a team of ten. Each of us has unique talents. My specialty is electronic communications. I'll start out by having my best guy tail Owen, to get a feel for his habits and hobbies."

"Your guy will have a lot of downtime. Owen's primary hobby is golf."

Carter chuckles. "We're used to it. I'll need your husband's work and home addresses."

I provide the addresses and hand over my key to the condo. "In case you need to get in for any reason."

"Thanks." Carter stands to go. "I'll be in touch in a couple of days. In the meantime, be aware of your surroundings and stay close to home."

His warning sets me on edge. Too distracted to focus on work, I change into my swimsuit and retrieve my kayak from the end of the dock. The water is calm and only a few boats occupy the sound. By the time I paddle across to Sandy Island and back, I'm feeling less anxious and ready to work.

When I get out of the shower, I have a missed call and a voice message from Sully asking about my meeting with Carter. Throwing on some clothes, I call him back, and we talk for over an hour. I hold nothing back. He's my same trusted friend from high school.

When we finally hang up, I slurp down a bowl of gazpacho for lunch before settling into work in my makeshift office. A new waterfront project inspires me, and I don't lift my head again until late afternoon when I notice Carrie getting out of her car at the main house. She doesn't look my way. She must not realize I'm staying in the guesthouse.

Slipping on my shoes, I cross the lawn and slip into the house through the front door. Hiding from my sister in a house with no walls isn't easy, but I manage to stay out of sight as I follow her around. She pauses briefly in every room, tilting her head back and forth as she studies the changes to the house.

We reach the second floor, and she makes a sudden turn. When she spots me, she startles with her hand pressed against her chest. "Geez, Ashton. You scared me to death. What're you doing creeping around behind me?"

"Wondering what you were doing creeping around my house."

"I was in the neighborhood and thought I'd drop by to check out the renovations. You completely changed the upstairs floor plan. I can't figure out which room is which."

"The front two bedrooms are the same, although mine now has its own bath. I reconfigured the back side of the house to have four bedrooms, instead of three, each sharing a Jack and Jill bathroom."

"Why do you need so many bedrooms when . . ."

"Go ahead! Finish your sentence. When I don't have any children. I'm an architect, Carrie. It's my job to maximize space." I don't dare tell her I dream of one day having my entire family share the holidays here together.

"Now that I think about it, having additional bedrooms might come in handy. I've been wracking my brain, trying to figure out why Mama left you the house, and I finally realize she wants us to share Marsh Point." Carrie roots around in her purse, producing a crumpled piece of notepaper covered in her scratchy handwriting. "If we split the calendar three ways, we would each get a month every quarter." She thrusts the notepaper at me. "I came up with a schedule. If we rotate the months, we'll each get to have Christmas here once every three years."

I back away from the paper as though it's contaminated with a deadly contagion. "I was considering using the house as a second home, but now I'm leaning toward living here full-time."

Carrie's face flushes red. "Why? Because you're getting a divorce? Because you drove your husband into the arms of another woman?"

I gawk at her. "Who told you that?"

"Gossip doesn't discriminate, Ashton. Even though I don't travel in your social circles, I still hear rumors about my family."

She puts herself down to make me feel sorry for her, but her *poor-me* talk only makes me angry. I've found it best to ignore her when she acts this way. "I'm aware of the rumors about Owen. Just so you know, we've separated, and I'm living in the guesthouse."

She turns up her nose. "Why? That place is gross."

"I gave it a good cleaning, and I'm finding it quite cozy."

Her eyes go wide. "Now that I think about it, this could work perfectly for all three of us. If you live in the guesthouse full-time, Will and I can share the main house." She extends an arm with her notepaper in hand. "This is my last offer. If you don't agree to it, I'm contesting the will."

"So, you're going to use your husband's hard-earned money for a lawsuit you'll never win."

My comment hits home, and she flinches. My sister blames me for everything wrong in her life. Just like it's my fault she never went to college, it's my fault she married a schoolteacher with a small salary that dictates their strict household budget.

Stuffing the notepaper in her purse, Carrie brushes past me and hurries down the stairs and out the front door. From an upstairs window, I watch her get in her car and hear the engine start up. She tears out of the driveway, nearly colliding with Dad's Mercedes as she passes him on his way in. The Mercedes—with Dad behind the wheel and Clyde perched in the passenger seat—skids to a halt on the gravel in front of the house.

I throw open the window and yell down to him. "Looking good, Dad!"

He grins up at me. "Feeling good, Ashton. I came by to check on your progress."

"I'll meet you downstairs." Closing the window, I take the stairs two at a time and greet them at the door with hugs. "This is a surprise. I was planning to visit you tomorrow."

Dad's face lights up. "You still can. Why don't you come for dinner? You can meet some of my new friends."

"I'd love that." I step aside so they can enter the house. "Come on in, and I'll give you the tour," I say, motioning for them to go ahead of me down the hall.

We meander through the house as I describe the improvements to each room. When we end up on the veranda, Dad says, "You're making smart changes, Ashton. Your mother would approve. I wish we'd renovated years ago."

"Mind if I walk out on the dock, Mr. Ernest?" Clyde asks Dad.

Dad waves him on. "Not at all. Take your time." He waits until Clyde has left the porch before easing into a rocker. "I'm glad he's gone. Gives me a chance to talk to you about something."

I sit down beside him. "What's up?"

"I'm grateful for everything Clyde has done for me. Thanks to him, I'm getting physically stronger every day, and I have a new lease on life. But I'm ready to be rid of him." Dad chuckles. "He's cramping my style, if you know what I mean."

I rock for a minute while I consider his request. "Let me talk to Gwen. Maybe we can start by cutting back to a few hours a day."

"I can live with that for a while. But my goal is to be on my own. I'm not an invalid, Ashton. Admittedly, I was in a dark place after your Mama died. But I've faced those demons, and I'm moving on."

I pat his arm. "I can see that. And I'm proud of you."

We sit for another minute in silence. "You just missed Carrie."

"Ha. You mean, Carrie just missed me. She damn near ran me off the road."

"She's threatening to contest Mom's will if I don't share the house with her and Will."

Dad presses his lips thin. "Yeah, she mentioned that to me. I told her to leave it alone. This is the way your mom wanted it. As usual, she refused to listen. I wouldn't worry too much about it if I were you. She doesn't stand a chance of winning."

"I hope you're right," I say, but I remain unconvinced.

After seeing Dad and Clyde off in the driveway, I place a call to mom's attorney and quickly explain the situation.

Virginia sighs. "Carrie's attorney warned me this was coming."

"Do I need to hire a lawyer?"

"No, I'll be representing the interest of your mother's estate. Carrie claims her mother made the decisions about her estate while under the influence of alcohol. But I have a half dozen witnesses who will testify Eileen was sober at all our meetings."

"I've already started renovating the house. Should I stop the construction?"

"Not at all. I wouldn't think another thing about this, Ashton. If it becomes a problem, I'll let you know."

I exhale a breath I didn't know I'd been holding. "Thanks, Virginia. That makes me feel better."

When I end the call, I turn to look up at my beloved home. I will fight with tooth and nail to keep this house. I'm not at all opposed to sharing my family's home. In fact, that is my goal. Problem is, my idea of sharing is entirely different from my sister's.

CHAPTER
TWENTY-SEVEN

Before I've even had coffee on Wednesday morning, I receive a text from my brother summoning me to the main house. *We need to go over some things.*

I respond. *Be there in a few.*

I change into workout clothes while my coffee brews. I'm strolling across the lawn toward the house when I spot Maurice, who is in the driveway overseeing a delivery of building supplies.

He calls out to me. "If you're here to see your brother, beware. He's in a foul mood this morning."

I give him a thumbs-up. "Thanks for the warning."

I find Will in the kitchen, studying the blueprints. He glances up at me and grumbles something that sounds like good morning. "Why are you putting the island here?" he asks, jabbing his index finger at the blueprints.

"Because that's the most obvious place for it. Do you have a better idea?"

"Not with this layout. And what's up with this wall of windows? Why do you want to look out at the lawn when the view is that way?" His arm shoots out with that same finger pointed toward the sound. "I suggest you scratch this plan and start over."

My jaw drops. "I will do no such thing. I'm eventually planning to put in a pool. I thought I mentioned that to you." I tap my fingernail on the blueprints. "These french doors open onto this small brick porch, which will then lead down to the pool deck. Ultimately, the wall of windows will overlook the pool."

"Whatever. It's your house." He rolls up the plans and stuffs them into the cardboard tube. "I don't get why you need a pool when you can easily swim in the sound."

Irritation crawls across my skin. I don't owe him any explanations. "We've worked on countless projects together, Will. You've never had a problem with my designs before."

"I just think you're spending too much money."

"Don't worry about it as long as you're getting paid."

I look more closely at my brother. He's strung as taut as a tightrope. "What's really going on with you, Will? Did you and Tracy have another fight?"

His face reddens. "That's none of your business."

His sharp tone makes me wince. "Sorry I asked. Yesterday, when you confided in me about your marital problems, I thought maybe you and I were on the verge of a breakthrough, that our bond was deepening into a genuine relationship."

"Don't hold your breath. That's never going to happen." He tucks the cardboard tube under his arm and leaves the house.

Anger sends me in the opposite direction, outside to the porch and across the yard to the dock. I walk to the very end and sit down with my legs hanging over the side. I sip coffee as I replay the scene with my brother. Will is right about one thing. I'm definitely spending too much money. Money I don't currently have. Now that Owen and I are separated, how will I pay the bills from Darby Custom Homes? Owen will have to either buy me out of the condo or we'll have to sell, which means I'll get half of the equity. With no other debt, I feel certain the bank would give me a line of credit to cover construction costs. Money aside, are my renovation plans too grandiose? But I'm an architect with high standards. If

I'm going to the trouble to renovate, I want a finished product I can be proud of.

The ringing of my phone startles me out of my reverie, and I accept the call from Mom's estate attorney. I have a suspicion why she's calling before she blurts, "Game on! I received notification of the will contest from your sister's attorney a few minutes ago."

I spring to my feet and pace circles around the dock. "I'm actually surprised my sister made good on her threat. Contesting the will is the only thing Carrie has ever followed through on in her life. What happens now?"

"We'll go through discovery. Which means we have to turn over your mom's financial records and other relevant documents that dispute Carrie's claim. The judge may require us to take part in mediation or settlement discussions."

"I'm not settling."

"I agree. We don't need to settle. We can easily win this case. But we have to go through the process, Ashton. I will keep you abreast of the developments as they happen."

I thank Virginia and end the call. Needing to blow off some steam, I kayak all the way to the mouth of the ocean and back. The exertion does little to improve my spirits. I've never felt more alone in the world than I do at this minute. I'm divorcing my husband, and my siblings hate me. The only family I have left is my father. I refuse to drag him into my problems when he's busy creating a new life for himself at Whispering Oaks.

I think about Susan, the woman I met at Palmetto Resort, and her new husband. The likelihood of me ever finding love again seems impossible.

I SPEND the day working at my desk. Sully calls several times, but I don't answer until late afternoon when I'm caught up enough on my work to talk.

"Finally!" he says with a loud sigh. "I was getting worried about you."

"I'm sorry. I've been working all afternoon, and I had my phone on silent." I lean back in my chair. "What're you up to?"

"A lot of work, same as you, but I can't complain. Have you heard anything from Carter?"

"Not a word. Should I be worried? He's only been on the case one day."

"He'll give you an update soon. Do you have plans for the holiday weekend?"

I've been so preoccupied by my problems, I failed to realize the Fourth of July weekend is upon us. "Honestly, I haven't even thought about it. What about you?"

"That's why I'm calling. My son is going to Sullivan's Island with some friends, so I'm footloose and fancy free. I remember Marsh Point is the best spot in town to watch fireworks. I was thinking maybe I'd invite myself down for a barbecue."

My heart skips a beat at the thought of seeing Sully again. "That sounds like fun. I accept your invitation."

"Great. I can't wait." He sounds as excited as I feel. "Since I'm inviting myself, I don't want you to go to any trouble. I'll bring some wine and whatever else you can think we might need."

Through the window, I spot our rusty old Weber grill in the carport. "Our grill hasn't been used in ages. I'm not sure it still works."

"Then hamburgers and hot dogs are out of the question. How about I pick up some fried chicken from Fancy Pantry?"

"I love that idea. A fried chicken picnic sounds patriotic." I notice the time on my computer. "I need to run, Sully. I didn't realize it was so late. I'm having dinner with Dad at Whispering Oaks. Let's talk again in a day or so and finalize our plans."

"Sounds good. In the meantime, be sure to let me know if you hear from Carter."

Ending the call, I change into a casual knit dress and drive out to Whispering Oaks. Dad is waiting impatiently in front of the main building.

"You're late, Ashton. We need to hurry. My friends are saving seats for us at their table." Taking me by the hand, he drags me through the lobby to the dining room. He's moving faster than I've seen him in years.

"I can barely keep up with you, Dad. What happened to your cane?"

He grins over at me. "I don't need it anymore. Thanks to Clyde, I feel twenty years younger. By the way, did you talk to Gwen about cutting back his hours?"

"I did. I'm sorry if I forgot to mention it. She'll begin scaling back his hours next week."

"Good." Dad's expression grows serious. "I admit I'll miss Clyde. But there's no sense in wasting money on care I don't need."

"We can always get him back if something changes," I say as we approach the cafeteria.

Lester's is the only face I recognize at the table. I sit down in the chair next to Dad, and he introduces me to his new friends. Annabelle, the woman on the other side of Dad, leans in close to him. "You didn't tell me your daughter is so beautiful," she whispers loud enough for me to hear.

Dad smiles at me. "Ashton takes after her mother."

Annabelle is an attractive woman with short gray hair, twinkling blue eyes, and a healthy glow from being outdoors. She's stroking Dad's arm, letting me know she has a crush on him.

Dad removes a flask from the inside pocket of his sport coat. He flashes me a naughty grin as he pours clear liquid, which I assume is vodka, into my sweet tea.

I lower my voice. "Are you allowed to have that in here?"

Dad winks at me. "Indeed. The administration turns a blind eye to this sort of thing as long as we don't cause trouble. After all, we're adults," he says and pours another splash into Annabelle's tea.

Like me, Dad has never been much of a drinker. After what we went through with Mom, I don't worry about him abusing alcohol. And he deserves to have some fun for a change. He's earned it after being devoted to my sick mother for so long.

The conversation during dinner is lively, and I enjoy these older people more than I do my own peers. I even agree to stay for a game or two of Bingo afterward.

Dad and I hang back from the others as we stroll toward the wellness center. "Annabelle seems nice. I think she's sweet on you."

A rosy glow appears on his cheeks. "I'm sweet on her too. She's fun and easy to be around. And she loves outdoor activities as much as me. Although I think she may be using me for my car." He chuckles. "But I don't care. Whatever works."

I laugh out loud. "Who are you? And what have you done with my father?"

His smile fades. "Do you think your mama would mind if I have a little fun?"

I loop my arm through his. "I don't think she'd mind a bit. In fact, I'm pretty sure she's smiling down on you right now."

I never realized Bingo could be such fun, and I end up staying until the end. When I walk Dad back to his apartment afterward, I ask about his plans for the Fourth, thinking I could invite him and Annabelle to join Sully and me for our fried chicken picnic. But he surprises me when he tells me he's going out of town.

"Annabelle's daughter's family has a house on Wadmalaw Island. We're going to drive up for the day and spend the night."

"Driving? You mean you're taking your car on a trip?" I ask, unable to keep the alarm out of my tone.

"Yes, but there's no need for you to worry. We'll be fine."

I nudge him with my elbow. "Of course I'm gonna worry. You'd better text me when you get there and before you leave to come back."

Dad frowns. "We've changed roles. You're now the parent, and I'm the teenager."

I grin at him. "A *love-struck* teenager."

He chuckles. "Maybe so. Feeling young again is good for the soul."

Night has fallen by the time I leave Whispering Oaks, and the road back to town is pitch black. The appearance of bright headlights in my rearview mirror alarms me. Based on the size of the headlights, the vehicle is bigger than a car, like a pickup truck or an SUV. When the driver rams my bumper, I grip the steering wheel and slam my hand on the horn. He responds by moving into the other lane and increasing speed until he's beside me.

I risk a glance at the black SUV, but tinted windows prevent me from seeing the driver. When I hit the brakes, the SUV drops back beside me. My heart pounds in my chest. Is he going to run me off the road? We play cat and mouse. I speed up. He speeds up. I slow down. He follows suit. When headlights suddenly appear from around the bend ahead of us, my tormentor steps on the gas and whips into the lane in front of me. He takes off, and I go after him, now determined to know the person's identity. But he's driving too fast for me to get a glimpse of his license plate, and by the time I reach town, he's nowhere in sight.

CHAPTER
TWENTY-EIGHT

I drive as fast as I dare on my way home, not caring if I break the speed limit. When I arrive at Marsh Point, I turn off the car and sprint to the guesthouse. As I'm unlocking the door, I realize I was in such a rush to get to Whispering Oaks I forgot to turn on the alarm when I left. Bolting the door behind me, I grab a kitchen knife and search the house from top to bottom, under the beds and in every closet. When I'm confident no one is hiding in the guesthouse, I shove a chest of drawers in front of the door and turn on the alarm.

Standing at the kitchen window, I watch for headlights in the driveway as I place a call to my private investigator. When Carter answers, I blurt, "Someone just tried to kill me. And I'm pretty sure it was Owen." The words spill from my mouth as I recount the event. "I'm scared, Carter."

"I know you are. Where are you now?"

"At home, in the guesthouse at Marsh Point. I've locked the doors, and the security system is on."

"Okay. Good. Now, let's back up a minute. You're certain it was a black SUV?"

"Positive. A Ford Explorer or a Tahoe would be my guess."

"But Owen drives a silver Lexus."

"I realize that, Carter. Maybe he borrowed a friend's car. Or rented one."

"Is it possible someone else may be trying to scare you?"

"No. My brother and sister want me dead, but they aren't murderers." I fill a glass with water and gulp it down. "I'm telling you, Carter, my husband is trying to kill me. He has motivation. If I'm dead, I can't divorce him and take half our money. And my life insurance is an added incentive."

Carter sighs. "I agree it sounds like Owen, but with tinted windows, you can't positively identify the driver. There's always a chance it was a random act of violence."

"That's too big of a coincidence considering, three days ago, I nearly died from anaphylactic shock when my EpiPen went missing."

"I'm aware, but we have to explore every possibility. I promise we will get to the bottom of it. Hang on a second." The line goes silent for an excruciatingly long minute. "Sorry about that. I'm texting with Aaron now. He's stationed in front of your husband's condo. According to him, Owen has been there all evening."

"Is he sure? Maybe Owen snuck out of the back door. I don't know how he did it, but I'm telling you, Owen is responsible. You're the investigator, Carter. You figure it out."

"And we will. Let me talk to Aaron. I'll call you back in a few minutes."

While I wait, I pace the kitchen floor's dated linoleum and sneak frequent peeks out the window. I've never thought about owning a gun before. I wouldn't even know how to shoot it. But right now, I wish I had one.

The minutes click slowly off the wall clock. Thirty minutes feel like thirty years. When Carter finally calls back, I answer on the first ring. The background noise tells me he's in his truck with his phone connected to Bluetooth.

"Well? What'd you find out?"

"You were right," Carter says. "It appears Owen snuck out the back door. When Aaron realized all the lights were off, he entered the condo with the key you gave me."

"And Owen wasn't there," I deadpan.

"Correct. We're pretty sure he's down the street at Harmony's house. Aaron saw two heads silhouetted in her bedroom. And guess what kind of car Harmony drives?"

I fall back against the kitchen counter. "A black Ford Tahoe."

"Close. A black Ford Explorer Because Owen felt the need to sneak out of his condo means he knows we're onto him. Which means I have to speed up my investigation."

I moan. "If he feels pressured for time, he might try to kill me again."

"I hope that's not the case, but we have to assume the worst," Carter says in a weary voice. "I'm thirty minutes away from Water's Edge now. When I arrive, I'll take over surveilling Owen and send Aaron to your house to protect you."

"Thank you." I slump against the kitchen counter as some of the tension leaves my body.

"Are you aware your husband has a private office in a shared office space building downtown?"

I straighten. "What? No."

"I just learned about it myself from Aaron."

My mind races. "Why would he need a private office when he already has two, one at Darby Custom Homes and one at the condo?"

"Because he's obviously hiding something. I spoke with a detective friend at Water's Edge Police Department. First thing in the morning, Detective Marlowe is going to contact a local judge about a search warrant."

"What if Owen tries to go to this office tonight?"

"Don't worry," Carter says. "I won't let him sneak past me."

"Like he snuck past Aaron earlier? I'm grateful for everything you're doing, Carter. But that should never have happened."

"I totally agree, and I've reprimanded Aaron. We made the mistake of underestimating your husband. I promise it won't happen again. You can trust us to take care of you, Ashton. Be on the lookout for Aaron. He'll call you when he gets to Marsh Point."

"Will do. And please let me know when you hear from Detective Marlowe about the search warrant," I say and end the call.

I make sure every lamp is on downstairs before heading up to my room. I take my time getting ready for bed, but when Aaron still hasn't called, I stand at the window in my pajamas waiting for him. Fifteen minutes later, headlights appear in the driveway, and his contact information flashes across my phone screen.

Accepting the call, I say, "I assume that's you in my driveway."

"Yes, ma'am. And I assume that's you in the second-floor bedroom window."

"Bingo," I say, and wave to him through the window.

"Try to get some sleep, Ashton. I'll be standing guard throughout the night. Call me if you hear any strange noises or just need reassurance of my presence."

"Don't worry, I will."

Climbing into bed, I nestle beneath the crisp sheets, but I'm too wired to sleep. I thumb off a text to Sully. *Are you awake? Can you talk?*

Seconds later, my phone rings. When I answer it, I burst into tears. And between sobs, I bring him to speed on everything that's happened.

"Try to calm down, Ashton. You've had a terrible scare, but you're in excellent hands with Carter."

I suck in an unsteady breath and dry my eyes with the bedcover. "Carter says Owen is renting an office in a building downtown. His detective friend is getting a search warrant in the morning."

"That's strange. He must be hiding something important to go to that much trouble."

The image of an office full of dead body parts pops into my brain, and I start crying all over again.

"What is it, Ashton?"

"Just my imagination getting the best of me."

"Do you want me to read to you?"

I smile through the tears. "I'd like that. If you don't mind." Growing up, my sisters and I had our own separate phone line. Sully and I used to talk for hours nearly every single night. After Mama's drunken episodes, he would read to me until I fell asleep. More often than not, he was still on the line when I woke the next morning.

"I don't mind a bit. What would you like to hear? The usual?" he asks, the usual being my favorite, Pat Conroy.

"Conroy would be great. But I can't handle any family drama tonight. Do you have a copy of *The Water Is Wide*?"

"Of course. Let me grab it, and I'll be right back." A rustling noise is followed by a long moment of silence. He comes back on the line and begins to read.

Placing the phone on speaker, I set it on the pillow beside me and snuggle deeper beneath the covers. His presence on the other end of the phone comforts me, and his deep voice lulls me to sleep before the end of the first chapter. When I wake at eight on Thursday morning, my phone's battery is dead.

Scrambling out of bed, I plug my phone into the charger on the dresser and cross the room to the window. Aaron's nondescript sedan is parked in front of the guesthouse, but there is no sign of Aaron. Slipping on my robe, I hurry down the stairs and throw open the door. He is sitting on the porch swing watching the sunrise.

"Good morning! Would you like some coffee?"

"I would love some coffee." He stands and stretches and follows me inside to the kitchen.

"Any word from Carter?" I ask as I measure out scoops of ground coffee.

"He texted a few minutes ago. All is quiet on the western front."

"You must be exhausted."

He rakes his fingers through his unruly sandy hair. "I'm used to it. I spent much of the night kicking myself for letting your husband pull one over on me. I would never have forgiven myself if something had happened to you on my watch."

I inspect Aaron's face. He can't be older than thirty. "Everyone makes mistakes," I say, even though his mistake could've cost me my life. "But if you learn from it, then it was a mistake worth making."

"Then the mistake was worth it, because I learned a lot." He tugs his phone out of his pocket. "Carter just texted with an update from Detective Marlowe."

I snatch the phone from him and read the text. *I'm outside Owen's office waiting for Marlowe to get here with the search warrant.*

I text back. *This is Ashton. Aaron and I are on the way. Send us the address.*

I hand Aaron back his phone. "I'm going to change. I'll be back down in five minutes," I say and dart up the stairs.

I'm suddenly terrified of what we might find in Owen's office. How is it possible I could've been so wrong about the man I married?

CHAPTER TWENTY-NINE

I've never noticed the nondescript four-story office building before, located off the beaten track on a downtown side street. We exit the elevator on the third floor to find Carter leaning against the wall with arms folded and head bowed, apparently asleep on his feet. Aaron nudges him, and he startles awake.

"I'm sorry. I nodded off for a minute," he says, rubbing his eyes with balled fists.

I chuckle. "In your line of work, you need to sleep whenever and wherever possible. Was there any sign of Owen during the night?"

Carter shakes his head. "He was still with Harmony when I left to come over here."

I narrow my eyes. "Come to think of it, if you're here, who's tailing Owen now?"

"Calvin, one of my top guys. He's fresh and alert, just back from vacationing in the Bahamas."

Or his brain is fried from drinking too many rum punches, I think.

The elevator doors part and a bald-headed mountain of a man

heads down the hall toward us. Although I would not want to meet this man in a dark alley at night, I'm grateful he's on my side.

Carter introduces everyone, and Detective Marlowe presents Carter with the search warrant. "I got the key from the building's manager on my way in," he explains as he opens the door.

To my relief, the scene inside isn't gruesome. In fact, the office is bare, with only a wooden desk and a straight-back metal chair. A small black backpack in the center of the desk appears to be the only personal item.

"Stand back!" orders the detective. He studies the backpack but is careful not to touch it. "I don't detect an explosive device."

We move closer as Marlowe empties the contents of the backpack. There's a small laptop computer, a US passport, a container of temporary blonde hair color, a rubber-banded wad of cash, and an EpiPen.

While I'd suspected my husband had intentionally caused my anaphylactic shock, seeing the evidence firsthand pains me greatly.

"Is that your EpiPen?"

"I assume so."

Marlowe unzips a side pocket and removes two velvet jewelry boxes.

"I believe those are mine as well," I say.

Marlowe opens the boxes one at a time. Carter gasps at the sight of the pearl necklace and pink diamond ring.

"Are those real?" Aaron asks, his green eyes wide.

"Yes. These pieces have been in my family for a long time. May I take them home with me?"

Marlowe shakes his head. "Not yet. I'm sorry. I have to keep them as evidence."

"Those jewels are priceless, Detective. You'd better keep them in a safe place."

"Understood." Marlowe closes the velvet boxes and picks up the passport. "Matthew Thomas Wilson. Is this your husband?" he asks, showing me the passport photograph.

I lean over to inspect the passport. "Yes, but that's obviously not his name."

"Good fake. Must have cost him a fortune." Marlowe tosses the passport on the desk and opens the laptop. "It's password protected. No surprises there."

"But you can hack into it, right?" I point at the laptop. "I'd be willing to bet the information regarding my brokerage account is on there."

"In addition to a lot of other stuff Owen doesn't want us to know about." Carter slides the laptop into the backpack, along with the other items. "We'll break into it. But it'll take some time."

I gulp back fear. I have a sinking feeling time is the one thing we don't have. "What happens in the meantime? Owen will go ballistic when he finds out you broke into his office."

"We'll watch closely for his next move," Carter says. "The next twenty-four hours are crucial to the case."

An attractive young woman with caramel skin and olive eyes appears in the doorway. "Am I interrupting something?"

Carter motions her in. "Not at all. You're right on time. Ashton, meet your new best friend, Cassi Mays."

I smile at Cassi. "Nice to meet you."

"Cassi, until further notice, I don't want you to let Ashton out of your sight."

She gives a curt nod. "Yes, sir."

My frustration with the situation rises to the next level. I'm so ready to have my life back. But for the time being, I'm at these people's mercy.

"Let's go, new best friend." I wave for Cassi to follow me as I walk toward the door. When we're alone in the elevator, I say, "I have a meeting with a client at eleven. If anyone asks, you're my intern for the summer." I give her the once-over. Although she looks young enough to still be in school, she's professionally dressed in a khaki summer pants suit and a crisp white blouse. "Have you been doing this long?"

"Long enough," she responds, which I take to mean not long at all.

Cassi drives me to Marsh Point in her black sedan and waits in the living room while I shower and dress. I'm leaving my bedroom when I remember the two pieces of jewelry I took to Palmetto Island. I grab them out of my top drawer. Even though I have a security system, with Owen on the loose, the jewels are safer in the bank than in my possession.

The Hausers are already seated in the boardroom when we arrive at my office. They seem satisfied with my explanation about Cassi being my intern, and we jump right into a discussion of my proposed plans for their new home.

We've been meeting for more than an hour when Cassi receives a text and quietly excuses herself. I feel certain it's news about Owen, and I'm impatient for an update, but the Hausers are full of questions, and the meeting goes on for another thirty minutes.

When we finally adjourn, Cassi is waiting outside the conference room. "I apologize for not rejoining the meeting. I've been texting with Carter, and I didn't want to be a distraction."

"You did the right thing. Let's go to my office," I say and lead her to the end of the hall.

Cassi goes straight to the window and stares out at the bridge. "Nice digs. I'm in the wrong line of work."

I close the door behind me and drop my things on my desk. "What did Carter say? Were they able to hack into the computer?"

Cassi turns away from the window. "Yes. They're sorting the content now." She takes off her suit jacket and drapes it over the arm of a chair.

"Do you have to wear that?" I nod toward the pistol holstered under her arm.

"I'm afraid so. My job is to protect you, which means being prepared for the worst." She eases into the chair. "They found child porn on the computer. Is your husband into that sort of thing?"

I scrunch up my face. "Not that I'm aware of. Adult pornography wouldn't surprise me, but child porn is sick. Then again, I'm learning a lot about Owen I never thought possible."

Cassi nods. "It may be a cover to throw us off. There are a few password-protected documents. Carter is working on those now. The Internet browser's history has been wiped clean. But there are ways of retrieving it. The process is tedious. These things take time."

My phone vibrates the desk with an incoming call. "This is my brother. I should take it since Owen works with him."

"Of course. Go right ahead."

I accept the call, and Will blurts, "Where's your husband?"

"I have no idea, Will. We're separated, remember?" I place the call on speaker and set the phone on my desk.

"Well, you'd better find him, because he just wired a hundred thousand dollars out of our primary account to an account in Nigeria."

My jaw hits the desk. "Wait! What? Can you say that again?"

"You heard me. I'm holding you personally responsible for this, Ashton. If you don't find Owen, you're on the hook for a hundred grand," Will says and ends the call.

Cassis's olive eyes are enormous. "Geez. Nice brother."

"He's angry. And I don't blame him." I bury my face in my hands. "I don't believe this. Things are getting worse by the minute."

Cassi gets up from her chair. "Excuse me a minute. I need to report this to Carter," she says, and leaves the office.

I spin my chair around to face the window. This is all my fault. I'll have to pay Will's company back. There goes my pool. I may not be able to finish the renovations in progress. Will may even fire me as his client, and I wouldn't blame him.

I don't hear Cassi come back in until she clears her throat. I look up to see her standing beside my chair. "We have a problem. Calvin followed your husband to work and watched him enter the building. Owen's car is still in the parking lot. At some point, he must have come out of the building in disguise. Harmony is missing as well. They appear to have vanished."

I leap out of the chair to my feet. "You've gotta be kidding me. And you call yourselves investigators."

Cassi places a hand on my shoulder. "You have every right to be upset, Ashton. But Carter is hot on your husband's trail. He's the best in the business, and he will find him."

I brush her hand away. "He'd damn well better."

"He will. I promise." Cassi glances at her watch. "It's almost two o'clock. Why don't we get some lunch?"

"I can't think about food at a time like this," I snap. I realize I'm being unfair to Cassi. None of this is her fault. "But you're right. We both need to eat."

We walk across Main Street to Custom Crust and order today's special—fresh tuna salad on toasted multigrain bread with a slice of juicy ripe tomato. I pay for our order, and we take our sandwiches to a table outside on the small patio. Making polite conversation, I ask Cassi how she got into the investigative business. Her answer makes me soften toward her more.

"I wanted to be a police officer like my father, who was killed in the line of duty. I was determined to follow in his footsteps, to finish the job he started, but then I got pregnant. Becoming a parent changed everything. I can't bear the thought of making my child motherless." She takes a sip of sweet tea. "I don't regret it though. I'm married to a wonderful man, and I love my daughter dearly."

"How do you manage the long hours your job demands?" I ask, popping a sweet potato chip into my mouth.

"I have the best boss in the world. Carter lets me work normal nine-to-five hours. And I enjoy the work. He has a variety of cases, not just domestic." Cassi takes a bite of sandwich and waits until she's finished chewing to ask, "What about you? Do you have children?"

I shake my head. "I never wanted children. I've been asking myself why a lot lately. I guess it's a good thing. I can't bear the thought of my children carrying Owen's genes."

We finish our sandwiches in silence. Cassi is good company, easy to talk to and content to go with the flow.

"Do you have other meetings this afternoon?" she asks on the way back across the street.

"No, I'm going to work from my office at home." Instead of going into the building, we head to her car in the parking lot. "If you don't mind, I need to stop by the bank on the way."

"I don't mind a bit," she says, unlocking her car doors.

Delbert Lewis accosts me in the lobby at the bank. "Mrs. Nelms! I was just getting ready to call you. I have an urgent matter I need to discuss with you." His gaze shifts to Cassi. "In private."

I give Cassi a nod, letting her know the gentleman banker is harmless. "I'll be right back," I say and follow him into his office.

He closes the door but doesn't invite me to sit down. "Normally, I wouldn't divulge information regarding our clients, but since Owen is your husband . . . And since you have joint accounts . . ." He hesitates, as though unsure whether to continue.

"What is it, Mr. Lewis? Owen and I are having some marital problems. If there's something I should know about my accounts, you need to tell me."

"Owen was in a couple of hours ago. He asked for the key to your safe deposit box. I didn't give it to him, of course, since you instructed not to allow him access." The banker casts a nervous glance at the closed door. "There's something else you should know though. He cleaned out your joint account. He asked for cash."

A chill travels my spine. "Are you kidding me? Last time I checked, there was nearly twenty thousand dollars in that account."

"Yes, ma'am. Twenty-one thousand and some change."

I stare at him, aghast. "And you just gave it to him?"

He tosses up his hand, as if to say what else could he do. "It's Owen's money, as much as it is yours."

Mr. Lewis is right. In the eyes of the law, Owen can do whatever he wants with the money. This is my fault for having joint ownership with a thief.

"I need to put something in my safe deposit box, Mr. Lewis."

"Of course. I'll escort you to the vault."

Mr. Lewis and I are in and out of the vault in less than five minutes. I wait until Cassi and I are back in the car to tell her Owen cleaned out our joint account.

"I'm so sorry, Ashton. Keep the faith. We're going to get your money back. Do you want to call Carter, or do you want me to tell him?"

"You can tell him. But wait until we get home," I say. I don't think I can stomach hearing her repeat the story to Carter.

We ride in silence, and when we reach Marsh Point, I make a beeline to the guesthouse, calling over my shoulder, "Make yourself at home. I'll be upstairs in my office if you need me."

Cassi hollers after me, "I'll be right out here on the porch if *you* need *me*."

I make a glass of sweet tea, drag myself up the stairs, and collapse into my desk chair. Forcing my troubles from my mind, I begin work on implementing the changes to the Hauser project we agreed upon during our meeting earlier. Around four thirty, when I look up to see Carter's black pickup truck and a police car coming down the driveway, my first thought is something bad happened. Did they find Owen? Is Owen dead?

I reluctantly leave my desk and go downstairs to the porch. "What's going on?" I ask Cassi, whose face is pinched in concern.

"I'm not sure. Carter didn't warn me he was coming."

Raising my hand, I shield my eyes from the sun as I look more closely at the pickup. "Someone's with him. It looks like Detective Marlowe."

The two men get out of the truck and make their way toward us with a uniformed officer trailing behind.

"We have a situation," Carter says in a grave voice. "Your brother has filed a complaint with the police accusing you of embezzlement."

The earth falls out from beneath me. "What're you talking about?"

Carter steps up to the porch. "Come inside with me, and I'll explain."

CHAPTER **THIRTY**

Carter and I enter the house, leaving the others behind on the porch. I show him to the kitchen and retrieve two bottles of water from the refrigerator, handing one to him.

"Thanks. I'm parched. It's hot as Hades today," Carter says, unscrewing the cap and gulping down water.

I lean against the counter as the reality of this latest development hits home. "I can't believe my brother is pressing charges against me. Are they going to arrest me?"

"They'd better not. Will lacks credible evidence to support his claim that you aided your husband in the embezzlement. Your sister was with him when he filed the complaint. I got the impression she's calling the shots. She's an angry woman. What did you do to her to make her so mad?"

"Carrie is upset because our mother left Marsh Point to me."

"I figured it was something like that." Carter finishes the water and looks around for a trash can for his bottle.

"Here. Give me that." I take the bottle from him and toss it into the trash can under the sink. "Have you had any luck finding Owen?"

"Not yet. We suspect Harmony is with him. Her Ford Explorer is parked in front of her house, but she's not answering the door."

"That's just great! We may never find them. Right now, they're probably boarding a plane to some faraway destination with a population of over a gazillion."

Carter points his index finger at the ceiling. "Assuming he has an additional fake passport from the one we found in the office. I doubt he'd be careless enough to use his own. And it doesn't sound like Owen and Harmony have been together long enough for him to have a fake passport made for her."

"I wouldn't put anything past him. My husband is turning out to be way more resourceful than I ever imagined." I take a big sip of water. "Why is Will so certain I had anything to do with stealing that money?"

"He claims you're strapped for cash because of the renovations."

"Seriously?" I throw my hands in the air, letting them fall back to my sides. "My brother must think I'm a total loser. Like I would help my husband steal money from my family's company when the whole town knows Owen's having an affair with Harmony."

"I agree. It sounds ludicrous. If it makes you feel better, no one believes Will. But the police are obligated to investigate. Detective Marlowe would like to question you. You don't have to speak to him without an attorney present, but that's your call."

Turning my back on Carter, I look out the window at the detective who sits on the porch swing, talking on his cell phone. Despite his size, he appears to be a nice enough guy. "I'll answer his questions as long as they are reasonable. But I reserve the right to stop if I feel threatened."

Carter gives his head a solemn nod. "Fair enough."

I brush past him on my way out of the kitchen. I stop in front of Marlowe, waiting until he ends his call. "I understand you want to ask me some questions."

Marlow gets to his feet. "If you don't mind."

"I mind. But I will in order to clear my name." I gesture at the main house. "We'll be more comfortable on the veranda."

We traipse in single file across the yard, and for the next forty-five minutes, Detective Marlowe interrogates me with a barrage of questions. He asks me about events that happened when I was a child that have nothing to do with the missing money. Events he clearly heard about from Will and Carrie.

Carter finally intervenes. "Enough already, Detective. This is a witch hunt."

I jump to my feet. "I agree. Either press charges or get off my property."

"I didn't mean to upset you," Marlowe says in a genuine tone as he closes his tablet. "I'm just doing my job. I'm satisfied you weren't involved in the embezzlement, and we won't be pressing charges." He hands me a business card. "If you can think of anything that might help us find your husband, don't hesitate to call."

Carter hangs back on the porch when the others head off to their cars.

"What happens now?" I ask.

"I have all my investigators on the case. You'll have round-the-clock protection. Cassi will be with you during the day and Aaron at night."

I realize this investigation could get costly, and considering Owen took off with all the money in our joint account, I probably can't afford it. "I'm fine here alone, Carter. I have my security system. Their efforts are better spent searching for Owen."

He tilts his head. "Are you sure?"

"I'm positive. Besides, you and I both know Owen is long gone from here."

"Unfortunately, I think you're probably right." He pulls me in for a half hug. "I'll be staying in Water's Edge until we solve this case. Call me anytime, day or night. I value my relationship with Sully, and he'll never forgive me if anything happens to you."

I watch the convoy of cars drive away before collapsing onto the daybed. Propping my head on pillows, I stare out at the water as my thoughts drift back to my childhood. I was close with my siblings when we were growing up. The atrocities we experienced strengthened our bond. But my going away to college sparked a chain of events that drove us all apart. Will, Carrie, and I are now virtual strangers to one another. The thought of my sister and brother ganging up on me hurts.

I try to imagine how things might have been different. If Savannah hadn't disappeared? If Bert's accident hadn't happened? If our mother hadn't been a drunk? We can't change the past, but we can make the future better. But how do I do that if my siblings hate me enough to want me in jail?

Sometime later—a couple of hours, maybe longer—I drag myself back to the guesthouse and turn on the security system. Even though it's still daylight out, I crawl into bed and power off my phone. Carter knows where to find me if anything urgent comes up.

I fall into a deep sleep, and when I wake at ten the following morning, my new reality crashes down on me. Owen stole a hundred thousand dollars from Darby Custom Homes, and my siblings are blaming me for the theft. As they blame me for everything else wrong in their lives.

Unable to face the day, I open the top drawer of my nightstand and remove my sleeping pills. I just had the prescription refilled, and the bottle is full. I take a pill and sleep the rest of the day. For the next thirty-six hours, I sleep, wake, pop a pill, and go back to sleep. When I wake late Saturday afternoon, I drive myself to the store and load up on red wine. If Mama found solace in a bottle of booze, maybe I can too.

CHAPTER THIRTY-ONE

Back at Marsh Point, I take two bottles of wine to the rockers on the veranda and settle in for the evening. My goal is to get smashed. I want to understand what my mother found so appealing about being drunk, what she experienced every day of her life. Maybe getting drunk will help me remember the past.

I don't bother with a glass. I drink straight from the bottle. I'm a lightweight, and it only takes several long pulls to give me a buzz. I close my eyes and let my mind wander back to my childhood. The memories are dim at first, but the more I concentrate, the more vivid they become. I hear Mama screaming at us, telling us we are worthless, that we will never amount to anything, that we aren't worthy of the Merriweather name. She routinely called Carrie a fat, lazy slob and Savannah a spineless coward. She told Will he was weak like his daddy, that he would never be a true southern gentleman like her father. And when she was too drunk to take care of my siblings, when the burden of cooking and bathing and homework fell to me, she said I would make a lousy mother. I was an impressionable girl at the time, and those insults shaped my future.

The wine is the magic key to my memory vault. By the time I

reach the end of the first bottle, the vault door has burst open, and the memories are washing over me like waves pounding the sand during a storm. I remember the fire, the flames, and the smoke and running across the lawn to the guesthouse, hollering like a banshee for my father. Mama's angry tirades terrified us. We ran from her, hiding in closets and under beds. When she found us, she wore us out with our father's leather belt. I took many of these lashings for my siblings while they escaped to the freedom of the outdoors.

I remember Will as a toddler, howling and squirming in my arms while Mama slapped welts on my bare backside and legs with the belt. Where is our father? I'd wondered. We haven't seen him in weeks. He's not living in the guesthouse.

The sound of laughter drifting through Mama's open bedroom window draws me inside. Darkness has fallen, and Maurice has cut the power out inside the house. I slip back in time as the light of the moon guides me up the stairs. The laughter grows louder as I approach the top. I recognize the woman's voice but not the man's. Mama's bedroom door is ajar, and I peek around the doorjamb. A naked man I've never seen before is doing things to Mama I'm too young to understand. Things I can't bear to think about now, as an adult.

I slide down the wall to my bottom. I've opened the second bottle, and I guzzle down the wine. Who was that man? What was he doing in our house? As memory after memory unfolds, I close my eyes and bang my head against the wall. There were many men. Not the sort of people my parents typically socialized with. Men with scruffy beards and tattoos and dirty clothes. My mother was a whore. My father must have known what was transpiring under this roof. Why didn't he divorce her?

I drain the last drops of wine from the second bottle and curl up in a ball on the floor outside Mama's room. I wake up at dawn in a puddle of my vomit. I clean up my mess with the worker's rags I find outside in their supply trailer. Staggering back to the guesthouse, I strip off my clothes, take a long hot shower, and dress in drawstring shorts and a tank. I go downstairs to the kitchen to make myself food but open another bottle of wine instead.

I spend the day stumbling around the house and grounds, reliving one traumatic episode after another. I consume more wine than I thought humanly possible. I'm drowning my sorrows. Like mother, like daughter.

When night falls, I return to the guesthouse to sleep. But every time I close my eyes, more voices and visions flash before me. Opening my eyes, I notice the sleeping pills on my nightstand next to an uncorked bottle of wine. Sitting up in bed, I unscrew the cap and dump several pills in my hand. I pop the pills into my mouth and swallow them down with a swig of wine. Tilting back my head, I pour the rest of the pills into my mouth and swallow them down with wine. I slide back down in bed and close my eyes. When the reality of what I've done hits home, I sit bolt upright in bed and rush to the bathroom. Sticking my finger down my throat, I vomit into the toilet. I do this again and again until I think all the pills have come up. But I have no way to be sure. Nor do I really care. If it's my time to die, then so be it. I have no idea how to go on living anyway.

I WAKE on the bathroom floor to the sound of loud knocking on the door. Assuming it's Carter with an update, I hurry downstairs to answer the door. I'm surprised to see May May on the front porch with one of Mama's journals tucked under her arm.

"You look awful, child." She waves her hand in front of her nose. "And you smell like a brewery. I've never known you to tie one on. What's wrong, sweet girl?"

I burst into tears. "Everything's wrong, May May. I think I tried to kill myself last night."

The color drains from her face. "What do you mean, you *think*?"

"I was drunk. The memory's kinda fuzzy. But my new bottle of sleeping pills is empty. I vaguely remember puking in the toilet."

May May shakes her head, confused. "This isn't like you, Ashton. Are you saying you *want* to die?"

"No. Yes. I don't know. Maybe. My life is ruined." In between sobs, I tell her about Owen's embezzlement and subsequent disappearance. "To make matters worse, Will and Carrie are accusing me of helping Owen steal the money."

"Oh, honey." May May takes me in her arms. "You're going through a lot right now. But you'll survive. These are things other people are doing to you. None of this has anything to do with who you are inside."

I push her away. "I had a breakthrough, May May. I finally remember the past. And that has *everything* to do with who I am inside."

"Well now, that's different. But I won't let you commit suicide on my watch. First, I'm going to sober you up. Then you and I are going to have a nice long chat." Setting Mama's journal on the kitchen counter, May May takes me by the arm and marches me up the stairs to my bathroom. She turns on the shower and waits for the water to get hot.

"Now get yourself cleaned up. I'll be right outside if you need anything. And don't you dare lock this door," she says, and exits the bathroom.

I lather my body in liquid soap and scrub my skin with a loofah sponge until it's raw. When I get out of the shower, I wrap myself in a towel and open the door. As promised, May May is standing right outside. She hands me a fresh change of clothes. "Get dressed."

I follow her orders, and we go downstairs to the kitchen together. I sit at the island while she makes me a scrambled egg, bacon, and cheese sandwich.

"When's the last time you ate?" she asks, placing the sandwich on the counter in front of me.

"I don't remember. Days ago." I take a big bite. "Thank you. This is really good."

"You're welcome," she says, pouring two cups of coffee, handing one to me.

I notice the gray clouds through the window. "I didn't realize it was supposed to rain."

"A tropical disturbance is coming through. We're expecting rain and wind straight through the holiday tomorrow."

"So much for the fireworks." I couldn't care less. I'm not in the mood to celebrate Independence Day. I eye the journal she left on the counter. "Is that one of Mama's?"

May May follows my gaze. "That's her last journal. I brought it with me, thinking you might want to read it. But considering everything you've recently been through, I'm not sure now is the best time. I found it very disturbing. Your mama was more mentally unstable than I realized."

"Tell me about it," I grumble. "I've been remembering some unsettling things about the past. No wonder my brain was protecting me from them."

May May rests a hand on my shoulder. "I understand. I wish I could forget some of what I read in your mama's journal." She gives my shoulder a pat before removing her hand. "We'll talk more after you finish eating."

I inhale the sandwich—I was hungrier than I realized—and we take our coffee out to the dock. The rain hasn't yet set in, but the temperature is cooler than it's been in months.

I stare across the sound at Sandy Island. "I used to love rainy days at Marsh Point. I wonder if I ever will again, if I'll ever love this property the way I once did."

"Your emotions are raw now, but once you come to terms with your past, the awful memories will fade."

"I'm not so sure, May May. I don't even know if I can live here anymore. All my fond memories of this place are now tainted by the awful images inside my head. I wish I could make them go back where they came from."

"You needed to set those memories free in order to truly understand who you are. Now that you've experienced them for a second time, you can begin the process of healing."

We sit on the edge of the dock with our feet dangling over the side. "Did you know about Mama's lovers?" I ask and watch closely for her reaction.

She presses her lips thin. "I had my suspicions before. She writes a lot about them in her journal."

"Who were those sketchy men?"

May May looks away, as though unable to meet my eyes. "I'm afraid they were drug dealers."

I sit upright. "What did you say?"

"Eileen exchanged sex for drugs. For a brief time in her life, she was addicted to some terrible drugs. Fortunately, she kicked that addiction during her second visit to rehab."

I slouch back down against a piling. "That makes sense. The worst of my memories happened during that time, right after Will was born. Did you know she used to beat us with Dad's leather belt?"

May May's eyes glisten with unshed tears. "No, sweetheart. I never would have let you kids suffer such brutality. I would've jerked y'all out of that house so fast your little heads would've spun like the tilt-a-whirl at the county fair."

Her analogy makes me smile. "I believe you."

May May moves over until our legs are touching. "Reading Eileen's journals really got to me. I can't imagine what you must be feeling after your breakthrough."

"Right now, I'm pretty numb. And I'm grateful to not feel anything. But I'm sure that will change. How much do you think Carrie and Will remember about the past?" I've never discussed our childhood with my siblings, except when they're accusing me of abandoning them.

"That's a good question. Those two are buttoned up tight when it comes to their emotions. I'm pretty sure they remember more than you though."

"I've always felt I didn't deserve to have children of my own because I'd let my siblings down. Because I'd failed them. But it's because Mama told me I would be a lousy mother so many times I believed her."

May May sighs. "And she felt awful about that. She mentioned it in her journals. She carried a lot of guilt to her grave."

I let this sink in. I'm curious to know what else is in the journals, but not curious enough to subject myself to more terrible memories. "I don't think I could've forgiven Mama if I'd remembered the awful things she did to us. I certainly wouldn't have nursed her through her illness."

May May reaches for my hand and squeezes. "I'm not so sure about that, Ashton. You have a bigger heart than anyone I know."

"What about Dad? Even though he wasn't living with us, he had to have known what we were going through."

May May stares down at the water. "You'll have to talk to Ernest about that."

"You mean there's more I don't know?"

"Unfortunately. But it's not my place to tell you."

I study her face, wondering what is causing her pained expression. A strong hunch warns me this has more to do with May May than my mother.

I swing my legs onto the dock, tucking my knees beneath my chin. "Did Mom say in her journal why she left me the house?"

"She hinted at it. Of all her children, she knew you loved Marsh Point the most. She knew you would restore the house to its original glory and cherish your time here."

"But that's a given. There must be something more."

"The house is a gift, a thank you for holding the family together during her darkest days. But she also believed you were the one person who could bring the four of you kids together again."

I rest my head on my knees. "From the time I was a little girl, she expected too much from me. And now she expects the impossible. How do I cure my family of the damage she caused?"

May May lets out a loud humph. "There is no cure for what's ailing your family."

"Maybe *cure* was the wrong choice of words. But you know what I mean. How do I mend us, May May?"

She presses her forehead against mine. "With the love only a mother can give."

CHAPTER
THIRTY-TWO

I remain on the dock for a long time after May May leaves. She was hesitant to go, but I assured her I wouldn't hurt myself. When she asked again if I wanted to read Mama's journal, I told her definitely not. I can't stomach any more of my mother's drama.

When the rain sets in, I move up to the veranda where I spend the afternoon cozied up with a blanket on the daybed. I never intended to commit suicide. I took the pills during my rock bottom moment. But I survived. The arduous task of bringing my family back together gives new purpose to my life. I failed my siblings once. But I've been given another chance, and I won't fail them the second time.

Now I need to figure out how to get through to them. My friends have often discussed the tough love of being a strict parent. I won't spoil my siblings by giving in to their every wish. I will share the house with Carrie, but only on my terms. She'll have her own bedroom, and she'll be welcome at Marsh Point any time. But I won't vacate the premises so she can have the place to herself. If she wants to spend time here, we'll do it as a family.

Darby Custom Homes is closed today and tomorrow for the holiday. I'm curious whether the work crew will show up on Wednesday morning. If my brother fires me as his client, I'll hire a builder I know from Beaufort who's as skilled at renovating historic homes as Will. I'll take out a loan from the bank. I'll have to postpone construction on the pool, but I will finish the main house before Thanksgiving. Then I'll invite my family and my closest friends for a feast to celebrate.

Realizing I haven't received an update about my husband, I dash in the rain to the guest cottage for my phone. The battery is dead, and I have to charge it for a few minutes before it powers on. I scroll through the long stream of texts from Carter. He has checked in periodically over the past few days, but he has nothing of interest to report. His team is still looking for Owen and still attempting to break into the laptop.

I charge the phone a few more minutes while I brew a cup of lavender tea. Then, grabbing my raincoat, I hurry back over to the veranda.

Optimism builds inside of me as dark clouds from the tropical depression slowly move in from the south. I've just witnessed the first streak of lightning off in the distance when Tracy comes running around the side of the house. On her heels is Will, yelling for her to stop and talk to him.

As he passes by the porch, I call out to Will. "What's going on?"

"Mind your own business," he hollers back at me.

Tracy sprints down the dock, lowers the boat, and jumps in. I've never seen her drive the boat before, and I don't know if she even knows how. Will leaps into the boat as she's speeding away from the dock. As they pass by heading north, I can see them fighting over the steering wheel and hear them screaming at each other, although I can't make out what they're saying.

I jump off the porch and run over to the shoreline, but the boat has rounded the bend out of sight. I have no way of going after them. I should call someone. Hattie! She lives nearby, and her husband has a fleet of boats.

When she answers her cell, I quickly tell her what happened. "Can you get Brad to go after them?"

Hattie gasps. "Are you insane, Ashton? There's lightning all around us. I'm sure they're fine. But if they haven't come back by the time the storm is over, we'll go looking for them."

A lightning bolt splits the sky, and a loud clap of thunder vibrates the earth, sending me sprinting back to the porch. When I hear Hattie's muffled voice calling my name, I realize I'm still clutching the phone. "Sorry! That was a close call. I'm scared, Hattie. This storm is nasty."

"I know, honey. Try to calm down. I'm looking at the radar. The storm is moving quickly. It'll be out of here soon."

"All right. I'll call you back in a few."

I pace the porch, chewing a hangnail while watching the coastline for sign of Will's boat. The wind picks up, and the blowing rain drives me inside. The storm seems endless. I stand at the window, my fear mounting with every beat of my pounding heart. My panic skyrockets when I notice a gray boat—at least thirty feet long, probably larger—with a small cabin and deep hull pass by.

I call Hattie back. "This is bad. I saw a rescue boat heading to the mouth of the sound."

"What makes you think it was a rescue boat?" she asks.

"It looked official. Besides, no one else would be out in this storm."

"Good point."

Over the wind, I hear the rumble of engines out in front of the house, and a swarm of figures dressed in orange crowd the veranda. "I've gotta go, Hattie. The rescue team is here." I end the call and walk out onto the porch.

A large man whose orange helmet covers all of his head and much of his face says, "Evening, miss. We received a call for help from"—he consults his phone—"Will Darby. Does he live at this address?"

"He doesn't live here, but he's my brother. I saw him a little while ago when he went out on his boat with his wife. He hasn't come back, and I'm freaking out."

"Which way did they go?"

"North." I toss my thumb over my shoulder. "Toward the ocean. What did Will say to the emergency operator?"

"The coverage was spotty, but she heard enough to understand his wife had fallen overboard, and he couldn't find her."

I clamp my hand over my mouth. "Oh god," I say into my palm. "This can't be happening."

Another boat, similar to the one that passed a few minutes ago, pulls up to the end of the dock, and the rescue team marches single file down the boardwalk.

"I'm going with you," I say to no one in particular and hurry after them with my head ducked against the wind and rain. My flimsy raincoat offers little protection, and by the time I reach the boat, my hair is dripping and my clothes soaked through.

We pack like sardines into the small cabin. I'm squeezed in the middle, and I can only see the gray steel of the ceiling and floors. The boat picks up speed, and we ride about a half mile. The sound is rough, and more than once, I grab onto the man standing next to me to keep from falling.

Someone yells, "There he is!" And the captain cuts his engines as he pulls alongside Will's boat.

When the rescue workers file out of the cabin to prepare for their search, I move over to the window where I can see my brother hanging over the side of his boat, staring down at the water.

The team leader, the man who spoke to me on the porch, boards Will's boat and attempts to console him. But my brother is deranged, screaming and flailing his arms as he gestures at the water. Whatever the leader says to Will appears to calm him. The leader places a supportive arm around Will as he helps him climb out of his boat and onto ours.

The cabin door bangs open and Will staggers in. When he sees me, he flings himself into my arms, and I comfort him like I once did when he was a boy awakened from a nightmare.

"This is so bad, Ashton! I'm so scared. They've gotta find her."

"Don't worry. They will," I say with feigned confidence.

"She was so upset," Will cries. "She was driving like a maniac. I tried to take the steering wheel from her, but she kept pushing me away. Instead of going bow-first into a huge wave, she turned away from it. The wave crashed into the side of the boat, and the impact thrust her over the side."

"She's a good swimmer," I say, even though I don't know if my sister-in-law can even dog paddle.

"She*'s* an excellent swimmer. I should've found her by now. I'm terrified she hit her head when she went overboard."

I'm aware the captain and first mate are listening to us. I can't imagine what they must be thinking. This doesn't look good for Will. Especially not with his history.

"Come with me," I say, and walk my brother to the far back corner of the cabin. In a loud whisper, I say, "Tell me everything. Where are the girls?"

"Tracy took them to stay with her parents in Savannah. Can you believe that? She took my children away from me without telling me," he says, his voice escalating.

I put my finger to my lips and cut my eyes at the captain. "Shh. It's okay. Try to calm down."

Will inhales several deep breaths. When he speaks again, his tone is softer. "When I got home from work, the girls were gone, and my suitcase was waiting by the door. She discovered a mental health institution in Atlanta that specializes in anger management issues. She threatened to leave me if I didn't check myself in."

"And you refused," I said deadpan.

He nods. "I told you the other day. I'm not one to talk about my problems."

I remember what Will told me the other day about Tracy. *She won't let up. She's like a gnat, buzzing around my head.* Despite their differences, taking his children to another state without telling him seems extreme.

The first mate brings us a blanket, and we huddle together at the window, both of us lost in thought. Will has retreated into his shell. He's told me all he's going to tell me about his marital problems and the boating accident.

The storm moves out and the waters calm. When dusk sets in, the rescue workers resort to using high-powered floodlights to search the inky waters. My legs ache, but there's nowhere to sit down.

Around ten thirty, the captain announces he's taking us back to dry land. I'm surprised Will doesn't argue. He's now a zombie, and I can only imagine what's running through his mind.

Back at Marsh Point, I try to coax him into coming with me to the guesthouse, but he insists on waiting on the veranda.

"I feel closer to her here," he explains.

"In that case, I'll get us some coffee. Is there anything else you need?"

"Just bring me back my wife," he says with a quivering chin.

When I touch his arm, he shrinks back. He needs time alone.

"I'll be back in a few minutes," I say and leave the porch.

On my way to the guesthouse, I notice both Will's and Tracy's cars in the driveway out front. Tracy must have left their house angry, and Will took off after her. If only he'd given her a chance to calm down. But no *if only* will bring Tracy back. My thought surprises me. At what point did I start assuming she was dead?

I use the potty—I've been holding my pee for hours–and rummage through my drawers for a dry T-shirt that might fit my brother. I should notify my family about Tracy, but I don't want to upset Dad at such a late hour, and my sister's melodrama will only make matters worse. I call the one person whose calming presence will be welcome.

When I explain the situation to May May, she says, "Dear Lord in heaven. I'm on my way. I'll be there in fifteen minutes."

"I'm making coffee. I'll wait for you in the guesthouse."

When the coffee maker finishes spitting black brew, I fill a thermos and wait on the front porch for May May. She arrives with a basket of warm cheddar biscuits. "I was just taking this batch of biscuits out of the oven when you called. I figured neither of you have eaten dinner."

I smile softly at her. "Thanks, May May. I'm not hungry but Will might want one."

As we cut across the lawn to the veranda, I relay what I know about the accident. Will bursts into tears when he sees May May, his loud sobs breaking my heart into pieces.

When he finally stops crying, Will changes into the dry shirt I give him and accepts a biscuit with his coffee. Positioning her rocker close to his, May May holds his hand and strokes his arm while offering her reassurances that everything will be okay.

Around midnight, Will moves over to the daybed, and I convince May May to go sleep in the guest cottage. I stay awake all night, keeping vigil beside my sleeping brother. For his sake, I need to be alert when we receive the dreaded news I'm now certain is coming.

As the first rays of sun break on the horizon, I hear the rumble of engines and see the first of the fleet of rescue boats as it comes into view. Leaving Will sleeping, I hurry to the end of the dock to greet them. The team leader tosses me a line from the bow.

"Did you find her?" I ask in a hopeful tone.

He gives his head a solemn shake. "I'm afraid I have bad news. A fisherman on his way out to the ocean discovered her body about thirty minutes ago."

CHAPTER THIRTY-THREE

News of Tracy's accident spreads throughout the community with lightning speed. When death comes to a family in a small town, death comes to the entire town. Tragedy striking a member of the Merriweather clan is an even bigger deal. Fourth of July festivities and fireworks are canceled. They would have been anyway because of the storm. We've no sooner returned to Will's house after identifying Tracy's body at the hospital than friends begin arriving in droves with food, flowers, and condolences.

Will sequesters himself in his bedroom, refusing to see anyone, including the minister. Carrie and I forge an unspoken truce as we greet guests and catalog their offerings for thank-you notes to be written later.

I haven't spoken to my father in private since my breakthrough, and I'm furious with him for allowing our mother to abuse us as children. But I put those feelings aside when I place the dreaded call. Because he's visiting Annabelle's daughter on Wadmalaw Island, he hasn't heard the news of Tracy's passing. He's made such dramatic improvement these past couple of weeks, and I fear this will cause him a setback. I'm grateful when Annabelle offers to drive him home to Water's Edge.

Tracy's parents, Loretta and Clarence Beaumont, arrive with my nieces around two o'clock. Caroline and Sophia are understandably confused by the absence of their mother and the presence of so many people in their home. When Caroline has a major tantrum, May May packs them up and takes them away to spend the night at her farm.

I've only met the Beaumonts once before, at Tracy and Will's wedding. Loretta is every bit as overbearing as I remember. I'm certain she's distraught over losing her only daughter, but she doesn't let her grief show. She takes over organizing her daughter's funeral as she once organized Tracy's wedding, like a drill sergeant issuing commands to everyone around her. Her husband, who is well-versed in avoiding his wife, slips outside to the porch. My heart breaks for Clarence, watching him rocking back and forth with his head bowed, struggling to accept the death of his only child.

But my poor brother can't escape his mother-in-law. Loretta makes it clear she blames him for the accident, and Will endures her wrath by going along with everything she decides. Will claims Tracy wanted to be cremated, but Loretta insists on a proper burial. She reluctantly agrees to hold the church service on Thursday at Tracy and Will's Presbyterian church in Water's Edge, under the condition that they bury Tracy in a private graveside ceremony in the family plot in Savannah afterward.

Loretta is a large woman, big-boned and tall. Despite being in her late sixties, she has toned muscles from Pilates and lap swimming. She dresses impeccably in designer clothes, and she wears her silver hair in a chic bob. She takes command of the kitchen, barking out orders to Carrie and me as though we're the hired help. After lunch on Wednesday, when I hear Loretta fussing at my brother from all the way down the hall in his bedroom, I decide I've had enough of Loretta Beaumont.

Marching down the hall, I enter the bedroom and close the

door behind me. "Shh! We have company, and I can hear you in the kitchen. What's going on?"

"We're having a disagreement about what Tracy will wear to meet her maker. Not that it's any of your business." Loretta snatches up a black tweed suit from the clothes spread out on the bed. "This is the most appropriate garment she owns."

Just looking at the suit makes me sweat.

Loretta tosses the suit back onto the bed. "It's not ideal, but it'll have to do. I can't very well take my dead daughter shopping."

Will crumples, his chin hitting his chest. "I never even saw Tracy wear that suit. She loved bright colors."

I rifle through the clothes on the bed until I find a familiar dress. "This is perfect." I hold the emerald-green midi dress up in front of me. "When I visited her boutique recently, Tracy told me this was one of her all-time favorites."

Will appears relieved. "I remember. She made me take her out to dinner to show it off."

Loretta looks at the dress in disgust. "I can't believe my daughter would own such a tacky garment."

I stare down my nose at her. "You obviously aren't aware of your daughter's success. Tracy had an amazing style. Every woman in town, young and old, shopped in her boutique."

Loretta puffs out her cheeks like a blowfish. "I will not bury my daughter in a dress one might wear to a beach party."

I move closer to Loretta, letting her know I'm not afraid of her. "Well, you don't get to make all the decisions. Tracy was Will's wife."

"Not for long. She was going to leave him," she says with a smug smile I want to smack off her face.

I glare at her. "Tracy gave him an unfair ultimatum."

Loretta stares past me at my brother. "He was abusing her and the girls."

"He most certainly was not."

Irritation twitches the nerves under Loretta's skin. "Your brother has anger management issues."

I cough up a laugh. "Don't be ridiculous. He's not angry. He's grieving. He just lost his mother. And Tracy was pressuring him to go for therapy when all he wanted was to be left alone. Everyone copes differently, Loretta. Surely you know that."

Loretta folds her arms over her chest. "Fine. She can wear the dress. No one will see her anyway."

"Except her maker," I say under my breath as Loretta storms out of the room.

Through glistening tears, Will says, "Thank you for defending me. I owe you one." He takes the dress from me. "I need to run. They are waiting for this at the funeral home."

I wish the circumstances were different, but I'll take the brownie points whenever I can get them.

HOURS LATER, I stand beside Will as we look down at Tracy in her mahogany coffin. The funeral director has arranged a private viewing for family only prior to the visitation, which is scheduled to begin in a few minutes.

"She would've hated this," Will says. "So many times, she told me she wanted to be cremated. She was adamant about it. Now that I think about it, she talked about her funeral plans a lot for someone so young. Do you think she had a premonition about dying?"

My throat swells at the possibility, and I choke out a *maybe*. "You had to compromise to make her mother happy. Wherever Tracy is now, I'm sure she understands that."

Will fingers the coffin's ruffly lining. "I doubt it. Tracy despised her mother. She resented Loretta for her strict upbringing. Which is why I can't believe she took the girls to Savanah to stay with her."

When I hear Will sniffle, I realize he's crying and step away from the coffin to give him some privacy.

A few minutes later, the funeral director calls my family into the adjacent visitation room, where for three hours we greet the seemingly endless line of friends and acquaintances. A large majority of these people have already been to the house, already expressed their condolences, but I don't fault them for wanting to console my family.

By the time the visitation ends, my cheeks hurt from fake smiling. I'm helping my exhausted father find somewhere to sit down when I notice Loretta pull the funeral director aside for a private word. I park Dad in a chair and inch closer to eavesdrop.

"My husband and I will drive ourselves and our granddaughters to Savannah for the graveside service," she tells the director.

My blood pressure hits the roof, and I insinuate myself into their conversation. "The girls won't be attending the funeral, Loretta. They're entirely too young. My sister's teenagers are staying with them."

Loretta looks down her nose at me. "Says who?"

I dig my thumb into my chest. "Says me. Says Will. Says anyone with a brain."

"Then we'll need a separate car for my husband and me," Loretta says, her eyes on the funeral director.

I appear confused. "But why? Won't you be staying in Savannah after the funeral?"

"We'll have to come back for the girls." Loretta lifts her chin high. "They'll be staying with us for the foreseeable future."

"Oh no, they won't," I snap.

"Tracy left them in our care, and they will remain in our care until further notice," Loretta says in a haughty tone.

The funeral director ducks his head and slips quietly away.

"You have no right to take them to Savannah, Loretta. As their father, Will has legal custody of them."

Across the room, Will hears his name and joins our conversation. "What's going on? Is there a problem?"

I glance over at my brother. "Your mother-in-law is planning for Caroline and Sophia to live with her after the funeral."

Will's glare pins Loretta against the wall. "Like hell you will. The girls are staying right here in Water's Edge with me. If you try to take them across the state line, I will have you arrested for kidnapping."

Loretta squares her shoulders. "You might as well know. I've already spoken with our attorney. Clarence and I are suing for custody."

I laugh out loud. "You've gotta be kidding me. No judge in his right mind would give an old bat like you custody over a child's own biological father."

"We'll have to wait and see about that."

"I'm not holding my breath. Now, I'm going to ask you to leave. I've had about enough of you to last the rest of my lifetime." As I take her by the arm and walk her to the door, I understand what it feels like to be a mama bear. I will do whatever it takes to protect my brother and nieces from that miserable old shrew.

CHAPTER
THIRTY-FOUR

The church is standing room only for Tracy's funeral. And there's not a dry eye in the sanctuary when my brother delivers the eulogy. As far as I can tell, he's speaking off the cuff. I certainly never saw him working on his comments. Who knew Will had such a way with words?

After the ceremony, my family follows the flower-laden coffin single file up the aisle. I spot Sully in the balcony on my way out, but I can't find him in the sea of people in the fellowship hall afterward. The director only allows us a few minutes at the reception before he whisks us away in the limousine to Savannah.

Bench seats face each other in the back of the funeral car. The six of us ride in silence. Dad, Will, and me opposite May May, Carrie, and Carrie's husband, Tom. Our vehicular procession comprises two police motorcycles, followed by the hearse and our limousine, with Tracy's parents' Audi bringing up the rear. As our convoy passes through town, Will's staff salutes us from in front of Darby Custom Homes, and a wreath made of the same white flowers as the coffin spray adorns the door of Tracy's boutique.

We drive an hour for a ten-minute ceremony performed by a minister we've never met. Afterward, we wait in the limo while

Will says goodbye to his wife. It saddens me to think of my brother and his daughters so far away from Tracy. They won't be able to pop in routinely to check on her gravesite. They'll have to drive sixty miles to place a pumpkin on her grave at Halloween and hang a wreath on her tombstone at Christmas.

Everyone falls asleep before we even cross the Savannah River, except for Dad and me. Carrie is drooling on Tom's shoulder. Tom's head is resting against the back of the seat. May May is cuddled up to the window. And on the other side of me, Will is snoring softly with his mouth open.

Dad whispers to me. "You've been distant these past few days. Is something wrong? Are you angry with me?"

I'm not in the mood for a confrontation, but I can't deny I've been giving him the cold shoulder. "I'm just going through some stuff with Owen," I say, keeping my tone low so as not to wake the others.

"Your sister mentioned something about that."

I roll my eyes. "Of course she did."

Dad pats my thigh. "For the record, no one thinks you stole money from the company."

My gaze falls on my sleeping sister. "Carrie does."

Dad shakes his head. "Carrie doesn't count."

This almost makes me laugh. I angle my body toward his. "After Owen disappeared, I retreated to Marsh Point to lick my wounds. I remembered some events from my childhood I'd forgotten. I found some of them confusing."

A deep V appears between his eyes. "Like?"

"Like Mom beating welts on us with your leather belt. And the awful things she said to us, insults that were so bad they shaped the adults we became. And the men she had sex with in exchange for drugs. Where were you when we needed you, Dad? I remember you living in the guesthouse for a while when we were little. You came back for a brief period after the fire, but disappeared again after Will was born. Where did you go?"

Dad looks away, staring out the window at the thick forest lining the highway. "What good will dredging up the past bring, Ashton?"

My heart thumps against my rib cage. I'm close to giving him a piece of my mind. "Make up an excuse, Dad! Even a lame one is better than me believing you intentionally neglected us."

"Since you put it like that . . . But I warn you, you might not like what you hear." His eyes glass over as he travels back in time. "The truth is, I was having an affair. Your mother literally drove me into the arms of another woman." He looks over at May May. "A wonderful woman, who was as lost in the world as I was at the time."

"You mean, May May?" I ask, and he nods solemnly.

I jerk my head back as the enormity of this revelation hits me. "Did Mama know?"

He shakes his head. "You're the first person I've ever told. We never meant for it to happen. May's husband had recently died, and I was considering leaving Eileen. We were two friends who found comfort in each other's arms at a difficult time."

"But what about her children? Surely, you didn't share her bed in front of them."

Dad appears indignant that I would ask such a thing. "Of course not! I would never do anything to compromise her virtue. I slept in the guest room. Liza and Billy were old enough to understand I was having problems at home."

"And this went on for years?" I ask, even though I already know the answer.

He holds up two fingers. "Until your mama . . . until she, you know."

"No, Dad, I don't know. Otherwise I wouldn't be asking you."

He narrows his haunted eyes. "Are you saying you don't remember the overdose? Your mama nearly died."

Memories from that night flash through my mind. Men in dark uniforms wheeling Mama out of her bedroom on a stretcher.

"It's all coming back to me now. The paramedics worked on her for a while. They pumped her chest and used the defibrillator paddles on her."

"Her heart had stopped," Dad says.

A shadow in the corner of Mama's room comes into view. "She wasn't alone that night. A man was with her. He had enormous feet and dark, hairy legs. And there were more men in uniforms. The police. They took the man away in handcuffs. And Carrie was so upset. Why was she so inconsolable?" I cover my mouth. "Oh my god! She's the one who found Mama passed out." I look over at my sister, who is now awake and staring daggers at me. "Do you remember?"

"Of course I remember, Ashton. It was the most defining moment of my life. I wasn't blessed with selective memory like you."

"I can't control how my brain works, Carrie."

A dazed expression appears on Carrie's face. "The man with her was the one we called Uncle Roy. She always made us call them uncle. There was Uncle Toby, Uncle Nelson, Uncle Jackie. I'd had a bad dream and wet the bed that night. I tried to tell Mama, but she wouldn't wake up. I went and got you, and we called 9-1-1."

"Your mama went to rehab for six months," Dad says. "When she came back, she was better. At least for a while. She started drinking again, but fortunately, she never went back to drugs."

"Weren't we the lucky ones?" Carrie says in a sarcastic tone. She closes her eyes and leans her head against the seat. A few minutes later, she snorts and mumbles something incoherent in her sleep.

I whisper to Dad, "Do you think she heard what you said about your affair?"

"No. I'm pretty sure she was sleeping."

"I've often sensed friction between you and May May, but I never would've suspected an affair."

"Our guilt consumed us after the overdose. Our selfishness

nearly cost Eileen her life. May May and I agreed to always put our families first. Our relationship is complicated, but our bond is deep. Not because of our affair, but because of our devotion to your mother."

We ride for a while in silence. My heart hurts thinking about Dad and May May sacrificing their own happiness for their families. I think back to the day at Whispering Oaks when Dad was feeling sorry for himself, and May May set him straight. They have a long history of friendship. What's stopping them from rekindling the romance they once shared? May May has always been like a mother to me, and I love her dearly. I would like nothing more than to see them together.

I nudge Dad's arm. "Is this thing between you and Annabelle serious?"

"Nah." He chuckles. "I'm too old for a serious relationship, honey. But I enjoy the companionship."

"Did you love May May?"

His face softens. "I still do. She's the most amazing woman I've ever met."

"Then what's keeping you two from being together now?"

Dad doesn't hesitate, as though he's given the idea a lot of thought. "Your mama's only been dead a couple of months."

"What's a couple of months when you spent most of your lifetime with the wrong woman?"

Dad hunches a shoulder. "Good point." He pauses for a long minute. "I'm afraid of rejection."

I rest my head on his shoulder. "You have to try, Dad. I'd hate for you two to grow old alone when you can grow old together."

CHAPTER
THIRTY-FIVE

Back at Will's house, I walk my dad to the car. I give him a hug. "Thanks for confiding in me, Dad. I'm glad I don't have to be mad at you anymore. But think about what I said. It's senseless for you and May May to live separate lives when you two still love each other. After all you've been through together, you deserve happiness."

Dad kisses my cheek. "Thank you for your kind words, sweetheart. But I'm not at all sure May May still loves me," he says and drives off in his sporty convertible.

Tom goes home with his teenagers, and Will locks himself in his study, leaving me in the kitchen with May May, Carrie, and my nieces.

I spread my arms wide at the empty house. "What do we do now?"

"Now comes the tough part of losing a loved one. Our friends are going about their business as usual, leaving us to pick up the pieces of our broken lives," May May says.

"Right. I remember that empty feeling after Mama died." I open the freezer door and remove a box of frozen chicken nuggets. "I'll make the girls some dinner."

While Caroline and Sophia eat the chicken, the three of us organize the contents of the refrigerator, storing casseroles in the freezer and throwing away leftovers that are past their prime. We've moved on to freshening up flower arrangements when Will enters the kitchen with a glass of whiskey in hand.

"Thanks for everything, but y'all can go home now," he says.

I glance over at the girls, who are now coloring quietly at the table. I remember what Tracy said the day I visited them several weeks ago. *He's uneasy around them, like he's afraid he'll break them.* My brother's eyes are swollen and bloodshot from either whiskey or crying, probably both.

"Why don't I take the girls home with me for a few days?" I suggest.

"Or I can. My teenagers can help take care of them." Carrie's tone is unenthusiastic. We're all exhausted from the past few days. But she has her own family to worry about. Will and the girls are my priority now.

"No, let me. If that's okay with you, Will?"

Will looks at his daughters as though they are strangers. "I don't care what you do with them," he says and retreats to his study.

"That's my cue to leave," Carrie says, grabbing her bag and hurrying out of the house.

I kneel beside the table. "Say, girls. How would you like to spend a few days with me at Marsh Point?"

Caroline's little bottom comes off the chair. "Yippee! Can we go for a ride in Daddy's boat?"

Last I checked, the police had impounded Will's boat as part of the accident investigation. "I don't think so, sweetheart. But I'll take you out in my kayak. And we can go swimming off the dock. Maybe we'll spend a day at the Sandy Island Club. We might even spot some sea turtles."

The girls are both on their feet. "Can we go now?" Caroline asks, pulling me toward the door.

"In a few minutes. After we pack some clothes." I turn to May May, giving her a hug. "Thanks for everything. I don't know what we'd do without you."

She palms my cheek. "I'm always happy to help, sweetheart. I can come home with you now if you need me. Although I think you've got this."

I smile down at my nieces. "I do! We'll be fine. I'm looking forward to having them to myself for a few days."

After seeing May May to the door, the girls and I pack everything they'll need for the weekend in their matching pink suitcases. Securing their car seats into my back seat takes some ingenuity I'm unprepared for, but I find a YouTube tutorial that provides adequate instructions.

"Can we ride with the top down?" Caroline shouts and Sophia adds, "Puh-lease, Aunt Ashton."

"You've got it." I push the button to lower the convertible top. Just hearing them say my name will get them anything. A few weeks ago, they barely knew who I was.

"Do you have a TV at Mush Point?" Caroline asks.

"It's Marsh Point. And yes, we do. Although we're going to cut back on your screen time. You two have been watching way too much television these past few days."

"Aww," they cry in unison from the back seat.

"There's way more fun stuff to do at Marsh Point than watch television," I say to them through the rearview mirror.

"Like what?" Caroline asks.

"Like string crabbing and looking for shells on the beach at low tide."

"That sounds like fun," Caroline says with a swift kick to the back of my seat.

At Marsh Point, I show them the bedroom they will share and help them unpack their tiny clothes into the dresser. I give them a bath, wash their hair with liquid soap, and help them into their pajamas. Taking care of children comes naturally to me.

Despite what my mother thought, I would've made a good mama.

I tuck them into the queen-size bed and read them three books of their choice. After a lengthy discussion about monsters in the dark, we decide to leave the bathroom light on, and I kiss their foreheads goodnight. I'm almost out of the room when Sophia's little voice asks, "When's our mommy coming home, Aunt Ashton?"

I ease back down to the edge of the mattress. There's no point in lying to them. They'll eventually find out. And Will certainly isn't in any shape to have this conversation with them. "She's not, sweetheart. She's gone to live in heaven with God."

Big tears appear in her eyes. "Who's gonna take care of us?"

"Your daddy, of course."

Tears stream down her face. "But he doesn't know how."

I smile. "Yes, he does, sweetheart. He's just never had to because your mommy has always taken care of you. You girls will need to show him how things are done." I wag my finger at them. "And don't take advantage of him, because he's smarter than you think. He knows you're not supposed to eat cake for breakfast."

This elicits giggles from both girls.

"Other people will help like May May, Aunt Carrie, and me. I'm redoing the big house next door. I'll give you a tour tomorrow. You'll have your own bedrooms here, and you can come and stay with me anytime."

"I'd like that," Caroline says, and Sophia smiles. "Me too!"

With a heavy heart, I go downstairs to the kitchen and set the kettle on the stove to boil. As I wait for my lavender tea to steep, I think about my nieces. They're so young. All the pictures in the world won't help them remember their mama. Tracy was the center of their universe. The days and weeks ahead will be difficult as they adjust to their new world. But I will be here to help when they need me.

I freeze when I hear a soft knock at the door. I'd forgotten to turn on the alarm. Am I still in danger? Who could that possibly be?

"Ashton, it's me, Sully."

Relief floods through me at the sound of his voice. I swing open the door and step into his outstretched arms. The years fall away, and we're back in high school. He feels so solid. So familiar. My rock.

"I looked for you today in the fellowship hall," I say to his chest.

"I didn't hang around for the reception. I didn't want to talk to you in a room filled with people. I wanted to wait until we were alone." He pushes me away, his hands still gripping my arms. "How're you holding up?"

"I'm okay. A little tired. Tracy and I weren't close, but seeing Will go through this breaks my heart. His daughters are staying with me for the weekend. I just put them down. I should check on them." I gesture at the door. "Come on in."

As I head toward the stairs, I say, "I'll be back in a flash. I was just making some tea if you want some. Or there may be a beer in the refrigerator." I'm not a fan of beer, but I think I remember seeing one at the back of the refrigerator, leftover from a previous occupant. I'd dumped out all the wine after my bender last weekend. I don't plan on ever drinking again. I scared myself. My self-destructive behavior reminded me too much of my mother.

Caroline and Sophia are nestled deep in peaceful slumber, their cherubic mouths forming perfect Os as if caught mid song in a celestial choir. I return to the kitchen to find Sully gulping down a bottled water.

"Sorry," he says, gasping for breath from the exertion of guzzling water. "I didn't realize I was so thirsty."

"No wonder. Today was a scorcher." I retrieve a beer from the refrigerator. "Don't you want something stronger?"

"I can't. I need to head home to Charleston in a minute." He shows me his empty bottle. "But I will take another water if you can spare one."

"Sure thing," I say, replacing the beer for a water. "Do you have time to sit a spell on the porch?"

"Of course. That's why I came. I couldn't leave town without seeing you first."

We go outside to the porch swing, leaving the door open so I can hear the girls if they need me.

"Even if you weren't close to Tracy, she was still your sister-in-law. Her death was a tragedy that affects your entire family."

"I know. I feel for the girls. They're so young, and I'm not sure Will knows what to do with them."

"Right. Girls are way different from boys. He'll figure it out. He has no choice."

"That's true." My brother will be forced to step up, but at what cost to him and the girls?

"I'm coming back to Water's Edge on Monday to install the Mathesons' kitchen. Maybe we can grab a bite of lunch."

"I'd like that. I'm impressed, Sully. You work fast."

"I have a large team of efficient cabinet makers."

"Good to know. I've finished my designs for the kitchen and bathroom cabinets." I hold up my teacup in the direction of the main house. "Would you be interested in giving me an estimate?"

"Absolutely," he says with a wide grin. "Email me the plans. I'll get you a number right away."

The thought of working together makes fizzy bubbles float around in my belly. Our friendship bond is strong, as though the past thirty years never happened. But this spark of chemistry between us is new. Or maybe it's always been there, and I was too preoccupied with my family problems to notice. It's too soon after my breakup with Owen to start something new anyway. But when the time is right, Sully Brown will be at the top of my list of prospects.

I sip my tea. "I haven't heard a word from Carter in days. Have you?"

"I spoke to him earlier. He didn't want to bother you until after the funeral. He's currently in Texas, tracking down a lead on Owen. He said to tell you he'll be in touch soon."

"Wouldn't it be wonderful if he found Owen? If he arrested him and somehow got my money back?"

"Don't give up hope, Ashton. It's not out of the realm of possibilities."

"Maybe not," I say, but with each passing day, my glimmer of hope grows dimmer. On Monday afternoon, when I meet with Cedric Morton, I'll file for a divorce based on abandonment. And first thing on Tuesday morning, I'll see Delbert Lewis about a loan to pay for the renovations. I'd rather be in my shoes, putting my life back together, than in my brother's.

CHAPTER THIRTY-SIX

I wake on Friday morning to find two pairs of piercing blue eyes staring at me from the side of the bed.

"She's awake," Sophia whispers to her big sister.

Caroline sends an elbow to her sister's rib cage. "I can see that, dumbo. Now we have to make her get out of bed."

The girls clamber onto the bed and begin jumping up and down on the mattress. "Wake up, Aunt Ashton!" Sophia yells. And Caroline adds in a singsong voice, "We wanna go outside and explore."

"All right." I throw the covers back. "But I can't do anything until I've had my coffee."

Sophia giggles. "That's what Mommy always says." Her face falls. "Do you think she's drinking coffee in heaven?"

I smile. "Of course! I can't imagine heaven without coffee."

Tears well in Caroline's eyes, and she inserts her thumb into her mouth.

"Oh, honey. I'm so sorry. Come here." I pull both girls down, tucking one under each arm. "It's okay to feel sad about your mommy. We'll have ourselves a good cry, and then we'll find a way to make us feel better."

"How?" Sophia asks, her blue eyes wide.

"Let's see," I say, tapping my chin. "Comfort food and exercise are options. Retail therapy always lifts my spirits when I'm feeling down."

Caroline removes her thumb from her mouth. "What's that?"

"It means you buy stuff. The stuff doesn't *fix* your problems, but it distracts from the thing that's making you sad."

"What kinda stuff?" asks Sophia.

"In your case, I'd suggest buying stuff we can do outside. Fishing rods and string crab devices." I try to remember what I saw in the kid's section the last time I was in Coastal Hardware. "Sidewalk chalk and hula hoops."

Sophia's eyes grow even wider. "Can we buy those things today?"

"You bet! As soon as the store opens. First, we'll eat some comfort food." I give Caroline a squeeze. "How does that sound to you?"

A sad smile spreads across her lips as she nods her head. "Good."

"Then what're we waiting for? Blueberry pancakes for three coming up!"

An hour later, we've eaten and dressed and are headed to the hardware store when Caroline spots Maurice in front of the main house. Both girls tear across the yard, calling his name. When they reach him, they throw their little arms around his massive legs, hugging him.

He strokes their golden heads, cooing to them softly. "I've missed you, girls."

Sophia tilts her head back to look up at him. "Our mama died, Maurice."

Caroline points at the sky. "She's in heaven with Jesus and God."

"I know, sweet angels. And I'm as sorry as I can be about that. I've been saying my prayers." He pries their hands off his legs and kneels down to their level. "If ever you need anything, you come find Maurice. Do you understand?"

They bob their heads in unison. Caroline says, "Yes, sir. We understand."

He straightens and looks at me. "Morning, Miss Ashton. How're you holding up?"

"Good. We're taking it one day at a time, aren't we girls?"

"We're going to the hardware store to buy stuff," Sophia says, and Caroline adds, "Aunt Ashton says retail therapy will make us happy when we feel sad."

Maurice laughs out loud. "I'm a firm believer in retail therapy myself."

I shrug. "Whatever works."

"Can we go inside the house, Aunt Ashton?" Caroline asks.

"Sure. But be careful where you walk and don't touch anything."

Maurice watches them go. "Bless their little hearts. I had a meeting with Mr. Will this morning. He didn't look so hot. I really feel for him." He turns his attention back to me. "Your brother asked me to rush things up on the project. He wants everything finished by summer's end. It'll be tight, but we can make it work. Cabinetry might be the only thing that holds us up."

I remember what Sully told me last night about his efficient team. "I've been working with a cabinet contractor from Charleston on the Mathesons' project. He may be able to meet our deadline. Did Will say why he wants to finish early?"

"No, ma'am. He didn't say."

I'm curious about Will's motivations, but I won't look a gift horse in the mouth. Having the house finished will make it easier for me to help Will with the girls.

I join my nieces on the second floor, and we spend a ridiculous amount of time picking out their bedrooms. I offer for them to have their own rooms, but they insist on sharing. I'm running out of patience when they finally choose the large rear corner room with a partial view of the sound.

Before they can change their minds, I usher them quickly out of the house and drive them to town with the top down. Coastal Hardware has been selling kids' toys since I was a child. Not the cheap stuff you buy at Walmart, but the old-fashioned quality items that last. We load up a cart with toys and games to entertain them. I'm stunned when Caroline tells me she's never owned a bicycle.

"Mama was afraid we'd fall and hurt ourselves," Caroline explains.

"That's why you always wear a helmet," I say, wondering how anyone could get through childhood without a few skinned knees.

Not only do I buy bikes with training wheels for the girls, I buy a blue cruiser with a basket for myself. When we return to Marsh Point, we spend the rest of the morning riding bikes on the street in front of the house.

"I really like retail therapy, Aunt Ashton," Caroline tells me over hamburgers for dinner.

"Me too," Sophia says, rubbing her tired eyes.

Our activities of the next two days bring back fond memories of happy times with my mama before her addiction hit hard. I don't hear from anyone in my family until just after lunchtime on Sunday. The girls are practicing with their hula hoops in the yard, and I'm in a rocker on the veranda, scrolling through emails on my iPad, when Dad and May May come strolling around the corner of the house. I nearly fall out of my chair at the sight of their clasped hands.

I stand to greet them. "This is a surprise. In more ways than one."

Dad is grinning like the cat that swallowed the canary. "I took your advice and invited May May to lunch yesterday. We talked for hours, and we've decided to give our relationship another chance."

"That's amazing. I'm so excited for you two," I say, pulling them both in for a group hug. "You deserve some happiness."

The girls spot their grandfather and run toward the porch calling, "Grandpa! Grandpa!"

He bends at the waist to speak to them. "Hello, girls. Are you having a good time with Aunt Ashton?"

"Yes!" Sophia cries.

"Guess what, Grandpa?" Caroline says. "Aunt Ashton taught us how to string crab."

"You don't say." Dad's eyes twinkle as he looks over at me. "And guess who taught Aunt Ashton how to string crab?"

"You did!" Caroline says. "Aunt Ashton told us."

"Wanna see?" Sophia asks.

"You bet," he says, as the girls take him by the hand and drag him across the yard to the dock.

I call after them, "There are some chicken necks in the cooler on the dock."

Dad responds with a thumbs-up.

I motion May May to a rocker. "We have a lot to talk about."

"Indeed, we do." May May lowers herself to a chair. "I imagine you're sore at me."

I sit down next to her. "How could I be upset with you? After Mom overdosed, you sacrificed your own happiness to hold my family together. I was shocked when Dad first told me, but your relationship is the missing puzzle piece that helps my memories make sense. You were both going through a difficult time, and you needed each other."

May May's eyes are cloudy with tears. "I don't view it as a sacrifice, sweet girl. I loved your Mama as much as I love Ernest. But it hasn't been easy. My feelings for him never went away. Seeing him all the time didn't help."

"I don't imagine it did." I chuckle. "There are some heartbroken women at Whispering Oaks today though."

May May smiles. "We're taking things slow. Holding hands is about all of us old folks are capable of."

"I don't believe that" I say, nor do I want to think about my father's sex life. "You've always been like my second mama. Maybe one day you and Dad will make it official."

May May laughs. "Let's not get ahead of ourselves. For now, we're just getting to know each other again."

Squeals of laughter get my attention, and I look toward the dock. "It does my heart good to see him so happy."

May May and I join Dad and the girls, and for the next hour, we watch Sophia and Caroline pull in crabs until their bucket is nearly full.

"The girls informed me they don't eat crab. Y'all should take these home with you," I suggest to Dad and May May as we make our way back to the house.

Dad looks at May May. "What do you think? Shall we steam them up for dinner?"

May May's face lights up. "I would love that. I can't remember the last time I picked crabs."

The girls insist on carrying the bucket, and May May walks ahead with them to help load it in the car.

Looping my arm through Dad's, I rest my head on his shoulder. "I'm thrilled for you. There's no one I'd rather see you with than May May. I hope Annabelle wasn't too disappointed."

Dad waves off my concern. "Annabelle is fine. She's already moved on to someone new. There was no chemistry between us anyway."

I laugh as my Casanova father helps his new girlfriend into the passenger seat. The two have no sooner taken off in his convertible than Will appears in his truck.

"Daddy! Daddy!" the girls cry as they run over to greet him.

Will scoops them up, one in each arm. His face is set in a scowl, and dark circles rim his eyes, but he appears genuinely happy to see his daughters.

"Did you have a good time with Aunt Ashton?" he asks, kissing each of them on the forehead.

"Yes!" Caroline says. "She bought us lots of toys."

"And bikes!" Sophia adds.

"And she's giving us our own room in the house. Wanna see it?"

"I'd love that," he says, setting them down.

The girls run ahead of us into the house, leaving Will and me standing awkwardly together in the driveway. I long to hug him, but as usual, I can't read his vibe.

"Thank you for keeping them," he says, kicking at the gravel.

"It was my pleasure. They're good company. And they really love it here. How're you holding up?"

He flaps his hand in a so-so gesture. "I needed to face my demons. But now it's time for the girls and me to pick up the pieces of our lives."

We enter the house and stand in the front hall. "Maurice says you instructed him to finish the renovations by summer's end. I'm thrilled, but curious why. Are you starting another project?"

"I have a few new projects starting in September. Mainly, I wanted to thank you for all you've done for me this past week. You were there for me the night of the accident, and you defended me to Tracy's mother." He chuckles. "That took real guts."

"I took great pleasure in giving her a piece of my mind."

Will's face turns serious again. "I didn't deserve your kindness after I accused you of stealing from me."

I shrug. "You were under a lot of pressure from Tracy."

"That's no excuse. You were under a lot of pressure as well. And I turned on you."

"Let's forget about it." I hold out my hand. "Truce."

"Truce." Ignoring my hand, he pulls me into his arms. The embrace is brief, but it's a start.

We walk to the kitchen. "Cabinets could be our only potential delay in finishing by Labor Day," he says.

"I sent my plans to Sully on Friday. He's working up an estimate."

Will scrunches up his face. "Sully who?"

"Sully Brown, my old friend from high school. He owns Regal Woodworks, the cabinet contractor in charge of the Matheson project."

"Oh, right. I vaguely remember him. Did you two date?"

My cheeks burn as I shake my head. "We were just friends."

"Because you were too busy taking care of us to have a boyfriend."

I move over to the open space where the crew has taken out the exterior wall and are preparing to put in windows. "I've been facing my own demons lately, Will. And I owe you an apology for abandoning you. I had an opportunity to save myself and I took it. I'm trying to forgive myself. I hope one day you will forgive me as well."

"There's nothing to forgive. It wasn't your job to take care of us. It was Mom's. And she failed." Will comes to stand beside me. "I don't know why I've been so hard on you all these years. I looked up to you so much when we were young. You took care of me, and you protected me, and I felt betrayed when you left and didn't come back. Not even for Christmases."

As the realization comes to me, the words tumble out of my mouth. "I couldn't face the disappointment I knew I'd find in your faces." Out of all my siblings, Savannah would've been my ally. She would've forgiven me. But she was gone.

When we hear the girls calling us from a distant part of the house, we leave the kitchen and walk toward the stairs, pausing at the bottom. "I know how you feel about the house, and I hope you don't mind me giving the girls their own room. I told them they can stay here with me anytime." A mischievous smile curves the corners of my lips. "I have plenty of extras, if you'd like to pick out a room for yourself."

He runs a hand across the smooth mahogany banister. "I

might. I'm softening toward this old place. We exorcised the demons when we took it down to the studs."

I laugh out loud. "That's exactly how I feel. We're giving the house a blank slate to start over."

"If ever there was a family who needed a fresh start . . ."

Warmth fills my chest. At long last, Will and I have declared a cease-fire. "I'm here for you, Will. Whatever you need, whenever you need it, just name it."

"I will definitely be taking you up on that offer. I have absolutely no idea how to go on with my life without Tracy."

"In divorcing Owen, I'll be starting a new chapter of my life as well. Maybe we can begin our journeys together."

"I'd like that." Will motions for me to go ahead of him up the stairs. "Coincidentally, Carrie paid me a visit yesterday. She tried to coerce me into supporting her will contest, but I told her I wanted no part of it. I get the impression her case is crumbling."

"Ha. She never had much of a case to begin with." We reach the top of the stairs. "Marsh Point isn't *my* home, Will. It's *our* family's home. It belongs to all of us. I would love to share it with Carrie, but I won't turn it over to her without a fight."

CHAPTER THIRTY-SEVEN

Sully and I are at the Matheson house late on Monday afternoon, overseeing the installment of kitchen cabinets, when I receive a call from an unknown number. I almost don't answer it, but my intuition tells me it's important.

"Ashton, this is Harmony. We need to talk."

My grip on the phone tightens. "Where's Owen?"

"I'll tell you when we meet," she says with an edginess to her voice.

I glance over at Sully, who is watching me suspiciously. "Who's that?" he mouths.

"Harmony," I mouth back and put the call on speaker.

"Is Owen with you, Harmony? Are you aware the police are looking for him?" I'm not sure how much Harmony knows about the situation, and I don't want to scare her off. Owen is the perpetrator. She's merely the accomplice.

Harmony lets out an audible sigh. "I was afraid of that." She pauses and I can hear her breathing. "Look, whatever trouble Owen is in has nothing to do with me."

"I need to find him, Harmony. He stole a lot of money from my family and me. Do you know where he is?"

"I know where he was this morning. I have no clue if he's still there."

My heart races. "Then every minute counts. I'm not talking to you unless the police are present, and if you want to avoid going to jail for being an accomplice, you'd better tell us everything you know."

After another long pause, she says, "Fine. I'm at my house."

I end the call and click on Carter's number. When he answers, I quickly explain the situation.

"Finally, a breakthrough! I'm with Marlowe now. We'll meet you at Harmony's. Whatever you do, Ashton, do not enter the house until we get there."

"I'm at a client's house on Sandy Island. You'll beat me there. Don't *you* enter without *me*."

"Deal. See you in a few."

I drop my phone in my purse. "I've gotta go," I say, and race out of the house.

Sully is on my heels. "I'll follow you," he says, and remains glued to my bumper across the Merriweather Bridge and through town to Mariner's Landing.

When we arrive, Carter is waiting with Detective Marlowe in Harmony's driveway. Carter rings the doorbell, and when Harmony answers, he provides the introductions.

Marlowe flashes Harmony his credentials. "Owen is wanted for embezzlement and attempted murder charges. You need to tell us everything you know about Owen's location."

Harmony bites down on her lower lip, as though trying to decide whether to talk to us.

Marlowe's face tightens. "We believe Owen was driving your Ford Explorer at the time of the attempted murder. Unless you want to be charged as an accessory, you'd better start talking."

The color drains from her face. "I understand," she says and steps out of the way so we can enter the house.

Harmony's home is decorated in a feminine style that doesn't appeal to my taste but seems appropriate for a romance writer. I sit next to her on the white velvet sofa with Sully and Carter on either side in club chairs and Marlowe in a straight-back chair in front of us.

Harmony places a hand on my arm. "I'm so sorry, Ashton. I'm not a home wrecker. Owen told me you two had been separated for over a year. He's so charming and handsome, I fell hard for him. I had no idea he was such a jerk."

I retract my arm from her touch. "He's a jerk *and* a thief."

Carter leans in close. "We're wasting time. Where is he, Harmony?"

"In a cabin in the woods in a remote part of the Virginia mountains. I marked the location on my phone. I took the rental car when I left. Unless he hiked out, he may still be there," Harmony says, and hands her phone to the detective.

Marlowe studies the location. "The cabin may have seemed remote, but you were only ninety minutes from Washington Dulles Airport."

"Did Owen mention leaving the country?" Carter asks.

"He didn't say anything about it to me, but I found a fake passport in his suitcase. I took a picture on my phone."

Marlowe pinches the screen out to make the image larger. "Matthew Charles Morris." He looks over at me. "Does that name mean anything to you?"

I shake my head. "Never heard of it."

Marlowe uses his phone to call his coworker. He provides the cabin's location and fake passport name and barks out orders for the person on the other end to contact the Virginia State Police.

Ending the call, he returns his attention to Harmony. "Start at the beginning and tell us everything."

Harmony falls back against the sofa. "There's not much to tell, really. Owen invited me to go with him to the mountains for a few days to get away from the heat."

"Didn't you think it was strange for him to rent a car for the trip?" Carter asks.

"Not really. He told me he was having his truck serviced while he was gone. Everything was fine the first few days, and then he started getting weird on me."

Marlowe frowns. "How so?"

Harmony stares down at her clasped hands. "He started acting secretive. He was constantly on the phone, and he always took his calls outside so I couldn't hear. We were gone longer than planned, and I was eager to get back to my work in progress. I can't write in strange surroundings." She gives me a look, as though I'm a fan interested in her writing process. When I stare blankly at her in return, she continues, "He kept saying he needed a few more days, but he wouldn't say what for. When he went out to get food for dinner last night, I snooped around in his stuff. And that's when I found the fake passport. Along with a handgun."

"What'd you do then?" Carter asks.

"I freaked out. I knew I had to get out of there. He was in a rotten mood when he came back to the cabin, and for the first time, I was afraid of him. I ground up two of my sleeping pills and put the powder in his bourbon. I waited until I was sure he was asleep and took off in the rental car."

"What time was that?" Marlowe asks, thumbing notes into his phone.

"Hmm." Harmony glances up at the ceiling. "Around one o'clock this morning. I would've driven straight through, but I got sleepy and had to pull over in North Carolina for a nap."

"Do you have any idea who he was talking to during the many phone calls?" Marlowe asks.

Harmony shakes her head. "None."

"Owen was driving your car the night he tried to run me off the road," I say. "Were you with him?"

"No! Of course not!" She narrows her eyes. "Although I remember which night you're talking about. He's only driven my car once, when his battery was dead, and he ran out to get some ice cream. Although now that I think about it, he was gone awhile, and the ice cream was melted by the time he got back."

"Is there anything else you can think of that might be important?" Marlowe asks, eager to leave.

"Not right now." She smooths her bleached-blonde hair back. "But I'm too tired to think straight. Something might come to me tomorrow."

Marlowe hands Harmony her phone. "I'll give this back to you in case Owen tries to get in touch. But if he does, I need you to call me right away."

"Yes, sir. Am I in trouble?"

He sets his dark eyes on her. "Have you done anything wrong?"

Harmony gulps loudly. "I don't think so."

"Then you have nothing to worry about."

We all stand to leave. I sense Harmony wants another word with me. Maybe she wants to apologize again. But I'm not buying her innocent act. She was at The Nest when I caused a scene. She knew Owen and I were still together. As far as I'm concerned, her apology is worthless. I won't be the one to ease her guilt.

I gather with Sully, Carter, and Marlowe in front of the house. "How long before we hear anything from Virginia?" I ask.

"Shouldn't be too long," Marlowe says. "A couple of hours, maybe."

"Let me know as soon as you hear anything, no matter how insignificant."

Marlowe salutes me. "You've got it."

Sully walks me to my car. "I'm staying with my parents tonight. Do you want to grab an early dinner at The Nest while we wait for word on Owen?"

"I would love that. Alone is the last thing I want to be right now." I open my car door. "I'll meet you there."

Monday nights are slow at The Nest, and we have our choice of tables. Sully chooses one by the front window. When the waitress arrives for our drink orders, Sully asks for a beer, and I order sweet tea. I sense a long night ahead, and I need to keep my mind clear.

"Do you think they'll find Owen?" I ask once the waitress has gone.

"I certainly hope so. Knowing the name on the fake passport will definitely help track him down."

"Unless he's already boarded a plane to Timbuktu. Then I'm screwed."

"Try not to go there, Ashton." Sully reaches for my hand. "I need your advice. Do you mind if I change the subject for a minute?"

I glance down at our clasped hands. This feels like more than a friendship gesture. "Please! I would be grateful to talk about something else for a change."

"My parents have decided to move to Whispering Oaks. Apparently, their friends are having a blast, and they don't want to miss out on the fun. They've offered me their house, and I'm thinking of moving back."

I furrow my brow. "But your life is in Charleston."

"What's left of it. I've been renting an apartment since I split up with my wife, and I lost all my friends in the divorce. As for my business, my management team is extremely capable, and my son will come on board when he graduates from college next May. I'm thinking of opening a smaller shop here."

"Good! This town needs a quality cabinet maker."

"Spending time in Water's Edge these past few weeks has reminded me of how much I love this sleepy little town. But I don't want to grow old alone, Ashton. I know it's too soon for you to date, but I'd like to know if there's hope for us down the road. As a couple. More than friends."

I look away from him, not sure how to respond. "I don't

know, Sully . . . I care about you. If it doesn't work out, our friendship might suffer."

He cocks his head to the side. "We'll never know until we try."

My phone vibrates the table with a call from Carter, and I snatch it up. "Have you heard anything?"

"Local authorities arrested Owen trying to board a plane to Brazil," Carter explains. "We're working out the details with them now. Someone will drive him back to Beaufort tomorrow. I'll let you know as soon as I hear more."

"Oh thank god." I end the call and drop the phone on the table. "They got him," I say, burying my face in my hands.

CHAPTER THIRTY-EIGHT

Carter summons me to the police station at ten o'clock on Tuesday morning. He greets me outside the main entrance and shows me to a small office with a metal desk and two-way mirror, looking into the interview room. We've been waiting only a couple of minutes when a uniformed officer ushers in my husband, takes off the handcuffs, and forces him into a chair. Owen rubs his wrist. He looks dreadful with mussed hair, rumpled clothes, and beard stubble on his face. Seconds later, Detective Marlowe enters the room and pulls up a chair opposite him at the rectangular table.

"You've been a very busy man, Mr. Nelms. The list of charges against you is long."

"Yo, dude!" Owen says. "This is all a big mistake. Let me talk to my wife. Ashton can explain everything."

Planting his elbows on the table, Marlowe leans in closer to Owen. "I am not a *dude.* But I would love to hear how the charges against you for fraud, embezzlement, and attempted murder could be construed as mistakes."

"For starters, my wife gave me permission to manage her money."

"Did your brother-in-law give you permission to wire a hundred thousand dollars out of Darby Custom Home's operating account?"

"I had an investment opportunity. I couldn't find Will to get his permission. I didn't think he'd mind. I didn't want him to miss out on this golden opportunity. I have his money. I swear." Owen's hand shoots up. "I'll give it back to him. I was planning to give it back anyway."

"And your wife's money? Did you invest it in this same golden opportunity?"

"No, sir. I tripled her principal in the stock market. I moved the money to a separate account for safekeeping." Owen looks and sounds terrified. He's never called anyone *sir* in his life. I almost feel sorry for him.

Marlowe squints at him. "You're saying you moved the money, not the stock portfolio."

"That's correct. Per Ashton's instructions, I sold all her stocks."

"He's twisting the situation," I whisper to Carter.

"Don't worry. Marlowe doesn't believe him."

"Look, Detective." Owen stretches his arms out with palms up on the table. "Let's cut a deal and save everyone a lot of time and trouble. I'll give back the money, and we can forget any of this ever happened."

With a straight face, Marlowe says, "I'll need to see the money first. Where is it?"

I cut my eyes at Carter. "What's he doing? He's not seriously going to make a deal, is he?"

"No," Carter says with a chuckle. "He's playing Owen. He's trying to get your money back."

Owen lets out a sigh. "I can point you toward it."

Marlowe sits up straighter in his chair. "Then start pointing."

When Owen bends over to take off his running shoe, Marlowe jumps to his feet and runs around to his side of the table with his handgun aimed at my husband's head. "What're you doing?"

"Don't shoot! I'm just taking off my shoe. Here, I'll show you." Owen peels back the shoe's insole and removes a small black thumb drive, handing it to Marlowe. "There's only one file on there. It contains links to the banks, account numbers, and passwords. Everything is there, including the money from Darby Custom Homes."

"Sit tight. I'll be right back." Marlowe exits the interview room, and a few minutes later, he joins us in the small office with a laptop. He turns both over to Carter. "You're the expert. See if this is legit."

Carter sits down at the metal desk and inserts the thumb drive into the laptop. Marlowe and I peer over his shoulders as he clicks on the spreadsheet. Two banks are listed with links, passwords, and usernames. The first account he accesses reveals a balance so high Marlowe lets out a low whistle. And the second balance is a hundred grand, the amount Owen stole from Darby Custom Homes.

"Looks like you got your money back, Mrs. Nelms," the detective says.

Carter emails a copy of the file to himself and hands Marlowe the thumb drive. "I assume you'll need this as evidence."

"You're not releasing him, are you?" I ask.

"Not a chance in hell. He's going to prison for a very long time. Let's see how he explains the attempted murder charges." Marlowe leaves the laptop with us and returns to the interview room.

Owen looks up at him. "Can I go now?" he asks in a hopeful tone.

"Not just yet. Why don't you tell me how your wife's EpiPen ended up in your possession?"

Owen has his answer ready. "We went on a picnic one day recently over to Sandy Island. She never leaves home without her

EpiPen. She put it in my backpack, so she wouldn't have to take a purse."

I roll my eyes. "He's lying. We never went on a picnic to Sandy Island. And I'm certain I had the EpiPen with me the morning before the allergy attack."

When Marlowe asks Owen about nearly running me off the road, Owen denies knowing anything about it. "You can't prove that was me driving the Ford Explorer. It's my wife's word against mine."

"He's right," Carter says. "Fortunately, we can get him on other charges."

Marlowe folds his arms over his chest. "Let's talk about your travel plans. Why were you going to Brazil? And why were you using a passport in the name of Matthew Charles Morris?"

"I already told all this to the cops in DC. I was in the Delta Sky Club before my flight, and I accidentally picked up another traveler's passport by mistake."

"Then why hasn't the other traveler come forward? And don't try to tell me he hasn't noticed the passports were swapped. He wouldn't have been allowed on his flight with your passport."

Owen shrugs. "I can't answer that. Maybe he got called away from the airport on an emergency and had to cancel his trip."

"That's a likely story. You were using a fake passport like the one we found in your secret office." Pushing back from the table, Marlowe opens the door and calls for an officer. When the same uniformed policeman appears, he orders him to take Owen down to booking.

"Booking? But what about our deal?" Owen argues as the officer handcuffs him again.

A smirk appears on Marlowe's lips. "We never had a deal. You can't fast-talk your way out of this kind of trouble, Mr. Nelms. You're going to prison for a very long time."

I turn to face Carter. "Is that it?"

"That's it. I've emailed you a copy of Owen's file. If I were you,

I'd go straight to your bank and have the money wired back into your account."

"I'm on my way there now." I give Carter a hug. "I don't know how I'll ever be able to thank you."

He gives me a warm smile. "It was my pleasure."

Carter walks me out of the police station, and we part on the front steps. I hurry to my car, my phone pressed to my ear as I call my brother.

He answers in a glum mood. "What's up, Ashton?"

"I got our money back from Owen," I say when he answers. "I'm heading to the bank. Meet me there so we can get it transferred back into our accounts."

"I'm on my way," he says.

We arrive at the Savings and Loan at the same time, and Delbert Lewis places us in the capable hands of a young, tech-savvy banker. A short time later, our money is being wired back into our accounts.

"I'm sorry again for accusing you," Will says in the parking lot afterward.

I smile. "It never would've happened if I hadn't married such a jerk."

"Well, he's out of your life for good. Considering the circumstances, you should be able to get a speedy divorce."

"Let's hope so." When we reach my car, I turn around to face my brother. "How're you holding up, Will?"

His shoulders slump. "Not great. Caroline has started wetting the bed again, and Sophia cries incessantly for her mommy. I'm working with a service to hire a nanny, but I don't know how much that will help."

"A nanny will offer stability. I'm happy to keep them again for a few days if you need a break."

"Thanks. I may take you up on that offer. But we have to work through these issues eventually."

I hug his neck. "You're gonna do great. Just take it one day at a time."

His eyes glisten with tears when he pulls away from me. "I don't know about great. Right now, I'd be satisfied with just surviving."

My heart breaks for him as I watch him trudge across the pavement to his car. He has a long road ahead of him, and it's my job to support him. I will plan a weekend for the girls at Marsh Point soon. Will needs some time to himself, and getting the girls out of the house, away from the memories of their mama, will be good for them.

I have work piling up in my office, but I'm in the mood to celebrate, and there's only one person I wish to celebrate with. I stop by Custom Crust for sandwiches to-go and drive across the Merriweather Bridge to Sandy Island. The installation crew has gone to lunch, and Sully is alone in the kitchen, studying the blueprints. He smiles when he sees me in the doorway.

"How'd it go at the police station?"

"I got my money back! I've just come from the bank. Will and I have wired our funds back into our personal accounts. Owen has been arrested. I hope he stays in jail until his trial." I hold up the bag of sandwiches. "And I brought lunch, if you're hungry."

"I'm starving. I was just getting ready to run out for a bite." His eyes travel to the covered porch. "Let's sit outside."

"Yes! Let's. It's a nice day."

We exit the house through the sliding glass doors and sit down on the steps. I hand him a California BLT and a bag of barbecue chips.

"You surprised me last night when you suggested we try being a couple. But I've been thinking a lot about it today. You and I have always shared something special. Maybe it *is* the romantic kind of special. Like you said, there's only one way to find out."

His face lights up. "Really? Do you mean it?"

I bob my head. "I'm game to give it a try. Otherwise, we'll

never know what might have been. I love the idea of you opening a shop in Water's Edge and us working together on projects. I look forward to doing all the things we used to do together. Spending Sundays on the water, sitting by the fire on cold evenings, and going for long walks on autumn afternoons. But . . ."

"But what, Ashton?"

I meet his eyes. "But I don't want to lose you as a friend if it doesn't work out."

He tucks a strand of my hair behind my ear. "We're friends first and foremost. I can't make any promises, but I don't think anything will change that. Even if we decide we're not a match made in heaven."

I grab hold of his hands. "There are no guarantees in life. But I believe taking a chance on us is a chance worth taking." Unexpected tears fill my eyes as a deep sense of calm settles over me. When we were teenagers navigating a confusing world, Sully, even more so than Hattie, had been my person. Even though we lost touch for over thirty years, our connection is still powerful.

CHAPTER
THIRTY-NINE

Late afternoon, I arrive back at the guesthouse to find my sister waiting on the porch.

"I hear Owen was arrested," Carrie says.

"That's right. They caught him trying to board a plane to Brazil with a fake passport."

"I guess he wasn't such a good guy after all."

An awkward silence settles over us, and I wait for her to say she's sorry for accusing me of embezzlement. When no apology comes, I unlock the door and turn off the alarm. She takes a tentative step across the threshold, as though afraid of what she might find inside.

"This place is foul," she says with upturned lip.

"What's foul about it? Outdated, maybe. But I've grown accustomed to the retro vibe, and I find it rather cozy."

She follows me into the kitchen. Dropping my purse on the counter, I pour us two glasses of sweet tea.

Carrie leans back against the counter, sipping her tea. "Will you move back to your condo now that Owen is in jail?"

I haven't gotten that far in my thinking. The burden of cleaning out Owen's possessions and putting the condo on the market will now fall on me. "I'll eventually sell the condo. I was never happy there. Marsh Point is my home now."

"Speaking of Marsh Point, I'm hoping we can reach an agreement so we won't have to go to court."

I work hard to keep the irritation out of my voice. "We tried that, Carrie. It didn't work. Mama's attorney says the judge will probably require us to take part in mediation."

"The lawyer's fees could get expensive," she says.

You started this, I think. She's so transparent. Her husband is clearly putting pressure on her to drop the lawsuit. Thomas's teacher's salary won't cover the cost of a lengthy court battle. "I'm listening. What did you have in mind?"

Carrie stares down at her tea. "The same solution I suggested before. That we split time in the house."

"And as I've said before, I'm willing to share Marsh Point. You can have a suite of rooms in the main house, and you're welcome to stay here anytime. But I'll be here too. This is my home."

"What about the guesthouse? Are you planning to renovate it?"

I know where she's going with this, but I play along with her anyway. "Maybe. After Will finishes the main house. The renovations won't be as elaborate. We'll paint and do a modest upgrade on the kitchens and baths."

"Why don't you give me this house?"

"What do you mean by *give*?"

She drains her tea and sets the glass down on the counter. "You know, deed the house and this sliver of land to me."

I bite my tongue. This unconditional love thing requires an enormous amount of patience. Why is she so desperate to own a piece of this property? It's not because she loves it so much. Is there something going on in her marriage I don't know about? "You may use the guesthouse as your own second home. But I will not give it to you."

Carrie's face flushes red. "But—"

I hold my hand out. "That's my final offer, Carrie. Either take it, or I'll see you in court."

"I'll take it," she says and storms out of the house without shaking my hand.

Snickering to myself, I refill my tea and wander over to the main house. The workers have begun hanging sheetrock, which sends tingles of excitement all over my body. I imagine the walls washed in a warm sand color with the elegant new trim I've selected painted white.

I wander out to the veranda and stare out over the marsh. My phone rings, and I accept the call from Hattie. "Rumor has it Owen is in jail."

"That's right," I say, and fill her in on the events leading to his arrest.

"You poor thing. You shouldn't be alone. I can come over if you want me to."

"Thanks. But I'm fine. I'm not alone."

"Really? Who's there with you?" Hattie says in a suspicious tone.

"Friendly ghosts. But don't worry, I've chased away all the demons." I chuckle. "Goodbye, Hattie. I'll call you in a few days, and we'll have lunch."

Leaving the porch, I stroll across the lawn to the edge of the water. I've come full circle. I've been on a long journey—college and career building and marriage. But I've found my way home again, and I will never leave.

Marsh Point is the source of my strength. The memories, good and bad, are a part of that strength, but the physical property—the house, dock, and marsh—makes my heart beat and the blood pump through my veins. I gave up the opportunity to have my own children, because my job here was incomplete. My purpose in life has always been taking care of my siblings. After the dust settles, I will hire Carter to find my sister. I will never stop looking for her. I will never stop trying until the four Darby children are back together.

I HOPE you've enjoyed *Long Journey Home.* Look for more in the Marsh Point series coming soon.

Please consider leaving an honest review at your favorite online retailers and book-related social media platforms. Recommendations from like-minded readers helps other readers discover new authors and titles. If you're looking for more action-packed Southern family drama, you might consider my latest stand alone novel, *Scent of Magnolia* or my newest series. Virginia Vineyards is a family saga featuring the Love family with characters you'll love and those you'll love to hate.

ACKNOWLEDGMENTS

I'm forever indebted to the many people who help bring a project to fruition. My editor, Pat Peters. My cover designer, the hard-working folks at Damonza.com. My beta readers: Alison Fauls, Anne Wolters, Laura Glenn, Jan Klein, Lisa Hudson, Lori Walton, Kathy Sinclair, Jenelle Rodenbaugh, Rachel Story, Jennie Trovinger, and Amy Connolley. Last, but certainly not least, are my select group of advanced readers who are diligent about sharing their advanced reviews prior to releases.

I'm blessed to have many supportive people in my life who offer the encouragement I need to continue my pursuit of writing. Love and thanks to my family—my mother, Joanne; my husband, Ted; and my amazing children, Cameron and Ned.

Most of all, I'm grateful to my wonderful readers for their love of women's fiction. I love hearing from you. Feel free to shoot me an email at ashleyhfarley@gmail.com or stop by my website at ashleyfarley.com for more information about my characters and upcoming releases. Don't forget to sign up for my newsletter. Your subscription will grant you exclusive content, sneak previews, and special giveaways.

ABOUT THE AUTHOR

Ashley Farley writes books about women for women. Her characters are mothers, daughters, sisters, and wives facing real-life issues. Her bestselling Sweeney Sisters series has touched the lives of many.

Ashley is a wife and mother of two young adult children. While she's lived in Richmond, Virginia, for the past twenty-one years, a piece of her heart remains in the salty marshes of the South Carolina Lowcountry, where she still calls home. Through the eyes of her characters, she captures the moss-draped trees, delectable cuisine, and kindhearted folk with lazy drawls that make the area so unique.

Ashley loves to hear from her readers. Visit Ashley's website @ ashleyfarley.com

Get free exclusive content by signing up for her newsletter @ ashleyfarley.com/newsletter-signup/

Made in United States
Troutdale, OR
11/09/2023

14432962R10166